Uncle Jack

A NOVEL

Uncle Jack

A NOVEL

Peter Somerville-Large

SOMERVILLE PRESS

Somerville Press Ltd,
Dromore, Bantry,
Co. Cork, Ireland

First published 2016

Designed by Jane Stark
Typeset in Adobe Garamond Pro
seamistgraphics@gmail.com

ISBN: 978 0 9955239 06

Printed and bound in Spain
by GraphyCems, Villatuerta, Navarra

To Christopher
for help and encouragement
over many years of writing.

CHAPTER ONE

The year was 1994 and I arrived in Australia more or less a remittance man.

Back in Ireland I had lived with my Uncle Jack at Mount Jewel, a house in County Louth, some miles north of Dublin. My uncle claimed that it was the fourth biggest house in Ireland.

Over the years various attempts had been made to find me a career. I had failed to get into university, and the attempt to find me a place in Sandhurst had also been unsuccessful. I rejected the opportunities offered to me by my uncle and his friends – training at a hotel beside the Blackwater where fishermen flocked, employment at a garden centre which would lead to a directorship, a job in a wine merchants which I might take over one day. Working with wine was a career gentlemen could aspire to, and was not considered to be trade.

All I wanted was to stay at Mount Jewel and help to run the estate, which in due course I would inherit. This did not seem to be possible, not while Uncle Jack was in charge.

'I'm sick of you hanging around the place. Why don't you go to Australia?'

'Australia?'

'You could stay with Desmond.'

'Who?' In the twenty years of my life Uncle Jack had never once mentioned Desmond.

'Cousin. Seduced a maid...' I watched a smile come over his leathery

7

face. 'Long time ago. Poor devil, after the frolic, he was given a single ticket to Sydney.'

'What happened to the maid?'

'Ended up in a Magdalen home.'

'Your cousin? You keep in touch?'

'Ever hear of Christmas cards?'

Australia seemed a good idea. There was the romantic idea of living in a wilderness and becoming a jackaroo. I could ride reasonably well; one of the few occupations I indulged in during long winters at Mount Jewel was hunting.

'Toughen up your character.'

So letters were exchanged, and Uncle Jack paid my plane fare. When I left he presented me with a bundle of fifty pound notes. They were in a sealed envelope given with the instruction that I wasn't to open it until I arrived. I opened it as soon as I was on the plane. The notes were enclosed with a letter on the familiar blue crested paper which contained the usual clichés about the Australian character and how their soldiers had proved themselves during the First World War. Uncle Jack also mentioned cricket and the horrors of Kerry Packer and the coloured clothes he made cricketers wear.

After I reached Sydney I made my way to Cousin Desmond, who lived on the north shore. I took a green and white ferry from Circular Quay and was carried across the great harbour to Manly. I went up on deck and sat back in the sunshine before the ferry backed away from the pier. Engines throbbed and propellors churned up water into a creamy wake as the opera house slid past and the bridge they called the Coat Hanger receded. Past the towering north and east heads framing the open sea. People waved from small yachts and it seemed that everyone was on holiday. Coloured spinnakers billowed in the wind as yachts raced each other and the sun beat down from a cloudless sky.

Before I reached Manly I decided I wanted to stay in Australia for the rest of my life. To hell with Mount Jewel.

I took a bus which rolled beyond the northern suburbs past Avalon and Barrenjoey towards more great beaches and headlands. From what I had gathered from Uncle Jack, I expected a corrugated shack hidden in trees, and Cousin Desmond's opulent house overlooking the water came as a surprise. Enveloped in soft green forest, it had its own private pier and a yacht moored within easy reach. A Porsche was parked outside.

A tall muscular old man, naked to the waist, pulled himself out of a hammock. A dragon and a snake wrestled across his chest and other tattoos covered his arms like sleeves. In between the tattoos Cousin Desmond was a shining mahogany colour from sunburn. He carried a tin of beer kept cold by a fur jacket around it.

'Ye're Jack's nephew…and how is the old bastard?'

'Well enough.'

'What are you doing living with that old crock?'

'My parents died when I was a small boy.'

Before he spoke again a beautiful oriental girl appeared on the balcony.

'Hey, Divina, come over and meet my cousin from Ireland. First, bring out a couple of bottles of bubbly. This calls for some celebration.'

Holding champagne glasses we stood on the deck with its view of the bay and Desmond's catamaran glinting in the sun.

Divina opened another bottle.

'You love it here, Divina?'

'I love very much.'

'Where do you come from?' I asked.

'Philippines. Not good place.'

I wondered what had happened to the Irish maid whom Desmond had seduced all those years ago. How long had the poor creature languished in the Magdalen home to which she was condemned, scrubbing linen, her back raw from blows from nuns? Desmond must be happy enough replacing her with this slim oriental mistress less than half his age.

I watched Divina feeding the birds who flew down from the surrounding trees, bullying cockatoos with puffed up yellow crests and glimpses of yellow feathers under their wings like hair under human armpits.

'You try. They not hurt you.'

'Sure?'

'Not move hand.'

A curved yellow beak helped itself to a nut. It would be worth losing a finger to gain such a beautiful girl as Divina.

Desmond went back in his hammock. After she poured him more champagne she settled down in his lap.

He began to talk. Heavens, how he talked. I suppose you could call it boasting. It took an hour for me to learn his life story and how he had made his money.

After Desmond left Ireland, he arrived in Broome in a cattle boat.

'Bloody storm – they threw the cattle overboard.' In due course the boat docked. 'Lines of empty bottles beside the harbour...Japanese diving for pearls.' He had wandered around western Australia looking for work. Jobs had not been easy to obtain in those days.

'Choice between going to a gold mine or an asbestos mine. Lucky I chose the right one.'

Divina brought him another drink. Desmond was back on beer. A warm breeze rustled the trees and the yacht bobbed up and down on the water. Divina climbed into his lap again.

'Now listen carefully,' he said, swinging her back and forwards on the hammock, 'The first thing you must know about Australia is that there are no free lunches or other handouts. It's up to you to survive whatever way you can. Isn't that right, Divina?'

'Is right.'

'And the next thing, every Australian is a born gambler. That's how I made my money.'

He talked about the partner he had worked with, who was descended from a convict who had stolen a loaf of bread.

'They all did that. Every convict ever transported to Oz was guilty of stealing a loaf or maybe even two.'

He mentioned the two aboriginals he had worked with, Midnight and Five to Twelve.

What was his job?

He had supplied much of New South Wales with one armed bandits.

'...Pokies...Choice between them or opening some brothels. I found machines easier to manage than women...'

'...The country is filled with miserable sods who leave their wives and kids starving while they waste their salaries pulling down the lever to try and get the one two three. The government makes no effort to put a stop to it; half its income is derived from pokies. So I felt it was O.K. to fall in with the business. Called my firm Fun-n-Games. Still makes me money.'

'Do you ever play er...pokies yourself?'

'God, no. Leave that to the fools.'

Night was falling when he squeezed Divina's bosom. 'Hey, sweetheart, – go off and get us some grub.'

Divina shifted off his lap and went off to the kitchen to prepare tiger prawns with chilli and a big salad.

'You can stay here,' Desmond said.

'Are you sure?'

'No worries.'

So I spent several weeks in great comfort, lazing away the days, bathing, and sailing the catamaran, filled with lovely young girls, over to the Hawksbury river. Desmond was rather too old to pull ropes and heave up the anchor, so he liked to employ the odd muscular young fellow like myself to crew for him. He was not easy to work for, and I grew used to the fact that as soon as he stepped on board he changed from cheerful old bore into Captain Bligh. But I enjoyed eating sumptuous meals supplied by Divina and attending the frequent parties my cousin gave, where he invited a good many more bosomy young women.

None of Desmond's female friends were half as beautiful as Divina.

11

I discovered that Desmond might not bet on pokies, but he liked horse racing. He told me that he had a plan to put me on the road to financial success.

The name of the horse was Shining Angel and she had never lost a race. He thought I might like to place a bet on her.

'If you are certain?'

'I'm not some bloody oracle.'

I had hardly spent any of Uncle Jack's money. I changed it into crisp Australian notes.

'Is that all he gave you...mean old bollocks?'

If the horse won, the winnings would be enough to enable me to live in Australia for over for a year.

The race meeting was some miles from Sydney out in the bush. A band was playing and a crowd of bookies roared their heads off. It was only when I reached the racecourse that I realised that the animal on which I had placed all my money actually belonged to Desmond.

'She's a great little runner and the conditions are as good as you could expect.'

In the owner's enclosure we met Shining Angel and her shrivelled jockey who was wearing bright green.

'Emerald green for the emerald isle.'

Desmond handed me the ticket he had obtained from a designated bookie. 'The best I could get was seven to one – a bloody bargain.'

With Divina beside him, her hand keeping in place her big hat adorned with artificial flowers, my cousin paraded his horse. My heart was pounding, but it was too late to change my mind.

Soon the band ceased playing and all I could hear was the roar from other punters as they strained to watch the race. I stuffed the bookmaker's ticket into my pocket; at those odds I would not be short of money again for a long time.

'How's she doing?'

'Not bad.'

Desmond's voice was strained as he peered through his binoculars.

'Come on! Come on, you bitch!'

Punters were jumping up and down waving their racing cards and I could make out the colours of our jockey just in front.

'We've won! By a whisker!'

A whisker was as good as a mile and my relief was enormous. I watched the little jockey in his green shirt joyfully vault from his saddle.

There was a cackle from the loudspeaker. 'Photo finish!'

'Bugger that!'

Seconds turned into minutes and I was watching a black insect crawl across my cousin's hairy red nose.

The loudspeaker crackled again. I could not understand the voice that boomed from it.

'Shining Angel lost. Beggars Bush won! Bloody outsider!'

'Are you sure?'

'Of course I'm bloody sure. A bit of bad luck. It could happen to a bishop!'

It was the expression Uncle Jack used when something had gone very wrong. All my money.

Desmond said: 'It's time you looked for a job.'

Next day he threw me out of his house.

'See ya later.'

I managed to borrow a few pounds from Divina and found a scruffy room in Dee Why rented to me and other unfortunates by a jovial Chinese lady. We offered a prize to whoever trampled the most cockroaches during the week – corpses were gathered in a plastic bag. I won twice.

My first job with a building contractor lasted less than a week; he sacked me when I dropped a tin of nails on his head.

My next was with a shop that sold hardware; goods had to be removed from crates brought in from Europe by cargo ships. The problem was that after a series of crates was emptied of plastic boxes, waste-paper bins, and such like, and carefully laid out along designated shelves, there was a long wait for the next load. We had to look busy, so there would be a period of emptying the stuff back off the shelves and into their crates and then back again.

Boredom drove me to become Santa Claus in a shop in the Corso at Manly. Christmas was approaching; it was warm work, particularly as there was a heat wave and Santa's costume and beard were not cool.

This all seemed to be far from my initial dreams of galloping behind cattle at some great ranch in Queensland the size of County Cork. I thought that after Christmas I would go north and look for work as a jackaroo.

It was almost a relief to receive a telephone call from my uncle's doctor back in County Louth.

The telephone was a public one in the hallway; upstairs someone was playing thumping music, Bruce Springsteen at his loudest, so that it was difficult to understand the long distance voice.

'The Colonel is in hospital,' roared Dr O'Shea from his consulting room in Drogheda.

'Anything wrong?'

'The usual.'

'Heart attack?'

'I'm afraid so.'

Nothing could be taken for granted, since on each occasion Uncle Jack went to hospital he came up with a range of symptoms that suggested he was very ill. Every time, just when it seemed the old boy might expire, within a day or two he would be back on his feet annoying everyone.

'He wants to get the best he can out of Voluntary Health Insurance,' I said.

'No, David, this time he is really ill. You had better come home.'

At the shop in Manly I got rid of the Father Christmas outfit with relief, since the temperature had risen to ninety-five degrees Fahrenheit. I bounced the last child off my knees – he was dressed in shorts – and told the last lies of the season. The shop where I had sweated and worked was sympathetic and sad when I told them that back in Ireland my uncle was dying. The people in the toy department did a whip around towards my airfare. I borrowed the rest of the money from Cousin Desmond whose reluctance to lend it to me I took to be an inherited family trait. He only handed it over on Divina's insistence and my sincere promise of repayment – was I not going to inherit something substantial? I had waited long enough.

CHAPTER TWO

I arrived back in Ireland in a blizzard. Mount Jewel was a palace of ice, the only warm place being the kitchen where Cook and the maids basked before the Aga drinking mugs of tea. They wore gumboots because of the damp of the kitchen floor. They picked them out from the box under the hatstand in the vestibule. The last time I counted, that box contained thirty-eight pairs.

The top floor of the vast house consisted of attics and a barrack room stretching the length of the facade, where eighteenth century squireens assembled before partaking in hunting and dancing and duelling and who knew? perhaps some discreet copulation.

On the floor below were countless bedrooms. I wandered around passing those which were locked after the person who regularly slept in them had died. Mostly men, mostly soldiers. An admiral who had fought with Nelson. One bedroom had belonged to my grandfather, another to my great-grandfather, others to officers who had fought with Wellington, or helped to lose the American War of Independence.

If you opened one of these rooms (the keys had been lost for years) you would find the uniform of the occupant who once slept here laid out on the double bed.

In the east bedroom the uniform included a hat with white ostrich feathers which an ancestor wore when governing some part of India, before he came home and died peacefully in Mount Jewel. Elsewhere in other bedrooms were feathered hats and white topis, generals' hats, and admirals' hats, worn by relatives who had spent much of their adult lives saluting parading soldiers or sailors massed on decks of battleships. All those hats would have been brushed spotlessly clean at the time their owners had died, but they must have gathered dust since then.

When Uncle Jack died one of my tasks would be to arrange his bedroom and then to close and lock it. His uniform with his medals pinned on it, would have been cleaned and ironed before being laid out on his bed. He would be one more ghost to wander around. Mount Jewel was lepping with them. They made the dogs bark, the two arthritic Labradors, Edward and Albert.

I came down into the hall past the stuffed lion and the tiger skin. In the study I gazed at the massive roll top desk where every month I used to watch Uncle Jack open the brown envelopes with details of dividends from numerous family securities. They were tidied away in drawers kept firmly locked.

Uncle Jack did not employ stockbrokers.

'Gamblers. All of them.'

He followed his money with the help of his dowser, which was a little medal on the end of a piece of black string. He would hold this diviner over a portrait of the director of Guinness or an article about General Electric and wave it gently.

'Are you paying a good dividend this year?' He claimed that the system worked as well as any portfolio devised by any stockbroker.

Once again, I found I was obsessed with what should be my birthright. I might be next in line to inherit the estate and I had waited long enough for this scrap of Irish earth which would belong to me. But would it? How much would Uncle Jack leave me, if anything? It had never been a question for discussion and I had never been encouraged to ask inappropriate questions. He might have willed his estate to the local hunt or the British Legion or Guide Dogs for the Blind or Save the Orangutans.

I was not even sure if I wanted to inherit Mount Jewel. I thought of Sydney and kept wondering if and when I would return.

It would be wonderful to be back in Australia, which was a genial place of warmth, instead of this cold house where rain was coming through the holes in the roof. If Uncle Jack were to die, which seemed likely, I might sell it straight away before departing for the Antipodes.

I rang the hospital in Dublin.

'You can come over after eleven o'clock but I'm afraid he won't recognise you.'

'There's no hope?'

'Very little. The worst could happen at any time.'

Good news.

I took Uncle Jack's Rover and drove up to Dublin. I walked through the front door of the hospital where people were not supposed to linger in case ambulances arrived shrieking with the sick. There was a huge crucifix in the hallway and maybe the grisly hallmark of Christianity offered comfort to some patients.

I had never seen a dead man or a dying one either except in films. What should I say to Uncle Jack if he recognised me? Should I hold his hand?

He was in a private ward. The green blind was drawn so that the only light from the windows had a ghostly quality. Beside the bed a machine monitored his condition, purring away, a wavering blue line indicating his heartbeats.

The young nurse who was sitting beside him wore a uniform with stiff collar and belt and puffed sleeves. In a few years time such gear would be replaced by trousers – frilly blouses would go with the advent of keyhole surgery.

The nurse took his pulse and consulted the watch upside down on her bosom.

'He's very peaceful,' she said loudly.

She probably said that phrase a lot. I assumed that was a euphemism for he's dying. I approached the bed. The poor old man was little more than a dried up husk. His skin was pallid, his face shrunken, his sparkling blue eyes shut. He was a gonner.

After I returned to Mount Jewel, I decided I had better start on the duties associated with my uncle's pending demise. I called in on A.P. Crowley, Merchants and Undertakers, a firm situated in a quiet back street of Mauricetown. Crowley had a garage for the hearse; wreaths were supplied and music played softly in the funeral parlour. He buried the local Protestant dead, and always had our trade. He disposed of my nanny who stepped under a bus during one of her infrequent days off. He buried the butler who shot himself. After that Uncle Jack only had female indoor staff.

He was small and squat and wore a dark suit and a coat with a black velvet collar.

I gave directions. 'Plain... wooden – simple brass handles.'

'I have it almost made,' Crowley said. 'Colonel Hilton ordered it after the bad storm. We chopped a big piece from one of the oaks that fell that time. I have it waiting. An hour or two will have it ready. Brass tablet. His name. Decorations.'

'That's all right, then.'

'We will miss him, Sir. He was a gentleman we could all respect.' I could hear the deferential whine in his voice.

But it seemed that Crowley and I acted precipitously. Things were not as they seemed when I rang the hospital next day. Uncle Jack had done yet another of his turnarounds.

'Colonel Hilton is fully conscious.' The matron's voice was chirpy.

I thought of Lazarus. 'I'll come up.'

'It's a miracle,' gushed the matron, who was big and blowsy in a stiff blue uniform.

If God was working miracles, why start on Uncle Jack?

'The doctors are astonished at the change in his condition. He is asking for his favourite brand of whiskey. Bushmills.'

My uncle was sitting up in that iron bed. There was colour in those lined cheeks that had been so pallid when I had seen him. They had taken away the ticking apparatus that had monitored his heartbeat.

'What are you doing here? You're supposed to be in Australia.'

'Dr O'Shea rang me.'

'All the way to Sydney? I hope he didn't ring you at my expense.'

'He said you weren't all that well.'

'I'm perfectly all right.'

The nurse who last week had taken his pulse and declared him peaceful, came in waving a thermometer.

'You had better leave your uncle now,' she smiled at me. 'Jack needs plenty of rest.'

My uncle growled, 'Call me Jack again and I'll get you sacked.'

'I'm very sorry, Colonel Hilton.'

He turned from her and stared at me with hooded blue eyes.

'How did you pay for your ticket back to Ireland?'

'I borrowed the fare from Cousin Desmond.'

'Rich, is he?'

'He seems to have had a successful business.'

'Doing what?'

'He's retired now. He used to supply the New South Wales government with gambling machines.'

'No different from being a stockbroker. Up to you to pay him back.'

I was told by the matron that my uncle had not fully recovered, and the doctors I spoke to were gloomy when it came to discussing what was wrong with him. Over the past decade he had suffered plenty of medical problems. There was something wrong with his bowel movements and he peed too often. I had once glimpsed his hernia which emerged from his navel like a rugby ball. I thought of it as in the film *Alien*. His blood pressure was high, his heart needed monitoring, he could easily have a stroke. He had a pacemaker the size of an alarm clock. Plenty of other things wrong – cataracts, hearing difficulties, aching joints, and a useless male organ.

'All part of life's rich tapestry,' he used to say whenever something new came up. He would talk about Churchill who, when he was eighty, had coronary thrombosis, a hernia, two strokes, three attacks of pneumonia and a condition known as senile itch. Like Uncle Jack Churchill smoked cigars – a quarter of a million over a lifetime.

'And he managed to live until he was ninety.'

'They make it as difficult as they can in this bloody place.' He waved his poor old bruised arm with its identification strip attached to his wrist, '...giving me a mass of pills – one is as big as a brick...all those doctors peering at you, thinking they know what's wrong. Black, khaki, every sort of wog. You'd think it was the United Nations.'

I had met numerous physicians as they swept into the ward. The chief doctor was Irish, known as Mister, too important to have the title doctor. Mister came in like a comet, and his cohorts, Arabs and Indians, trailed behind the tail.

Uncle Jack grumbled 'You saw the one supposed to look after me? Not the white man, of course.'

'Dr Patel?'

'Black as my hat. Not a word of English.'

'He speaks English perfectly well.'

'I need an interpreter. Notice his tribal scars?'

'He hasn't got tribal scars. He's Indian.'

'Back where he comes from he'd eat you.'

Uncle Jack was given his lunch, pale food under a tin cover.

'Garbage. They do their best to kill you. Every stiff they can produce means they get an allowance from the Department of Health.'

He nibbled at a snowy mound of mashed potato. 'Local padre came in last night.'

'Kind of him.'

'No it wasn't. Last thing I want is prayers said over my bed. Very

21

last, more than likely. I bet he was in here the day when I wasn't well. Can't even let you die in peace.'

They kept him in hospital ten days longer.

Back at Mount Jewel I wandered around the frosty fields of this part of County Louth which had been familiar to me since childhood. The estate had a wall which surrounded over a thousand acres.

Accompanied by the old Labradors I walked past the famine pot which Aunt Maud used to fill with pelargoniums and past the empty greenhouses where she had grown tomatoes during the war when Uncle Jack was away fighting – she had run the place far better than he ever did.

I went down to the front field and the cricket pitch, now grazed by sheep. Uncle Jack had kept a cricket team going among his men until the game had slowly died out in all the surrounding villages and there was no one left for the Mount Jewel eleven to play with. As far as I was concerned anything to do with cricket was watching paint dry. I could never understand any enthusiasm for the game – such as the hysteria shown by Australians.

I shivered with cold and began thinking what a pity it was that I had listened to Dr O'Shea and come back from Sydney. I needn't have bothered. I might have known that Uncle Jack would resurrect himself once again. This was the third time he had been in hospital on the verge of dying and had miraculously sat up and prepared to come home.

The dogs and I wandered down to the lakes. The larger lake had originated during the famine as a form of relief. The smaller was a similar artificial creation dating back to the beginning of the nineteenth century after an ancestor had been deported to Australia for abducting an heiress. When this villain, who managed to hang on to his money, acquired an estate in Sydney, he wrote back to Mount Jewel for some Irish earth blessed by St Patrick. He needed it to surround his house in order to keep out snakes. His relations obliged; here at Mount Jewel the earth was dug up near the river and the hole it created filled with water.

That had been the Hilton family's first encounter with Australia.

The bank of the smaller lake was spread with gunnera, brown and miserable in winter. I kept an eye out for the vicious swan – there was always an angry swan there. The current one could hardly be the same as the bird that had heaved itself out on the bank and chased me when I was eight years old. How long do swans live?

I trudged past the yew trees, the avenue of limes and the second oldest oak tree in Ireland. Uncle Jack had once made an expedition to see the famous oak King of Charleville – 'smaller than ours'. Past the wood with other oaks and hollies and a few sycamores where you could occasionally spot a red squirrel.

Past the dog's cemetery which was pretty full. Here was the inscription Aunt Maud had stolen from the Duke of Ormonde's dogs' cemetery in memory of a favourite Pekinese.

There are men both good and wise

Who hold that in a future state

Dumb creatures we have cherished here below

Shall give us joyous greetings

When we pass the silver gate.

Oh how earnestly I pray it may be so!

Edward and Albert who bounded ponderously before me would eventually lie there, and would be provided with headstones. Maybe a verse of poetry.

Between two Wellingtonias was the battered dower house. My father had been Uncle Jack's younger brother and my parents and I had lived there. A lot of the roof was off now, and there was nothing inside it but the disintegrating shell of the grand piano. One of the few memories I had of my mother was of her sitting in a long skirt and playing – Greig. Tum…tum tum…tum tum…I inherited none of her musical ability – Uncle Jack, Aunt Maud and I all had cloth ears. The piano with its nesting rats and mice had stayed in the empty tumbledown drawing room after the rest of the furniture was removed.

My parents died in a balloon crash – they were flying from the Nile towards Abu Simnel. This was bad luck, since going up in a balloon is considered one of the safest forms of air travel.

'Bloody fools,' raged Uncle Jack, 'going up together.'

Since my father turned out to be insolvent, no one ever knew how he had afforded that Egyptian holiday.

After those unfortunate deaths there appeared to be no one else to take me on except for Uncle Jack, Aunt Maud and a succession of nannies and governesses.

Later Aunt Maud and her Pekineses fled Mount Jewel. She was tired of the rows she had with Uncle Jack that echoed through big rooms.

The last straw had been my uncle's affair with Lady someone who rode side-saddle at the Meath hunt. He was a careful man, who always drafted his letters; unfortunately the draft of a love letter to this Lady someone which he squashed and tossed into a waste-paper basket was retrieved by my aunt.

A considerable part of my uncle's income still kept Aunt Maud in comfort in the south of Spain.

Over the years nannies and governesses tailed off, and then there were just the two of us, Uncle Jack and myself. That was my bad luck, since my uncle was a tyrant. Even before Aunt Maud's departure he had treated me badly. I remember the terror I had felt overhearing him say, 'He'll have to be put down'. I did not realise that he was referring to a dog.

There was scarcely a corner of the house where I hadn't stood facing some piece of peeling plaster for what he considered a piece of bad behaviour. Or, after a really disgraceful misdemeanour he would have me standing to attention for several hours in the hall under the Zulu spears. I much preferred the odd beating with a stair rod. When I went to school I was the only one of the boys in my class who dreaded the holidays.

Uphill to the twelve-acre field. The estate was run on what would now be considered organic methods. Patsy Massey, the steward, wearing his waistcoat and gold watch, supervised most of it.

Occasionally my uncle would sack someone. Did Marty Sullivan have to go because he bore a perceived resemblance to Gerry Adams? In the house Josie had been threatened with dismissal after she inadvertently revealed her passion for Bono. When Uncle Jack saw Bono on television he attacked the screen with his blackthorn stick.

Farm hands looked after the cattle and the horses, and counted the sheep. Their numbers had come down since the old days; in the 1920s twenty people had been employed on the farm, ten as gardeners, and there had been numerous servants in the house.

Now we were down to the three indoor female servants and half a dozen men outside the house. Among them, most importantly, was Massey, principally because he looked after the horses. Massey had been at Mount Jewel for many years, almost as long as Manzie Roycroft who was in charge of the poultry. I used to watch Manzie tying half a dozen of birds in a row on a string and beheading them; they flapped for fifteen minutes.

As a boy I was ordered by my uncle to collect eggs, a task that terrified me. Every morning I lifted up the hen's backsides with a shovel.

In Aunt Maud's time there were white peacocks to wake us at dawn on summer mornings – she gave them names of Greek gods like Hebe or Artemis. They were loathed by those living near the estate; either they kept people awake with their cries or they brought bad luck. After she departed all those great white birds disappeared, and it was assumed that the bad luck went with them. Manzie was suspected of eating them, but nothing was proved.

Manzie was also in charge of the walled garden. He grew a lot of cabbage. He told me convincingly that I had been found in the cabbage patch as a baby; much later I learned that I had emerged into the world in a nursing home in Hatch Street. Manzie grew high trellises of beans. 'You needn't grow peas,' decreed my uncle. 'Frozen are good enough.' So no peas for the wicked.

'We won't bother with flowers,' Uncle Jack said after Aunt Maud left. There were only the snowdrops, whose bulbs had been brought back from the Tchernaya valley by an ancestor who had fought there in the Crimean war. Plus the daffodils and narcissi in the fields falling down to the lake; the azaleas and rhododendrons, lilac, the little red tulips that shot up in May under the avenue of crab apple trees and all the stubborn dahlias and pushy Japanese anemones. And old roses like the Boule de Neige and a rambling cerise Souvenir de la Bataille de Marengo. Aunt Maud used to say their names with relish.

Back at the house I was served a sumptuous dinner by Josie and relaxed afterwards in the study before a large fire. Life at Mount Jewel was so enjoyable without Uncle Jack.

Alas, my uncle's health continued to improve, and the doctors got to the state of admitting there was no further reason for him to stay in hospital. He'd be home with a nurse who had been hired to take care of him.

It was my task to inform the men he was returning and would be resuming his military-style inspections. Their good humour vanished in an instant.

Once again the potholes in the avenue were filled up with gravel. The maids washed their uniforms and the dogs were shampooed.

CHAPTER THREE

'You know I like bacon crisp, not floating in a pool of grease.'
It was seven in the morning. My uncle was in his four-poster
bed, the dogs lying on the floor beside him. He pointed accusingly at
the tray which Josie had brought in after climbing up two flights of
stairs from the basement kitchen. She would have to come up again
with the coffee. She was very fit.

He dabbed at Cook's home-made marmalade. 'Toast is burnt.'

I was standing and watching. 'No it's not, Uncle Jack.'

'Is it too much to ask Cook to prepare a simple breakfast? I've a
good mind to give her the sack.'

Nothing had changed. He never fulfilled his threat about Cook,
knowing she could never be replaced.

But this was not the case with Nurse Cummins, who had been
provided by Dr O'Shea to look after him when he emerged from
hospital. Dr O'Shea never learned.

Uncle Jack persisted: 'Don't let that creature near me. I can't stand
her washing me or taking my temperature.'

Nurse Cummins performed her duties in exemplary fashion, giving
my uncle his pills, enough to fill a coffee cup each morning. Amiable
and middle aged, she did not object to emptying his chamber-pots, all
of which had floral decorations. They were numerous because of the
distance between his bedroom and the one bathroom on the first floor.

She dabbed herself with eau de cologne, but that did not justify

Uncle Jack considering her to be the scarlet woman.

'She wears lipstick. You just have to look at her.'

'Only a trace...'

'What do you know about women?'

He was twisting around in his bed, upsetting his tea which was in a cup almost as large as one of the chamber-pots.

Less than a week later a furious Nurse Cummins had departed. I was still wondering what had stopped her taking up Uncle Jack's pillow and ramming it down on his head. At least she managed to get a month's wages out of him.

She had been in attendance just long enough. By the time she left Uncle Jack was able to fend for himself. Every morning he was up and about, dressed in his Harris tweeds, hobbling around the big house with the aid of his blackthorn stick followed by his two decrepit dogs. Smoking a cigar, he would go up and down the divided stairs, across the big rooms to his study, and outside for the steady walk to the stables to consult Massey, the Labradors persisting in following his slow progress.

These dogs were preferable to past animals – Swift, the Borzoi that lay before the fire and guarded it so that anyone who sought warmth risked his great teeth in your leg. The mongrel, Rascal, usually had feathers in its teeth from the hens it had killed. Barney, the Alsatian, bit everyone until he went blind and could be more easily avoided. Bonzo, the Jack Russell ate four twenty-punt notes and a passport. All my uncle's darlings.

Maids at Mount Jewel had to be more highly paid than others in houses elsewhere if they were to stay; they soon got the knack of avoiding bad-tempered canines.

Always among the dogs there would be a gentle Labrador or two like the current Edward and Albert, good natured and glum. Very likely these would be the last lot of dogs that Uncle Jack would have.

Once again my uncle was annoying staff inside and out – why didn't others follow the example of Nurse Cummins? But Cook and

Josie and Bridget, were fond of him, even if they had been happier when he was away in hospital. They had been at Mount Jewel for years; Cook had come when Uncle Jack and Aunt Maud first married. The outside staff were loyal – he knew enough to pay them very well. So he strutted around the house and estate complaining, causing arguments, grumbling about the treatment of horses and animals, about his meals, and about Dr O'Shea who called in once or twice.

'Not more bloody pills, O'Shea.'

'We don't want you back in hospital. And take my advice, Colonel, and lay off the drink.'

My uncle lied, 'I only have a couple of shots of whiskey every evening'.

'And the cigars. It's a great pity you didn't follow David's example at Ballinrobe, and stop smoking altogether.'

Three years ago I had accompanied my uncle and Dr O'Shea to Lough Mask during the mayfly season. I was no fisherman, but since Uncle Jack was too mean to hire a ghillie, I was taken along to row the boat while they chased the trout. We ate nothing else, and any surplus fish Uncle Jack caught was wrapped in grass and sent up to Mount Jewel for future meals. Not fresh.

That first evening at Lough Mask, after supper – fried trout – when I lit up a Sweet Afton, Dr O'Shea gave me a lecture on the evils and perils of smoking.

'I'll try and give up one of these days.' I drew on the cigarette I could ill afford.

Dr O'Shea said: 'Look here, David, if you don't smoke all this week I'll give you as much drink as you like.'

I took him on, and for the next six days I indulged myself in as much alcohol as the good doctor would provide in the one pub in Ballinrobe that he and my uncle visited. Uncle Jack sat watching me, biting off the end of his cigar, while I drank glass after glass of Bushmills.

By the end of the week I was badly hung-over, but I never wanted a cigarette again. Or a Bushmills.

Dr O'Shea earned my untiring gratitude, particularly as I knew that he was as mean as my uncle.

Before we left Ballinrobe he presented me with a large limestone-riven boulder from the shores of Lough Mask.

'If you ever want a cigarette again, David, you pick that up and walk back from Louth to Mayo.'

In Sydney I had been regarded as a phenomenon – the Mick who didn't smoke.

But Dr O'Shea was never able to persuade Uncle Jack to follow the same course with regard to cigars. Cubans were the ones my uncle liked, Monte Cristo, La Gloria Cubana, Bolivar, Romeo y Julieta and the rest.

'The way you smoke you'll soon be puffing your last,' Dr O'Shea often told him. Just as often my uncle ignored him.

'Churchill smoked all the time. He was older than me before he pegged out.'

I received a letter from Crowley about the coffin. It used the phrasing 'unfortunately business is business' and ended 'I would be grateful if you could settle up when convenient.'

When I called into the undertakers in Mauricetown, Crowley told me in a soft muted tone about the small difficulty. After taking my order, the coffin had been finished with its special accoutrements and was waiting to be collected.

'We don't need it,' I protested.

Crowley gave the special smile that indicated sympathy for the bereaved and emphasised the good qualities of the departed. Especially departed gentry. He was on the verge of rubbing his hands together.

'I am sure our differences can be easily settled, Mr Hilton.'

We toured the workshop, passing cheap elm coffins that did not as yet merit a lid. They were rubbish compared to the beauty at the back, the single large body container hewn from the great oak tree.

'Now, look at this, Mr Hilton.'

It was a masterpiece. I could recognise its superior quality.

He stroked his work of art and smiled to himself. Uncle Jack was over six feet tall and there would be no problem fitting him in with room to spare.

We eventually agreed on delivery and sending the bill to Colonel Hilton.

Crowley's coffin arrived at Mount Jewel with the hefty bill. Uncle Jack complained bitterly, and gave me hell.

'You can pay for this.'

'I haven't the money.'

He had three of the men on the estate heave, first the coffin, then the huge lid, up the stairs to his bedroom. Over the following weeks he filled it slowly with shirts and socks and unpaid bills.

He had taken to Crowley's work of art.

After the clocks went forward Uncle Jack started to behave more oddly than usual.

At first I did not notice. Much of the time I was dreaming of summer in Australia, the ice-blue plumbago and agapanthus, Divina's lorikeet cheeping Top of the Morning – and the heat. Most of all I missed the heat and instead I had to endure the perpetual drizzle in County Louth, day after day.

At Mount Jewel spring was in the air as I half listened when my uncle told Massey of his daft plans of improving his model farm. Every worker would be given his own schedule which he would have to adhere to. Any shortcoming would entail a fine. A series of microphones would be installed along the fences in the fields through which he would relay orders.

He was also considering a new milking parlour with music which would make the the cows happy and produce higher yields.

'Jazz, not classical. When we get going you'll find them twitching their tails in time to the music.'

At the same time he cancelled the free milk bonus that the workers on the estate had obtained for years. That alone, should have given an indication that something was badly wrong with him.

'Mr Hilton, what's going on?' Massey appealed to me.

'I don't know.'

It was taking time for me – or Massey for that matter – to come to the conclusion that Uncle Jack was nuts.

I was walking across the lower fields when I was disturbed by the sound of cattle moving along the road outside the wall. It looked like all of the estate's herd of little black Kerry cows was trotting past, followed by our horses. I ran to the nearest gate which was open. Uncle Jack was standing there, his walking stick in his left hand, wiggling his right hand back and forth in the direction of the wandering beasts. (This was the way he encouraged animals to cross the road when he was brought up short in the driving seat of the Rover.)

'I have come to the conclusion that the best thing we can do is liberate our livestock.'

'But ...'

'They are on their way to Africa. They will be a lot better off there eating plenty of good grass and enjoying bountiful nature.'

It needed a day for the men to round up the animals. Meanwhile my uncle was persuaded by Dr O'Shea to take a good rest.

'Give him plenty of fresh air. You will be surprised how such a simple remedy often works. And salad.'

I had to escort Sergeant Brady, puffing and panting from climbing the stairs, into Uncle Jack's bedroom where he sitting up in bed wearing an ancient silk dressing gown and a scarf to keep out the cold.

'We can't have cattle and horses wandering loose along our roads, Colonel.'

Uncle Jack was studying an atlas. 'I am worried about the lions around Lake Rudolf...Put that thing over there, will you, Sergeant?'

The summons which Sergeant Brady carried, was placed in Crowley's coffin.

Hazel, the rector of the church down the road from our estate, called to Mount Jewel. She was full of good spirits and enquiries as to why we did not attend her services. She may have heard from the Bishop that before her appointment Uncle Jack had never once missed Sunday matins in the past forty years. As yet she had no idea that she was not beloved by him. From the first moment he heard of her appointment, the idea of being ministered to by a woman filled him with horror and rage.

Catholics may have failed to grasp the nettle and introduce women priests to their congregations, but the Protestant Church of Ireland had plunged ahead to the dismay of people like Uncle Jack. From the start, from the moment it had decided to introduce women into its sinking little concern, – years ahead of the Church of England – things had improved. This was because the instant they were given free rein, the Church began to be run by pushy ladies like Hazel. All over Ireland this new lot of bossy clergy persons was taking charge.

Since she had come to Mauricetown, Hazel had managed to attract a proper congregation. In the old days the previous rector, old Lambert, had difficulty in rounding a mere two or three gathered together to listen to his tedious sermons. They usually consisted of Uncle Jack and myself, in addition to one or two old women. But these days several dozen gathered to listen to Hazel's chirpy declarations about the advantages of Christianity.

Lambert's Sunday congregation could have been worse. For example, it was larger than than Cousin Nicholas services over in Leitrim. For many years in that far boggy place Cousin Nicholas had conducted services by himself. Every Sunday in his lonesome parish, he had gone through the ritual of morning service without one member of any congregation taking part.

Lambert had done only a little better than Cousin Nicholas. He recognised the fact and even suggested to the Bishop that St Michael's in Mauricetown should be dismantled. The building could perhaps be sold to the developer who had ideas of disposing of the pinewood pews where generations of our family had prayed amid the marble and brass monuments and turning the shell into a dance hall, a ballroom of romance.

Hazel had arrived in the parish just in time, full of good cheer. Instantly she won over hearts and minds, tracked down every Protestant in the district, persuaded them to come to church and saved St Michael's from destruction.

But Uncle Jack was not going to give her any credit.

'All my life I have been a supporter of the church and attended the Synod. And how have I been rewarded? This hag has been foistered upon St Michael's by that bloody Robert who must have become alcoholic when he came to that decision.'

Robert was the Bishop, who regularly turned up at Mount Jewel wearing his purple shirt. He was a big brawny man, well known for playing international rugby in his younger days. He had known Uncle Jack for decades.

'She's charming, Jack,'

'No woman in charge of a Church of Ireland parish can be considered charming.'

'My good fellow, some older parishioners like yourself might find this development difficult to accept. But it's God's will that we must go forward slowly step by step.'

'I've a good mind to become a Roman Catholic.'

Uncle Jack peered through the drawing-room window at the neat little figure climbing out out of a Morris Minor. Hazel wore a clerical collar, white and bright as her smile.

'Tell her I'm out!'

Too late. She knocked and the dogs barked.

'Cooee!' she called like people in Australia. Josie opened the heavy door and allowed her into the main hall.

'The house must be so difficult to heat,' she cried in the high voice that carried her sensible sermons to everyone of her listening congregation. Josie showed her into the drawing room where my uncle was trapped. He treated her with a politeness that gave away nothing.

Josie brought in scones and sponge cake and tea in the Crown

Derby cups spattered with pink roses.

Hazel drank with her little finger raised as Uncle Jack's frown deepened. She had a twinkle in her eye as she talked with relentless good cheer about parish matters and discussion groups and whether Uncle Jack might like to rejoin the vestry.

'I understand, Colonel Hilton, that you were a member when Mr Lambert was rector.'

Could she not interpret the fearsome glare on my uncle's face? Not at all. She continued chatting. She told him she did not like fox hunting or other blood sports. She mentioned that in her services she used a new version of the Bible – the King James, she considered was a wee bit old fashioned.

'I find my people, especially the young ones, prefer the New Living Bible.'

She was considering asking the Bishop if the gravestones in the cemetery could be flattened so that the lawn mower could get around more easily. Twice she told Uncle Jack how much the congregation had risen in number – it had tripled since the departure of Maurice Lambert.

'On most Sundays I preach to between twenty and thirty people!'

Uncle Jack hissed.

She stayed on until sherry was due, but not offered, and then mentioned she wished to powder her nose. It was my job to direct her to the lavatory which she called the toilet.

After she left Uncle Jack said, 'I bet she smokes. And I wouldn't be surprised if she didn't play golf.'

Two days after Hazel's visit I went to the study at six o'clock in the evening and found my uncle was not there. This was very strange. Normally he would have retired in here at exactly six o'clock for his medicine. Bushmills with a jug of water would be laid out on a silver tray by Josie. It was a regular moment of happiness for him, sitting in his armchair, smoking the seventh or eighth cigar of his day. Every evening, even in summer, the fire was lit, reflecting in its warm glow the lines of books and the prints by Snaffles.

'Uncle Jack?' I called out.

On the rent table, half hidden by letters and newspapers I caught sight of a smiling photograph of Hazel on the front page of the *Church of Ireland Gazette*. It was circled in thick black ink.

I looked out of the window to see if the Rover was parked in the drive as it had been earlier in the day. There was no sign of it.

Just to be sure I went to the garage and borrowed the van Massey used to go around the estate – as usual Massey had left the keys in the lock.

As I drove I became distracted. I thought of how all over Ireland the Church of Ireland was divesting itself of its architectural heritage. Here, in Mauricetown, against all advice, the Church Body had disposed of the previous gracious Georgian building which had housed clergymen and their families for over two hundred years. Mullins, the contractor who had bought the old rectory, pulled it down immediately. In its place he erected semi-detached houses.

A monkey puzzle was the only reminder of the original church estate, since Mullins chopped down all the other old trees, including an apple orchard, to make room for as many houses as he could fit in – a couple more than he had been given permission for. The planning authorities never bothered to come and count.

Some way apart of these two lines of houses stood the bungalow which was the new rectory. Hazel and her husband, Raymond, a retired bank manager, had moved in six months ago after Lambert had departed.

I had guessed right. As I drove past the new estate I saw my uncle's battered Rover parked near the first of the houses. Its sides were covered with dents which Uncle Jack refused to get mended.

In the gathering darkness I noticed his bald domed head sticking out of a ditch beside the monkey puzzle.

I ran over. 'What are you doing?'

'Be quiet. I am trying to burn the place down.'

Beside him were pieces of the *Irish Times* torn into strips.

'Bloody damp paper. Luckily I had a can of paraffin.'

He pulled me down beside him; he was surprisingly strong.

'The woman has to go.'

I looked over at the bungalow and noticed flame coming out of one of the rooms. A man in his shirt sleeves ran towards the open window carrying a hose spewing water.

My uncle said: 'I'll have to try again another time.'

CHAPTER FOUR

'How did they know it was Uncle Jack?'

Dr O'Shea said, 'Raymond saw him. He was too busy putting out the fire to apprehend him. And you left his car behind.'

Of course. After I had driven Uncle Jack back to the house, I had to go down with Massey to retrieve it.

'Was a lot of harm done?'

'Most of Hazel's books were destroyed.'

I imagined her library – hymn books with petunia-coloured edges, bibles – modern versions – theological books, Bishop Robinson's *Honest to God*, most probably a bound set of Dickens' works, *The Course of Irish History* and the *Encyclopaedia Britannica*. All wrecked by smoke and water.

'Is she OK?' I couldn't get the image out of my mind of Hazel lying prone, burnt to a crisp.

'Most luckily she wasn't there – attending to a sick parishioner. Your uncle acted like a maniac. But he is extremely fortunate.'

'In what way?'

'Hazel is a forgiving Christian.'

'How do you mean?'

'Naturally Raymond is seriously considering bringing a charge against the Colonel, but I believe Hazel has managed to dissuade him.'

'That's all right, then.'

'No, it's not all right. I don't think you realise, David, that Colonel Hilton is a very sick man. From now on he has to have proper supervision.'

'What do you mean?

'He will have to go to a home.'

'Home?' I was horrified.

'As in nursing home. A place where he can be properly taken care of.'

A thought immediately struck me. 'Not that looney bin, surely, that looks like a castle?'

On the outskirts of Mauricetown was a monstrous Victorian building whose style seemed as crazy as its unfortunate inmates. This masterpiece of Gothic horror, which had room for hundreds, perhaps thousands of lunatics, was what came into my mind after O'Shea's declaration. Numerous terrible asylums exist here and there in Ireland, indicating that there must have have been a good many mad people in this fair green isle during the nineteenth century. I had read that more than forty lunatics a month were admitted to Mauricetown when times were hard.

'Oh no.' O'Shea spoke reassuringly. 'Not at all. '

For the next quarter of an hour he took pains to persuade me that castellated palace with the iron grills on its windows was for the great unwashed. Not for the likes of high class maniacs like my uncle who had money and connections.

'I have in mind a far more suitable place.'

'Where?'

'Silver Meadows is where I send many of my difficult patients. It is an institution where the Colonel will be properly looked after. I have already rung the proprietor, Mrs Freebody, and told her about his particular problems. She will see to it that he is made comfortable.'

'How soon?'

'In the next couple of days. And David, there is no reason for you to blame yourself.'

Uncle Jack sat in his study beside the fire wearing his army greatcoat and a woollen cap; a scarf was wrapped round his neck, a cigar was in his hand. The dogs sprawled at his feet.

On either side of the fire were bookshelves up to the ceiling; many of the books were about Africa. Once he had spent a year in Kenya killing animals. He had come across Isak Dinesen – 'damn fool Dane' and Hemingway – 'loathesome'. He had avoided the excesses of Happy Valley and returned to Ireland where he resumed killing birds. Then came the war and the opportunity to kill Germans.

One of the most prominent shelves contained a line of the only fiction that my uncle ever read – the works of P.G. Wodehouse. Every one of them, all first editions.

'Why don't you try *War and Peace*, for a change, Uncle Jack?' I once asked, but that did not go down well.

My own reading was also largely confined to Wodehouse, although piles of old copies of the *National Geographic* had been obtained by Aunt Maud to teach me geography. Somewhere in the bookshelves was the bible presented to an ancestor by Oliver Cromwell; no one had found it for years. The family did not often talk about the period of the past that was linked to Cromwell, preferring to dwell on the dubious story that the Hiltons were descended from John of Gaunt.

Nor did we like to talk about the fact that certainly was true – our money had originally came from beer. Trade! Worse than slavery. Uncle Jack's friend, Trigger, was proud to tell people that his wealth had come from O.K. sugar plantations in the Barbados, and that his family had brought half a dozen slaves back to Ireland – he was related to one of them.

Trigger could boast, but we Hiltons seldom mentioned the brewery which had made the Hilton fortune.

'Leave that to the Guinnesses!'

Above the fireplace the old seventeenth-century portrait of Bartholomew glowered down, his armour painted painstakingly. That was the ancestor who came to Ireland with Cromwell and did not behave well at Drogheda. In his hand he carried a paper which read NULLA DIES SINE LINEA. It was the only Latin I knew. NO DAY WITHOUT WORK.

Beside the Spanish leather screen a corner cupboard contained the hoof of Parfait, the horse bred by my great-grandfather that had won the

Ascot Gold Cup. There was also some Satsuma porcelain brought back from Tokyo by great-uncle Hubert who had acted as consul or suchlike.

Great-uncle Hubert had also indulged himself in a group of torture scenes carved in ivory, which took up a whole shelf below the Satsuma pieces. A little fellow was having his head cut off by a miniature executioner; another was losing his limbs which were being carved off while a third was getting a whipping; streaks of painted bloodstains appeared all over his little back. Other miniature men suffered worse; some of the things being inflicted on them in ivory were very gruesome. No one in a hundred years had suggested putting these horrible pieces of ivory away or even selling them – flogging them might be the right word.

On a very high shelf was a shrunken Jivarro head. No one knew where it came from.

'What have you been doing with yourself?' Uncle Jack took the cigar out of his mouth and barked as I came in.

'Looking at Melissa – she's still lame,' I shouted.

'What does Flanagan say?'

'He hasn't been to see her yet.' The vet always took his time.

'Blackguard.'

The conversation changed to corrupt politicians, the price of whiskey and the fact the country was going to the dogs.

Uncle Jack wore a hearing aid, flesh-coloured and shining with ear wax. Bought at great expense, it was relatively new, since he had driven over his last one.

'The deaf are demonised. It's a racket. Why can't they make bloody batteries easier to handle?'

I could only agree, whenever I watched him trying to replace them with trembling old fingers. He was doing that now. At least he never asked me to do it for him, and fiddle with that horrible sticky object.

He lit another cigar. 'Did I ever tell you about Mountbatten?'

'No,' I lied.

The unfortunate late Earl was a pet hate. Once again I listened to my uncle's Mountbatten stories – the plot to get his nephew onto the throne... flashing his chestful of decorations – KG GCB OM GCSI GCIE GCVO DSO PC – all that stuff about the Kelly an exaggeration – show off – never stopped irritating his junior officers...always made the best of his royal connections...'

I said, 'The poor old man hardly deserved to be blown up by the IRA.'

Uncle Jack twiddled his bony fingers. 'I don't know about that.'

Outside the study window we heard a car drive up. Dr O'Shea had arrived. The dogs began their barking – they recognised his BMW and hated the doctor almost as much as they hated the vet. Then the sound of another vehicle. I looked out and saw an ambulance.

Josie let in the doctor who came across to the study where the dogs continued to bark angrily at him. It was O'Shea's task – not mine – to use persuasion about going to a nursing home. I got up to leave them since I assumed the decision was out of my hands.

'Stay, David. You'd better hear this.' So I evicted the dogs and sat at the window looking out at the rain and the ambulance, half listening to the doctor's coaxing voice. '...don't misunderstand me. Jack...what you did was serious...rector...arson...a true Christian...you need a good rest...Silver Meadows...Mrs Freebody...no, Jack...I know it will suit you...'

Uncle Jack's replies were protesting and negative. The bushy eyebrows met in their customary frown.

Josie had packed his things by the time two men in blue uniforms carrying a stretcher arrived to more hysterical barking from the dogs.

'We have the orders to collect the Colonel.'

'Who are these people?' My uncle glared at the doctor who was fiddling with his briefcase. 'What the hell are you up to, O'Shea?'

Dr O'Shea came over, took the glowing cigar out of his fingers and threw it into the fire. In his other hand he was carrying a hypodermic needle which he jabbed into the old man. It was the final betrayal.

They lifted him up and placed him on the stretcher. They were solemn men. I thought of bears, creatures with no facial expressions, but capable of hugging you to death.

'Lie down there, Colonel, and be a good boy!'

In the hall the stuffed lion my Uncle had shot in Kenya looked on, together with all the people in the portraits. Cook, Josie and Bridget were gathered at the top of the stone stairs that led to the basement to watch my uncle's departure. His angry face stared up from under the red blanket they tucked under his chin.

'What are you doing? Get back to work.'

He was carried past them, over the flattened tiger. I followed miserably, carrying his suitcase. The dogs howled.

Outside, the outdoor staff had rushed up in mackintoshes and gumboots to see what was going on. It rained on the ambulance. Uncle Jack lifted his head from under the red blanket and the raindrops poured down on his bald head.

'Come here, O'Shea!'

But Dr O'Shea was scuttling towards his BMW.

'If he doesn't settle we'll give him another injection' called out one of the uniformed men in charge.

The ambulance set off down the avenue. The rain eased, the light began to fade, and the rooks came home and squabbled in the oak trees. Tenants who paid no rent, Uncle Jack called them when he shot at them with his Purdey.

Three weeks passed on Dr O'Shea's advice before I paid my first visit to Silver Meadows. It was on impulse that I took with me a Supervalu bag containing *Carry on Jeeves* and a box of cigars, together with matches.

My destination was twenty miles from Mount Jewel, on the other side of the county. I had to ring up and ask for directions to what was described as a 'rest home'; even so I had difficulty tracking it up a country road. Past a pub and a couple of crossroads I found a wall and pillars, one of which bore the inscription SILVER MEADOWS NURSING HOME on a highly polished brass plate.

Through the gates I drove up to a three-storey Victorian mansion covered with Virginia creeper. Fake battlements at its corners gave the impression that it was a mini-version of the castellated asylum outside Mauricetown. The house was surrounded by smooth black tarmac and some desultory flower beds filled with floribunda roses.

When necessary, the building could be lit up by an imposing line of florescent lights.

I walked up a flight of steps and waited nervously until a white-uniformed Filipina nurse unlocked the front door, greeted me, and locked the door behind me after I had stepped inside. She led me through the hall which was very hot. I was reminded of Manly in mid-December.

On the grey walls were reproductions of bland blue Paul Henry paintings, the clouds and mountains, found in most dentists' waiting rooms. A corner opposite the front door was crammed with crutches and zimmer frames. Another corner contained a telephone booth. A glass vase of artificial white roses stood on a side table beside a book and pen for recording comings and goings. A round clock with Roman numerals had a loud tick which seemed to me to indicate that people did not have long to stay here. It chimed while I waited; you're dying soon, you're dying soon.

Beside the clock sat an old lady in a wheelchair who did not answer when I said 'Good afternoon'. The nurse took no notice of her but escorted me into Mrs Freebody's office.

Mrs Freebody sat at her desk on which were numerous photographs of herself, short and plump, receiving handshakes and scrolls at public functions indicating her fame and success. Behind them were three photographs of old women, who, from the huge cakes set in front of them, appeared to be celebrating their one hundredth birthdays.

A little apart, on its own, was a portrait of a bald man carrying a golf club. On top of the bookshelf behind the desk was an urn. Both photograph and urn concerned Mrs Freebody's late husband. The urn contained his ashes.

She stood up, shook hands, and greeted me with a smile. I was to find out that she smiled most of the time unless things were going badly wrong. Her teeth were white and even, and I assumed wrongly, that like those of most of the inmates of Silver Meadows, they must be false. Her cropped hair was blonde; she must have helped it to stay that way. She wore a navy blue trouser suit, and butterfly spectacles. When she raised her eyebrows above these spectacles you could see they were plucked pencil thin. Her eyes were blue as turquoise. She had a faint fair moustache.

I sat down on the chair she indicated and waited as the nurse brought in Nescafe.

'David? The Colonel's nephew? He has told me all about you.'

Had he, indeed? I put my hand on the radiator beside me and snatched it away; it was red-hot.

'You have recently been in Australia?'

'I returned when my uncle became ill.'

'There seems to be nothing physically wrong with him.'

'I'm glad to hear it.'

'He is settling down very well, but it will take time to make him feel at home. We are all doing our best to see he is comfortable.' The slight emphasis on 'all' indicated that this was a hard task.

'He's probably missing Mount Jewel.'

'No doubt. But most of my patients settle down and enjoy staying in Silver Meadows. Let us hope this will be the case with Colonel Hilton.'

For five minutes or so we discussed Uncle Jack and his feelings. After I drank the bitter coffee and nibbled a biscuit I was dismissed.

'Anastasia will take you to your uncle.'

The nurse led me outside past the old lady in the wheelchair, who once again remained silent when I said hello. We went down a corridor to the main room, which must have been a drawing room when Silver Meadows had been a private residence.

The nurse stood aside at the door. On the wall to the left were two portraits, one of Padre Pio, that old fraud, the other, an amiable representation of a waving John Paul II. Above the Pope a framed text said: LIFE IS TOO IMPORTANT TO BE TAKEN SERIOUSLY – OSCAR WILDE.

On the large chimney piece were two jugs of water and a line of glasses. A giant gilt mirror was there to reflect a wrinkled face if the person the face belonged to happened to be very tall. The fireplace below had a pleated piece of cardboard; it could never have been lit, since the surrounding radiators did the job of heating all too efficiently. The heat made the smell of a floral air freshener very strong. On a table was a pile of copies of the *Irish Times* and magazines.

The room was filled with old women some dozing and lightly snoring. A group were sitting round a television set which happened to be showing a race meeting; the screen was so large you could have parked a car in a horse's nostril. The sound was turned down so that no one could hear the commentary.

Beyond the television two old ladies were playing snakes and ladders. Three nuns sat in a line dressed in the sober dresses and cardigans that modern nuns wear, their lips moving as they read from their prayer books or missals or whatever.

Other old women were reading less edifying stuff, magazines mostly, *Image*, filled with beautiful young models, and the *Irish Tatler* which was dedicated to showing Hibernian society having fun. A few had their noses in books; a bookshelf near the door offered Daphne du Maurier and Agatha Christie. A woman in a pink dressing gown who wore a little white beard was reading a novel by Maeve Binchy with the aid of a magnifying glass. The book was almost too heavy for her to hold.

Others were talking loudly, quite loud enough for me to hear what they were saying. Many people in this room must have been deaf; a lot were wearing hearing aids. I passed by one couple; a woman in a long blue cardigan and slippers was knitting a sock and turning the heel while she shouted at her neighbour:

'Sixty years married, and he still hadn't learnt that I didn't like water with my whiskey.'

Another old dear in a dressing gown was saying:

'Cancer. Such a fuss she's making...'

The one, who wore a black eye patch declared to the other who wore two long grey plaits:

'I could no more do that than I could do ice dancing.'

Another, her face withered like an autumn leaf, a plaid rug folded neatly over her knees, seemed to be talking to herself, but I realised she was humming: 'I'll wait for the wild rose that's waiting for me...'

I felt a soft touch on my arm.

'Haven't we met before?' A mottled hand tugged. I sat down beside a trembling old lady with white hair in ringlets and listened to a quavering voice recalling a garden.

'You should see the magnolias in spring and the japonica and the plum blossom and all the pear trees. And the grove of white cherry.' She frowned and I was horrified to see her eyes were full of tears.

'I sometimes worry in case they have been cut down.'

'I'm sure they haven't!'

'Dick is such a difficult person, you know. I never really trusted him.'

Any men in this huge room? Anywhere? Was the feminine presence an indication of age difference and the premature demise we lads could look forward to? Was everyone in here insane?

It was a relief to see two old men at the far end of the room. They were sitting looking intently at some toy soldiers. One was Uncle Jack who was wearing his houndstooth jacket and regimental tie. His face was beaded with perspiration.

I was glad to recognise his companion. Sammy Griffin was an old friend; he and Uncle Jack had known each other during the war. Sammy was an amiable old boy whom I had always liked. He was short and had grown stout recently, as if he had been poured into a square mould. His hearing aid was even bigger than Uncle Jack's. He had a really bushy moustache; by comparison, my uncle's was trim. It had always worried me when I was a small boy that except for the fact it was white, Uncle Jack's moustache resembled Hitler's.

Like my uncle, Sammy was a colonel or ex-colonel. One of my governesses told me that the word 'colonel' had been used by a Dublin wit as a collective name for any old man associated with the Big House. These two, who could be another species among all those old women, were sitting at a table playing an elaborate children's game with toy soldiers which concerned the Battle of Waterloo. I knew from visits to Sammy's house, that this ancient Victorian children's game had come down through his family, and he had inherited it. He was very proud of it, and perhaps for that reason, he had brought it to Silver Meadows. My uncle was not an easy opponent. This afternoon he was shouting, and not only because Sammy was deaf. His voice was far louder than any of the old women's. Sammy had mixed up the Prussians with the Imperial Guard, and, worse, did not understand Wellington's strategy of forming squares. The little painted figures had become misplaced. Marshal Ney had fallen under Sammy's chair.

'You've knocked down the Duke!'

Sammy put his hand behind his hearing aid, lifted his head to one side and blinked. 'What?'

'YOU'VE KNOCKED DOWN THE DUKE!'

'He was riding a white horse.'

'Chestnut, you fool. Copenhagen was a chestnut!'

'What sort of horse did Napoleon have?'

'Marengo was a grey.'

'What?'

'MARENGO WAS A GREY!'

'I dislike grey horses. Ignorant punters at racecourses always bet on them because they can pick them out of the bunch when they are travelling.'

'Marengo did Napoleon very well. But he wasn't riding him at Waterloo. He rode a mare named Desirée. Also a grey. But he had stomach ache.'

'What had stomach ache to do with it?'

'HE SPENT MOST OF HIS TIME AT WATERLOO IN A TRAVELLING COACH.'

'Don't believe you. It's your move.'

By this time Waterloo was in chaos.

Uncle Jack looked up and saw me.

'Three weeks and you never bothered to come here and see me.'

'Dr O'Shea said it was better to wait until you had settled in.'

'Typical. I could be here for years among all these coffin dodgers for all he cared. Or you for that matter.'

I dug into the Supervalu bag I was carrying and brought out the cigars.

My uncle's scowl vanished, and for the first time in many years he gave me a big smile.

He was also quite pleased with *Carry on Jeeves*.

A gong sounded for dinner.

The old women got up slowly, many of them abandoning spectacles, hearing aids, magnifying glasses, books, knitting, fierce-looking knitting needles, shawls, rugs, and crumpled tissues. Supported on walking sticks and in several cases on crutches, they shambled off at snail's pace towards the dining room.

'Goodbye...goodbye.'

Uncle Jack and Sammy abandoned the fallen lead soldiers and politely brought up the rear of the shuffling procession.

In the hall the old lady who had been sitting there all afternoon continued to sit until the Filipina nurse came along and wheeled her chair towards her meal.

While I waited for the nurse to return and unlock the front door, I peered into the dining room. In the brochure describing Silver Meadows Mrs Freebody called it The Parlour. She had decorated a fairly gloomy room in much the same way as the dining room of any provincial hotel with two huge mahogany sideboards. People were seated, four to each table; a single flower in a slim glass vase was placed in front of each diner. Like the main sitting room it was suffocatingly hot.

Next day, back at Mount Jewel, it occurred to me that I had made a big mistake. Forget my uncle's beaming smile when I opened the Supervalu bag; how on earth would he be able to smoke those cigars? I couldn't imagine Mrs Freebody or her bevy of nurses giving permission for such an indulgence. Could he retire to his bedroom leaving the window wide open? Or the lavatory? I doubted either possibility. Even here in the house when he lit a Havana, the smell would waft the whole length of the drawing room, lingering around the grey watered-silk wallpaper. And Mount Jewel's drawing room was big – in the days when the family had balls a hundred people danced in it with ease, although when two hundred were invited to waltz under the cupids who fluttered across the plaster work ceiling, there was a squash.

If my uncle smoked for a minute anywhere in the interior of Silver Meadows, the premises would be pervaded with Havana and heat.

There was one remaining box of cigars in his desk in the sitting room. But I doubted if he would able to light up any of the ones I had given him.

However, I tried again. The following week I took the final cigars off his desk and drove down for my second visit.

The weather was bitter when I climbed out of the car at Silver Meadows. Uncle Jack was outside the building, wrapped in his army coat, striding down the cinder path. Here he was, smoking a Bolivar, keeping a lookout for any nurses or other sneaks.

Who was that tall and elegant woman walking beside him, holding his free arm? She looked totally unlike the poor bent old slippered creatures I had seen the first time I came to Silver Meadows. She might be just as old, but she was walking along firmly in high heels, dressed in a sable coat with matching hat.

Uncle Jack introduced her. 'Lady Marsden.'

'Call me Daisy,' she said.

I shook her cold hand, noticing that the knuckle duster ring she was wearing had a large mix of sapphires and diamonds.

'I was sorry to miss you when you were here last week. I was at the hairdressers.'

We stood and waited while Uncle Jack puffed away.

'It's getting chilly,' Lady Marsden – Daisy – said eventually.

Uncle Jack did not take the hint. Instead he growled at me: 'What are you doing with my car?'

'I have to use it first of all to come and see you. And for the cigars.'

'You're not driving up to Dublin to Fox's for them?'

I didn't answer, leaving him with the benefit of the doubt.

He kept us outside in the gathering evening frost puffing away at his Bolivar Royal Corona. Perfect for outdoors. On summer evenings at Lough Mask he used to smoke those Bolivars as he handled rod and line in the pursuit of trout.

A little blue cloud rose above us.

'A woman is only a woman, but a good cigar is a smoke,' grumbled Lady Marsden. In spite of her sable she was shivering. 'We'll get pneumonia.'

At last, when all three of us were quaking and trembling, even Uncle Jack acknowledged that it had become quite nippy.

We climbed to the front door and rang the bell; the same nurse I had encountered before let us in.

'Come inside, Lady.'

'Thank you, Maria.'

I wondered how and why the two of them were let go outside in the cold. Probably Lady Marsden was tough enough to be in charge of the nurses, and also of Mrs Freebody.

We walked passed the same old woman I had encountered sitting in her wheelchair and made our way into the overheated main room.

Lady Marsden took off her sable coat to reveal a neat tweed suit. A little regimental brooch in diamonds on the lapel appeared beside a pearl necklace.

'Bring the sherry,' she directed to the nurse who was keeping an eye on things.

'O.K. Lady.'

What was my uncle's new friend doing in this place?

We sat in the bay window where Uncle Jack had been sorting out Waterloo with Sammy, who joined us, looking despondent. Jealous?

51

The nurse brought in a bottle of Amontillado and three Waterford glasses.

'Make that four.'

'O.K., Lady.'

As she poured out the sherry my uncle's new companion looked at Uncle Jack with a smile. True love? And was true love the reason his voice had got clearer and his reasoning sharper? Whither the loss of memory?

CHAPTER FIVE

On my next visit to Silver Meadows I found all the inmates assembled outside on the tarmac in the cold. It was an awesome sight. Some were able to stand on two legs and shuffle about in their slippers, most tottered around on sticks, several used zimmer frames and two were lying on stretchers. A patient in a hospital gown, her hair a grey halo, was swaying like a toddler as she staggered between two helpful nurses. The old lady in her wheelchair who sat in the hall was being wheeled down the steps.

Nurses ran around calling out:

'Where is Mrs Dunphy?'

'Maria, did she ever get out of the bed?'

'O.K. Mrs Dunphy here.'

'It's all right, Maeve, you'll be able to go back inside very soon.'

'Don't worry, Maureen, your knitting will be quite safe.'

'You'll get your lunch. It will be served at the usual time.'

Mrs Freebody was standing in her blue trouser suit, her feet apart, at the top of the steps, a notebook in her hand; nurses hurried up to her with lists of names.

'Fire practice,' said Uncle Jack who was standing with Lady Marsden; she was resting on a shooting stick.

It took a half hour for all of the shivering inmates to be assembled and counted, before they were escorted back inside.

'How often are these practices held?' I wondered.

'Once a month, or there's trouble. At the worst, the place could be shut down,' said Lady Marsden sipping her Amontillado.

Uncle Jack said: 'A couple of old darlings go missing each time. When they find them they bury them under these rose bushes. And of course two or three will die of pneumonia.'

The next time I arrived a hearse was parked on the tarmac with its back door open. The grim reaper had swished once again. I noticed a discreet notice on the side of the vehicle: A.P. Crowley, Mauricetown.

A nurse appeared at the front door and waved to the two men in black gabardine coats who stood beside it smoking. They dropped their half-smoked cigarettes on the tarmac and stamped them out, more strewn tobacco butts to add to the bigger ones thrown about by Uncle Jack. Their faces assumed the solemn look of their profession as they climbed the steps and vanished into the house.

I waited in the car until they emerged lugging a coffin which they edged expertly down the steps. At the hall entrance Mrs Freebody, together with a group of her nurses, watched as the undertakers placed it into the hearse, closed the back door, climbed into the front and drove away.

For one moment – truly only one moment – I was filled with the idea that the corpse might be my uncle's. I did exactly not feel a surge of hope, but it occurred to me that at his age sudden death would be a merciful end to a long eventful life.

Sense came immediately. If he had died, straight away Mrs Freebody would have made me a long mournful phone call. I was sure that every time she had to inform relatives the news that the pale horse had cantered through her establishment and that their loved one had passed away in untimely fashion, Angelica Freebody would sound really sad.

She would be telling the families of the departed how happy and peaceful and beautiful the corpse looked. Come and have a look at her, or – very occasionally – him. Since it was a routine she had done for so many years, and the proprietor of Silver Meadows was an authority on end-of-life care, practice would have made perfect.

One more inmate had expired this morning, but not Uncle Jack. And not one of the old women.

'Poor old Sammy.'

Lady Marsden stood beside my uncle at the bay window, looking elegantly sad. Today the suit she wore was black.

'All very peaceful.'

'Poor fellow keeled over face first into his rice pudding.' Uncle Jack was absolutely back on form as far as his speech was concerned – perhaps because of Lady Marsden. I was beginning to wonder if there was any need for him to be staying longer at Silver Meadows.

'He insisted on eating his meals with his own forks and spoons decorated with his family crest. Didn't make the grub taste any better.'

'You'll miss him.'

'Always happening. They die like flies in here. One a week. Killed by horrible food.'

I protested, 'You told me the food here was good.'

'Tap the biscuits they give you and weevils come out. Half the people here have scurvy. '

Lady Marsden said sadly, 'Don't listen to him. The food here is excellent. The chef was trained at Ballymaloe.'

'Gourmet boot camp,' said Uncle Jack.

The two of them were allowed to go to Sammy's funeral.

Wearing his bowler hat, which at his request I brought down in the Rover, Uncle Jack insisted that he himself would drive to Westmeath. We made our way towards the little shoe box First Fruits church and the churchyard overgrown with long grass where Sammy would be buried. Lady Marsden sat beside him, wrapped in her fur coat.

Mrs Freebody also came to the funeral in the minibus belonging to Silver Meadows. She had made it a rule that whenever possible she would attend the formal departures of her inmates. Naturally she was an authority on obsequies, Catholic and Protestant, removals and requiem masses, the two bites of the cherry that Catholics have for their corpses. On this occasion she brought along a couple of nurses dressed in black like she was. Two frail friends of Sammy's – at least, two old women who said they were friends – also came along with her. The nurses had to help the both old women into the church and along a pew at the back, under the organ.

From his pew Uncle Jack declared: 'All those bloody nurses and carers – carers, what a word! – keep special black outfits for the funerals of the poor old stiffs who have died in Silver Meadows. Cupboards full. Use them every week. They get worn out pretty regularly.'

Others entered the church, mostly people who managed to survive in decaying big houses. There were several old men, all of whom were taking off bowler hats similar to the one worn by Uncle Jack. Bowler hats were *de rigeur* country funeral uniform, apart from the occasional topper.

I noticed Trigger, Gusty, Duffy, Rabbit and Beakey, friends of Sammy, and also of my uncle. Sammy's two balding paunchy sons were present. So were some ancient retainers from his old house. But most of the attendance was feminine. Both his ex-wives were there.

'The church is packed,' I whispered to my uncle.

'No one forgets Sammy,' he said at the top of his voice, 'because of what happened in Cairo.'

'Mmm?'

'He swung on the chandelier at Shephard's Hotel. Brought it down with a crash. Caused more fuss than El Alamein.'

That particular wartime incident was not mentioned in Sammy's fulsome eulogies given by the rector and one of the plump sons during the service.

I wasn't really listening. I sat wondering what hymns should be played for Uncle Jack when his time came. Not 'Abide with Me' which should be banned – the dreariest hymn in the book, what a wail, especially when it was played on a tape recorder as it was here. Nor 'The Lord's my Shepherd' – another hymn done to death, you might say. 'Fight the Good Fight', perhaps. Or that roar of Welsh thunder, 'Guide me Oh thou Great Redeemer'.

How soon?

After the service the plump sons helped to carry Sammy's coffin to the nearby hole in the ground. Better than the squeaking trolley pulled by all those busy undertakers, sad expressions stitched to their faces. Someone had scythed a way through the long grass to his grave.

One of Sammy's old retainers played 'Danny Boy' on a violin.

'*Nullus funus sine fidula*,' said Uncle Jack.'

'What?'

'No funeral without a fiddle.'

Afterwards a reception was held in the house nearby which had once been Sammy's residence, but was now a hotel. We spent some time there eating stale sandwiches and talking about the old boy's past life. Even though another veteran had bitten the dust, the occasion was cheerful. We did not have to undergo the hypocrisy of sympathy. We talked to plenty of people who would be joining Sammy very soon and others whom you only met on these occasions, like Mrs Bailey who had not missed a Protestant funeral in Louth in thirty years.

Uncle Jack said, 'She'll be at mine, you wait and see.'

Mrs Bailey smiled.

Mrs Freebody and her party did not attend the reception, since the frail old ladies she had brought down were threatening to provide other funerals and had to be hurried back to Silver Meadows. Rather to my surprise, Uncle Jack was pleased enough to follow them, together with Lady Marsden. I thought there was a possibility that he might want to come home to Mount Jewel.

'The hag has another funeral tomorrow. Three this week. Silver Meadows will be empty before you know it.'

On the way back Uncle Jack and Lady Marsden continued their reminiscences.

'While Sammy lived in that place breakfast was never served until after ten o'clock because he and his wives waited for the cook to cycle up the drive to prepare it for them.'

Lady Marsden recalled, 'Sammy was eighty-two when he underwent hypnotism to improve his croquet.'

Uncle Jack said, 'It didn't do him any good. His croquet was hopeless.' He added: 'Remember when he was married to Moira? The house was known as Gin Palace.'

'Moira had a glass of gin in every room. You might expect one in the drawing room or dining room. But they were also upstairs in every spare bedroom. In the lavatories.'

'You could sip a gin and tonic as you peed.'

'Amazing how she's still going strong when you think it's all alcohol in her veins instead of blood. She looked splendid at the service.'

'Still name dropping. All the wonderful famous people she knows. All those lords and film stars. Never stops talking about them even now.'

'Always a social climber.'

'She climbs with crampons.'

'Remember how Sammy had those dogs. At least nine, all a special kind of springer spaniel.'

'And they all stank an unusual springer stink.'

Uncle Jack mused: 'When I'm dead I don't want to moulder in the grave like John Brown, or Sammy for that matter. Make it a half hour at Glasnevin and into the oven.'

Lady Marsden said, 'I'd like to die surrounded by roses. And have a coffin like a basket. I've ordered one.'

'Hope you don't get to use it too soon.'

'And also an orchestra playing Beethoven's Fifth.'

'Inconvenient.'

'Not at all. I've arranged for that as well.'

As he speeded along my uncle said, 'There are now thirty old women at Silver Meadows and only one man.'

'You've quite a choice.'

'Have to leave out the nuns.'

If the weather was fine my uncle and Lady Marsden were usually to be found wandering around the miserable garden.

'Like Mountjoy jail, this place. Every time Daisy and I want to come outside we have to ask someone to unlock the door.'

He added, 'In my day there were very few places like Silver Meadows. When you were over the hill you hired a nurse or two and an extra servant to look after you before you pegged out.'

'Nonsense,' said Lady Marsden 'There were nursing homes galore.'

'Very few as ghastly as this one.'

I asked, 'Who is the old lady who is always sitting in the hall in a wheelchair?

'That's Sheila.' Lady Marsden said. 'She's been sitting there every day for the last five years.'

'She's not the only looney,' said Uncle Jack.

'You shouldn't call them loonies,' said Lady Marsden, 'even if they are not quite the full shilling. They are people with special needs.'

'Most of them crazy. Sheila stuck sitting in the hall day after day glaring at everyone who goes by. There's Paula always clutching her empty handbag, pretending it's full of money. And Annie making out lists and doing accounts for the shop she ran twenty years ago. And Lily passing the time until she dies singing songs by Percy French. Everyone of them round the bend.'

So was Uncle Jack.

When it was raining, Uncle Jack and Lady Marsden would be indoors playing bridge. They had found two regular partners, Paula with her empty handbag and Rosie who wore long grey plaits, old women who were still sane enough to know how to play. The bay window contained a table where the four of them sat.

'One no trump.'

'Two spades.'

They played for high stakes.

'Don't tell Mrs Freebody how high!'

What happened to Sammy's board game about Waterloo?' I asked.

'Mrs Freebody threw it out.'

In the evening before dinner was served, the four of them drank sherry and counted their winnings. It may have been because he loved Lady Marsden that my uncle accepted his glass of sherry without complaint and did not demand whiskey.

In the dining room Uncle Jack and Lady Marsden now sat at a table they shared with their bridge opponents. I assumed that he had ceased taking out his false teeth and putting them on a saucer beside him, the way he used to do at Mount Jewel. The saucer he used there was Chinese – Ming dynasty.

If he could play bridge, his short-term memory could not be that bad.

I said as much when I ran into Dr O'Shea who went to Silver Meadows regularly to check up on him. Their meetings, I learned gave him no pleasure. After thirty years the doctor and my uncle were no longer friends, since Uncle Jack had not forgiven him for putting him in Mrs Freebody's clutches.

Dr O'Shea told me ruefully: 'His rudeness, David, towards an old friend is hurtful.' I didn't say, 'Serve you right.'

'Couldn't he come home? He seems to be fine.'

'Remember what he tried to do to the Reverend Hazel? We cannot possibly afford to take any risk.'

Whenever I drove to Silver Meadows I carried reports from Massey about the estate. Uncle Jack would question me about the crops and animals. These days there was no more mention about setting them free to go to Africa; the instructions he gave me to relay to his steward were always sensible.

He seemed back to normal, sane and sharp, verging as ever on the disagreeable.

Every time I came to see him I brought with me not only the cigars, to be laboriously smuggled into his bedroom, copies of *Country Life* and the *Financial Times*, but books from his library whose names he gave me, which were either about Africa or novels by Wodehouse. I also brought cheques to be signed for the salaries of the staff of Mount Jewel. Following instructions, I obtained these from Dan Hennessy, Uncle Jack's solicitor.

Hennessy's office was in Drogheda in Laurence Street. He was on the second floor of a Georgian building whose rooms had been divided into small rectangular spaces; a few fine mahogany doors and traces of stucco work gave indications of past glory. To reach him you had to pass a chiropodist and a distributor of dental floss. Often a smell of burnt cabbage came up from the basement.

Dan Hennessy had a red jowly face and particles of snuff fell regularly from his nostrils onto his shirt and collar, difficult to tell apart from his dandruff. He must have been one of the last people in the country to take snuff, squeezing up regular pinches from a small blackened silver box on his desk which lay among an untidy pile of papers.

These were supposed to be sorted by his secretary, Miss O'Brien. She also brought him his Earl Grey tea in a mug and shortbread biscuits.

'I believe Jack is much better.' Sniff, sniff and another lot of the stuff would go up his nose, 'The Hiltons are a long lived family. Your grandfather didn't die until he was well into his nineties.'

Every week Hennessy handed over the cheques for my uncle to sign. Among them was some money for me after I persuaded him to provide me with a small salary. He slipped it in under a heading like 'oats' or 'nails'.

'We won't tell Jack.'

By now I realised that those who chose to come and live in Silver Meadows or were shoved in there by their relatives must be extremely rich to afford the exorbitant fees that Mrs Goodbody charged. Most inmates were widows of judges, solicitors, politicians, medical specialists and diplomats. The nuns had come after their convent had been sold for building. There were also a few Anglo-Irish relics from big houses.

Here was the race against time which every middle class senior citizen – female in most cases – had to face. Would the dosh from selling your house cover your evening years? Do you get evicted from Silver Meadows when your money runs out, and move down to the castellated horror at Mauricetown? But most of them were well off enough to enjoy – if that was the word – the comforts inflicted on them at Silver Meadows. Mrs Healy, for example, was the widow of a government minister who had made a packet of money during his time in government. He had been dead for ten years. Mrs O'Hara was the widow of a brewer in Guinness's, as Mrs Freebody kept reminding anyone who cared to listen, had outlived her husband by twenty-five years. Poor old men.

I got used to seeing a hearse waiting on the tarmac outside. Not only Crowley's – some came from far away, Dublin and Kells, and the odd one from across the border in Northern Ireland. Those hearses came to Silver Meadows almost as regularly as the postman's van.

Faces changed. Old ladies came and went (permanently); they would all die in due course, but two of them had been residents for longer than a decade.

I got used to hearing the old girls saying 'if anything happens to me' which was code for 'if I die'. Death's fetid breath was always at their backs. Whoever said eighty was the new sixty told a lie. Old age was preparation for a massacre, a discreet crossing out of names in phone books.

Uncle Jack, at present the only man in the place, acknowledged these truths cheerfully. Death was not a matter of 'if' but 'when'. The writing was on the wall.

If someone was mentioned as being 'not too well' it meant she was extremely sick. When the dying started to behave unreasonably, or developed paranoia, or were in pain, their departure was considered a 'blessing'.

People hissed the word.

Lady Marsden told me that Silver Meadows was considered an excellent old people's home and Uncle Jack had no reason to describe it as a hell hole.

Certainly Mrs Freebody seemed to be doing her best for her old ladies. They were offered visiting priests and comedians, outings on buses for the sturdy, sweet little nurses from the Far East, flowers changed every day, coffee and biscuits and people who were qualified to give them physiotherapy, conduct exercise sessions and cut their toe nails.

Doctors were constantly in attendance to deal with ailments, treating poor old creatures with sore backs who moved like sad tortoises, or painful hips which necessitated operations where steel balls were substituted for arthritic bits. The majority of the inmates of Silver Meadows were walking wounded as I could see from all the sticks and zimmer frames that were much in evidence.

Mrs Freebody provided ophthalmologists who offered cataract removals; vision was regained and many old women with clouded sight after suffering stoically, were turned into Hawkeyes. Ugh...The idea of being conscious and looking up while they sawed away at your pupil, seemed dreadful, although they were assured there would be no pain. There must have been truth in it. But since so many people underwent the procedure, medical terminology for torture session, it could not be unendurable.

Lady Marsden, who had undergone two cataract operations, reminded me: 'Remember Charlotte Bronte's poor old father – he had a cataract removed without an anaesthetic. And while the surgeon was doing it she was writing *Jane Eyre*. Without that surgeon we would not have known about Mr Rochester.'

Birthdays were constantly being celebrated at Silver Meadows. Relatives would bring in large bunches of flowers which would wither and die instantly because of the heat. Often balloons were provided. Cakes with candles appeared – not the full amount, but one for each decade, plus one or two extra just in case.

Wrinkled old mouths would be pursed and a puff or two of breath would be aimed at those candles. If necessary a nurse would stand nearby to blow as well. Numbers and names were written in icing, Happy Birthday dear Rose, eighty-nine, Happy Birthday, Mary, ninety-one.

Squeaky voices rang out in the dining room, singing their congratulations. If the celebrant was lucky, Mrs Angelica Freebody would be there to add to the sounds, singing in her own melodious soprano, Happy Birthday, dear Margaret, Happy birthday Dear Patsy.

In the first months Uncle Jack was staying in Silver Meadows an old lady reached a hundred.

'She could be older. You'd have to carbon date her to find out.'

The photographer from the local paper was invited to the party and his camera flashed – yet another smiling picture for Mrs Freebody's collection. The cake was extra large and dollops of sponge and icing were distributed to the general company before the happy chorus was sung for dear Catherine. Everyone watched, not exactly envious, while this really old girl was presented with a letter from President Robinson and a large cheque.

'Of course her children will take the money off her,' Uncle Jack said. 'When I reach a hundred I'm going to spend all of it straight away on ten year old Bushmills. And cigars of course.'

At Mount Jewel birthdays had never been celebrated and throughout my boyhood the only presents I ever received were provided by pitying nurses and governesses.

I did not know the date of Uncle Jack's birthday, or even his age, but presumably they were both on his medical notes. It was a total surprise for me when I arrived at Silver Meadows one day to find that he had reached a certain age.

The cake that was wheeled in for him was monstrous. There were one or two complaints later on that it was bigger than the one provided for dear Catherine, the hundred-year-old a couple of weeks before. It was studded with eight blue candles to indicate he was in entering his ninth decade. The cook, the one who had been trained at Ballymaloe had iced it with the inscription HAPPY BIRTHDAY COLONEL HILTON – EIGHTY TODAY. CONGRATULATIONS. How did she know his age? Mrs Freebody must have told her. Was he really as old as that? There was a representation of a rifle in brown icing. How did Mrs Freebody know about Uncle Jack's Purdey? He must have boasted about it.

How did the cook know what a Purdey looked like?

The bushy eyebrows drew together, the mouth beneath the white Hitler moustache turned down. But my uncle behaved impeccably. The manners were there; he listened politely as every little old lady in the room, together with Mrs Freebody, trilled the anniversary message. Happy Birthday, Colonel Hilton they sang like a lot of larks.

The following week there was a good deal of excitement when another man came to stay at Silver Meadows. The female residents were thrilled at this replacement for poor old Sammy. The eyes of many, and those of the nurses as well, followed the new crazy old fellow adoringly, not only because he was another man, but because he was a celebrity.

He was Sean Dempsey who for many years had fronted a gardening programme on television.

The exception to the enthusiasts who were so galvanised by the coming of the great gardener was my uncle. Apart from their sex, Dempsey and Uncle Jack had nothing in common; as far as I could make out they never spoke to each other. Perhaps Uncle Jack was jealous. Even Lady Marsden had seen Sean Dempsey on television telling Ireland what to do with its dahlias and roses.

Dempsey loved living in Silver Meadows. He did favours for worshipping old ladies, behaving as if they were his harem. He loved them all. They flirted and simpered, including the nuns. They loved him far more than they had ever even liked my uncle.

They liked Dempsey's jokes.

'I owe my age to cigarettes and whiskey and wild, wild women.'

He wore a trim beard, dyed ginger like his thin hair.

But the hearse waited. Heart transplants get you in the end. It took only two months for Sean to be gathered.

I learned the news from Uncle Jack whose voice was gleeful. 'He died at the dinner table.'

'Didn't that happen to Sammy?'

'I've told you before. It's the horrible food they give you.'

Dempsey's funeral was massive. A woman in military uniform came down from Dublin representing the President. His funeral mass, attended by hundreds, was in St Peter's church in West Street; Oliver Plunkett's severed head was nearby, watching. Many photographs appeared, not only in the *Drogheda Independent*, but in the *Irish Times* and the *Irish Independent*. Mrs Freebody cut them out, plus the obituaries, which she scattered in the front hall and among the unread newspapers in the main sitting room.

Once more Uncle Jack was the only cock among the hens.

Next time I called there was no old lady in the hall.

'Where's Sheila?'

'She won't be in her wheelchair any longer. When the nurse came to fetch her in for dinner last Wednesday, she was sitting there dead as a doornail.'

Uncle Jack continued, 'Mrs Freebody had problems with the dead from day one. She wasn't prepared for her first corpse. She needed the bed. Had to put the stiff in the phone booth overnight. Poor old dear was stuck in a sitting position by the time they came to get her out. No end of trouble unwinding her and putting her in her coffin.'

'How do you know this?'

'Mrs Macnamara told me.'

'Which is Mrs Macnamara?'

'She's not here. Died last Saturday. Didn't get up from watching television. *Coronation Street*.'

He added 'Rosie Bulger copped it yesterday.'

Lady Marsden commented: 'Rosie was only eighty-two.'

Lady Marsden regularly received a string of friends and so did Uncle Jack. Trigger, who seemed to have acquired a new wig, and Beaky called in to see him every few weeks; they had all stuck pigs in their youth in India. The old retired admiral, Gusty, came, together with his wife whom Uncle Jack disliked and was appallingly rude to.

Dan Hennessy called in a cloud of snuff with papers to sign relating to the running of Mount Jewel which were too secret for me to see.

Duffy Moffett arrived carrying a box of melting Black Magic chocolates.

Duffy was a lord. Mrs Freebody, overwhelmed by the presence of a belted earl, greeted him cringingly. His peerage was a United Kingdom creation since his grandfather had governed a part of Africa. This meant that Duffy was entitled to go to England and sit in the House of Lords on a scarlet bench, collecting a day's expenses whenever he wanted to. For forty years this daily allowance was his only source of income; when he became ill he arranged to be carried into the red chamber. He never once gave a speech.

Other inmates waited for their relatives to come and see them, relatives who had installed them in Silver Meadows for the rest of their natural lives. You could see nervous smiles and guilt in the eyes of sons and daughters who knew they should have their dear old mothers living with them instead of getting rid of them by placing them in Mrs Freebody's care.

Was it enough to take them out to a good restaurant for Sunday lunch before returning them at tea time?

I offered a meal in a hotel to my uncle and Lady Marsden. The cost could come out of one of Dan Morrissey's cheques.

'Some time, perhaps.' Neither of them wanted to be interrupted at their bridge.

They had to desist from card playing on Sunday mornings when the priest came and said Mass in the little oratory beyond the dining room.

Occasionally, not regularly, since she was busy with her congregation at Mauricetown, Hazel turned up for a short service for the two or three Protestants gathered together in Silver Meadows. Since it was best for all concerned that Uncle Jack was not present on these occasions, he was encouraged to retire to his room.

Hazel had benefited from his attack on her. The incident had not made the newspapers, but had spread all over the place by word of mouth. As a result her congregation has increased immensely. Plenty of people came to her services from Meath and Westmeath and as far as the north of Ireland.

I saw Mrs Freebody regularly, whenever she walked into the main room on her daily inspection tour. She would provide an enigmatic smile for each old woman, a raised plucked eyebrow above the butterfly spectacles, a pause to listen for any complaints, a respectful simper for the nuns, a special smirk for really valued inmates like Sean Dempsey, who had been smiled at all too briefly, and Lady Marsden and Uncle Jack.

'Damn woman is always inviting Daisy and I into her study to drink her foul coffee.'

'She doesn't have us in so often since you insist on calling Silver Meadows Death Row.'

I wondered if Uncle Jack knew how much he was paying for the privilege of being Mrs Freebody's client.

Lady Marsden continued to be immaculately dressed, preferring good plain tweed suits, her knotted gold chain dropping over her silk blouse, her high-heeled shoes well polished. Unlike other inmates of Silver Meadows, she never wore bedroom slippers.

'They are for those who have given up.'

She was always in good form, having had her vitamin injections.

'Everyone should have vitamin B12 injections. All the people here in Silver Meadows and others like Albert Reynolds, George Bush, Mikhail Gorbachev, John Major.'

The hairdresser who attended to her hair, thick and white and curly like a shampooed sheep, came up specially from Dublin. So did the woman who filed and painted her nails pale pink.

She moved in a mist of scent which was called Vol de Nuit.

'Night Flight,' Uncle Jack said, sniffing. 'What you need to get out of here.'

As far as I could make out Lady Marsden seemed to be that formidable creature, a good woman. And not only good, but nice, which was

unusual when you realised she was also a Christian. She terrified people
when she made them realise how horrible the rest of us were.

One afternoon she and Uncle Jack were strolling outside, my uncle
as usual half way through his cigar, keeping an eye open for any nurse,
or Vincent, the elderly man who worked the boiler, or even Mrs
Freebody herself. I took the opportunity to ask her why she chose to
come to Silver Meadows when she seemed so fit and well.

'I can't bear living on my own. I've tried housekeepers, but they
never worked out.'

'Sorry to hear it.'

'You can't imagine how awful it is to be alone in a house with
nothing for company except a television set.'

She added, 'Of course I waited until Rupert died before coming here.'

Rupert? Her husband?

'My King Charles spaniel.'

Once, when Lady Marsden was having her hair done Uncle Jack
told me more about her.

'...Daisy likes being the lady – on her writing paper she puts Lady
Elizabeth Marsden above her address. She was pleased enough when
Max got his K...

'Max?' That could only be her husband.

'Diplomat...English...All those phony diplomats who work for the
British foreign office get their K's in due course – unless they foul up.'

'Foul up?'

'Like Ronald, that friend of Max who let Idi Amin take charge in
Uganda. Cost him his knighthood. Or Tristam, who let down the
Americans in Somalia during Thanskgiving.'

'How?'

'Delegation of Yanks wanted to eat turkey. Stupid American tradition
eating two turkeys in a month around November and December.
Tristam trusted the blacks to provide the birds. When they were cooked
the Yanks found they tasted very odd. African turkeys, they were told.

Turned out the blacks had shot a couple of vultures.'

I had to laugh.

'Diplomatic incident. Tristam got the blame. Didn't go down well at the Foreign Office. No K for Tristam, poor bloke. Had to do with a sickly CBE. Lucky not to get an MBE like a fireman or a lollipop lady.'

'...Poor Daisy never had an easy time, Max would come home exhausted after a day's work. No libido whatsoever. She would even rather have had a better sex life than the right to call herself a lady.'

Since we were on good terms for the moment and I had just brought him cigars, I ventured to ask my uncle about his own libido.

'I've none – one of the things Maud objected to. After she left me she had a string of lovers in Spain. Dagoes. Marbella is full of them.'

I knew that this was not true and that poor old Aunt Maud had no companions apart from her Pekineses.

Uncle Jack told me more about his new girl friend.

'Notice her ring? Max paid a fortune for it. Daisy gets it on and off with the help of Vaseline.'

'...She can be a bore, always saying that people would rather admit to being rapists than lacking a sense of humour or lacking taste.'

Lady Marsden would never wear purple like the old lady in Jenny Joseph's poem. Her stick would not run down railings but help to push forward her feet in her well-polished shoes.

When they photograph old people in homes for television – an impudent invasion of privacy – usually the camera bears down on the old dears' feet and the slippers they are wearing, symbols of helplessness and approaching imbecility.

Lady Marsden was an exception.

When Mrs Freebody showed old people and their relatives around Silver Meadows to see if they wanted to come and spend what remained of their lives and what was left of their fortunes in this particular Chinese death house, she always let them peek into Daisy's room. Visitors could inspect her paintings, the patchwork quilt which she had made herself, the Regency chest of drawers, and the whatnot on which she had arranged her pieces of Worcester and Capo di Monte beside the little television where she watched the news and moaned about the state of the world as if it was the fault of Mrs Freebody. The little bathroom nearby was decorated with a couple of Redouté prints of roses. There was no bath of course, just a shower; baths were never provided in case someone got stuck in one.

CHAPTER SIX

Suddenly, overnight, everything changed.

I was invited into Mrs Freebody's office and seated opposite her, Nescafe was put in front of me. In front of her was a list of names. When I twisted my head I could see it must be a waiting list for rich oldies, poor things, destined to come and die here.

There were the occasional exceptions.

'We think that by next week your uncle can go home.' She appeared extremely pleased.

A long silence followed as the news sank in. I gazed at the beaming photograph of her late husband, clasping his mashie niblick. I knew by now (from Uncle Jack who managed to get all the information he could ever require about the institution where he was incarcerated) that Mr Freebody, in addition to being a superior golfer, had been the owner of a chain of slaughter houses. They had names which were rather similar to those they gave to retirement homes, Sevenelms or Woodlands.

'You don't call them slaughter houses, but meat factories,' Uncle Jack said. 'Like you call a brothel a lap dancing club.'

My uncle had also found out that one of Mr Freebody's meat factories had been situated beside the Boyne which ran regularly with blood. During the Troubles this fact had disturbed a number of English visitors and journalists who didn't think things were that bad.

'The Colonel has fully recovered.'

I knew anything was possible. A few, very few, inmates left Silver

Meadows and resumed what might be deemed normal life – living with relatives, or, far worse, living on their own, regularly checked by impatient social workers. Around their necks they wore an alarm to press if they fell down and couldn't get up.

'We think your uncle is quite capable of returning home. Especially, David, when you are there to keep an eye on him.'

So I was the reason she could be rid of Uncle Jack. It did not look as if I would be going back to Australia anytime soon.

'Are you sure he won't try burning another rectory or murdering someone?'

She gave a little laugh that sounded like tee hee.

'Oh, that's quite in the past. The Colonel has made a wonderful improvement. There is nothing to stop him returning to normal life.'

'I thought he had dementia.'

'Oh, nothing like that.' She did not quite say the Colonel is as sane as you and I, but that was what she meant.

I did my best to express delight.

'I know how fond you are of your uncle. Such a charming old fashioned gentleman!'

'Does he know?'

'I plan to tell him sometime in the next few days.'

'When will he be leaving?'

'Let us say this time next week. You will want to get the old place ready for him. I will arrange for a nurse to accompany him.'

A nurse would be far cheaper than the cost of Silver Meadows. But she wouldn't last long.

Driving back to Mount Jewel, I thought I would not tell the staff yet of Uncle Jack's impending return. I would give them another few days of happiness.

During this particular absence, the longest there had ever been, Patsy Massey had gradually allowed a really relaxed atmosphere to seep into the estate. The farm bell was not run at exactly eight o'clock, as Uncle

Jack had decreed it should every working day. It was now rung at nine or even ten o'clock, or not rung at all. The cows were milked any time; the horses were exercised in the usual way but at a leisurely pace. Manzie continued to look after the poultry in a desultory fashion. He had killed a lot of them. Indoors, Cook and the maids fed me scrumptious food and neglected to do the sweeping and dusting. I sang in my bath.

No more.

I took the dogs for their usual daily walk, going the rounds of the estate. Unlike humans, the dogs would welcome back Uncle Jack and would give him great howls of delight. They were the only creatures he loved. And they loved him. He had paid Flanagan something like five hundred punts to operate on Albert's hip.

It occurred to me, perhaps things might have changed and he might have become fond of Lady Marsden. Really fond of her. I indulged in a fantasy of Uncle Jack bringing her back to Mount Jewel. That, at least, would cheer the place up.

I picked mushrooms in the rath field and brought them back to the house where Cook fried them for me together with bacon. I ate them gloomily before going to the study where I sat drinking a tumbler of Uncle Jack's whiskey – the last of it – and watching a thriller on television, the sort he would never want to see.

Next morning I woke to despair – I could not put things off any longer. First thing I would have to find Massey and tell him. He would ring the bell and announce the bad news to the men on the estate. It was perfectly possible that they might want to leave.

Meanwhile I would tell the indoor servants who would have just enough time to sweep and dust and wash their uniforms. Probably one of them would burst into tears – that had happened before, when Uncle Jack returned from hospital in Dublin. Philly Brosnan, Bridget's boy friend would have to be told to stop making his visits to the kitchen.

There was a knocking on the bedroom door, a hammering. Bridget called out. 'Telephone, Master David.'

I switched on the light and felt for my dressing gown. By the time

I had walked down the stairs and across the hall to the study at least five minutes must have elapsed.

At first I could not recognise the voice, a high pitched sound.

Mrs Freebody was gasping. 'David, I would be grateful if you could come down to Silver Meadows immediately.'

'Has my uncle died?'

'No, no, he hasn't passed away. But something very serious has happened which I prefer not to discuss over the telephone.'

I took my time. I had breakfast, eating the rest of the mushrooms with more bacon and trying to imagine what was going on.

There was a storm as I drove down to Silver Meadows; rain thundered down on the roof of the car.

The expression on the face of the nurse who let me in was grim. In Mrs Freebody's study there was no smile or cup of coffee.

'A dreadful incident took place last night.'

'Uncle Jack?'

'This is not an easy thing to talk about.'

'You know your uncle's friend, Lady Marsden?'

'Of course.'

She leaned across the desk and took my hand. Her own was warm and fragrant and comfortable as she delivered the blow.

'I am sorry to have to tell you that shortly after dinner your uncle attacked her savagely.'

I thought of Hazel.

'There was no provocation.'

'What did he do?'

'He tried to throttle her.'

'My God.'

'Nothing like this has ever happened before at Silver Meadows.'

'How is Lady Marsden?'

'As well as could be expected under the circumstances. We had to remove her to hospital in Drogheda.'

It seemed the fracas had taken place as the pair of them drank their evening sherry . A member of staff witnessed what had happened.

'One moment they were talking amiably and the next moment your uncle had his hands around her neck.'

'Terrible.'

'The language the Colonel used was coarse and ungentlemanly. It took Nurse Teresa all her strength to release her from his hold. As you can imagine, the other ladies in the sitting room were greatly disturbed.'

'I wonder what provoked the attack?'

Mrs Freebody gave a heavy sigh.

'Lady Marsden managed to inform me. They were quarrelling over Lord Mountbatten who was a particular friend of hers when he was alive.'

There was no question of seeing my uncle at this stage – he was drugged, comatose.

'...No visitors. Perhaps in a week or two you may call on him briefly.'

Outside Dr O'Shea was getting out of his car, trembling so much that the case he was carrying rattled.

'First Hazel, and now this. It couldn't be worse.'

'Women get on his nerves.'

Both of us remembered that final argument with Aunt Maud.

I drove back to Mount Jewel where Josie served me boiled chicken for dinner. Manzie had dispatched another old bird whose laying was not up to scratch.

'How is the Colonel, Master David?'

I fiddled with a drumstick.

'He's very well.'

Lady Marsden was in a private room in the hospital. On the window sill were flowers sent by sympathisers, freesias gerbera, stiff iris, strelezia, and a weird green orchid, all stabbed into damp sponge. They were arranged in plastic vases or laid out in curved baskets. Get well cards were lined up in front – a dozen at least. In this Rousseau jungle there was no room for my own wretched bunch of flowers which I put in the sink.

Poor Daisy lay propped up on pillows and gave me a grimace that passed as a smile. She looked dreadful with the bandage wound round her throat. She had a black eye.

'I liked Jack very much...he made me laugh.' She croaked like a raven. 'But he's mad.'

'I suppose he is.'

'...Cracked...batty...cuckoo...lunatic.' She might have been reciting from a Thesaurus. She gave an alarming cough.

'You'd better not talk.'

As I left she squawked, 'Louis Mountbatten was such a nice man.'

The nurse who brought me down to the basement to see Uncle Jack was oriental.

'My name Maria.'

'What country do you come from?' Easy to guess, polite to ask.

'Philippines...'

'How long have you been in Ireland?'

'Three year.'

'Do you like it here?'

'Very much I like.'

I followed her down stone stairs to be greeted with a smell of damp. The passages, flagged with slate, were beaded with water. The same heat that filled the rooms upstairs pervaded these lower spaces which were in semi-darkness, lit by dim lights.

I could hear voices and a telephone rang. Doors opened and shut.

'Here Colonel's place.'

She led me to a cubicle surrounded by a curtain. There was a small set of open shelves for my uncle's clothes on top of which, laid out carefully in a line, were his ivory backed hairbrush and comb, a Bible provided by Mrs Freebody, and a plastic tumbler for his false teeth, with a tube of tablets beside it.

I noticed the sponge bag and shaving mirror.

'I shave Colonel,' Maria said.

When he lived upstairs my Uncle Jack had been allotted a pleasant bedroom of his own with a cupboard to hang his clothes, a chest of drawers and an arm chair.

There was no sign of him.

'Colonel in rest room.'

We followed another Filipina nurse who was pushing a wheelchair containing a sleeping old woman in a dressing gown. She wheeled her towards a thunderous noise. An automatic door opened into what must have been the kitchen in Victorian times. The walls were peach coloured, perhaps to attract a bit more light; there were dozens of chairs and a couple of battered leather sofas. Again, I felt damp.

This big room was in semi-darkness. Overhead was a paper Japanese lantern, but most of the light was of a flickering quality provided by an immense television set identical to the one upstairs. On one wall was a reproduction of Dürer's hands in prayer. On another a notice in large capital letters: LORD HELP ME TO REMEMBER THAT NOTHING IS GOING TO HAPPEN TO ME TODAY THAT YOU AND I TOGETHER CAN'T HANDLE. The curtains on the windows had a pattern of big flowers all larger than life; through the glass you could see lines of vertical iron bars. No escape.

Here was a dim imitation of the room upstairs with a similar semicircle of chairs around the set filled with dozing figures. I smelt pee. A woman news reader was reading to the sleepers items about carnage. Road accident. Knifing in Finglas. Bombs in Baghdad. Drugs, drugs, drugs. If you switched her off you would have heard a wave of snores.

The old women here down below, everyone of whom was asleep, were unfamiliar to me. Most of those up above, however much they came and went, and died, I had got to know well enough for a nod of greeting. But I recognized no one downstairs.

The sane upstairs, the loonies below. Or, more likely, moderately mad upstairs, raving mad downstairs.

Did the rejected come to the basement diagnosed as crazy, smuggled down before the relatively smart and sane upstairs caught sight of them? How many of them had committed some sort of violent breach of behaviour like Uncle Jack which condemned them to punishment? Had they all got dementia?

I wondered why Uncle Jack had not been cast down here in the first place when he first arrived at Silver Meadows. He had just missed out on murdering Hazel. He had been given his chance. At Daisy's expense.

An old woman woke up. She opened her mouth; there was a gap between her teeth the size of the entrance to a railway tunnel. 'Fuck!' she said.

Even in a country where the word falls from Irish lips like raindrops, old women are not supposed to be saying that. I wondered if there is an equivalent in Arabic and Hindustani. A Japanese never swears. Instead he is able to offer an antagonist a couple of words that are so humiliating that the poor guy he addresses wants to commit hari kari straight away.

Swearing is not mentioned in the Bible as a sin. Swearing may be a way of relieving stress. Chimps curse at each other and make rude gestures. Animals that do not curse go straight into attack mode.

Most curses are so ancient that their birth dates and inventors remain unknown. The practice appears to have a deep neurological significance – Parkinson's and Alzheimer's people swear long after every other word has gone.

'Colonel sitting there,' said Maria.

'Uncle Jack?'

He was fast asleep, his mouth open. I could hear the deep gurgle of his breath, in, out, in, out, and see the sudden twitch of his moustache when he moved his lips. Across his knee, half opened was a book – *Out of Africa*. He looked small and frail and his head was nodding over his regimental tie.

'I look after,' said Maria.

She bent down and knotted up his laces which were undone. The fact that the shoes were as well polished as ever did nothing to lessen his feeble appearance. She prodded him gently on the shoulder and he raised his head with a snort.

'You have friend.'

He gave a jerk and frowned in my direction.

'Hello, Uncle Jack.'

He shouted: 'Get me out of here!'

He looked around at the other figures whom you could just tell were alive from the way their chests moved up and down. Then he got up and made a shuffling move towards a far door which must have led into a basement yard. When he reached it he turned the handle; it was locked.

At the other end of the room the automatic door opened and a piercing voice called out:

'Jack! What are you doing?'

Two of the sleepers stirred and woke. Mrs Freebody came across and turned down the sound of the television.

'What a naughty boy you are, Jack! Come here at once! Maria, bring him back to his chair.' Maria took him by the elbow as Mrs Freebody caught sight of me.

'Oh, hello, David, you're here to see Colonel Hilton?' She stammered slightly.

Maria led Uncle Jack back to where he had been sitting.

My uncle picked up *Out of Africa* and threw it at Mrs Freebody. She caught it deftly.

'We don't want too much excitement, do we, Colonel?'

Another Filipina nurse was coming in with a trolley on which were a large dented tin teapot, thick white mugs, and digestive biscuits still in their packets.

'Tea time!'

'I want to go!' Uncle Jack cried out.

'Not quite yet, Colonel.'

Before I got into the car I walked around the house looking down at the basement rooms which I had never noticed before. They had bars on all the windows. The architecture of the house included an addition at the back – the kitchen must be there, and rooms where the nurses must sleep in between the times they were on duty – I had never noticed that either.

Did those who were condemned to the basement receive visitors at regular times like those upstairs? Celebrate birthdays? Did their relatives come and see them? How many descended down the steps to Hell? When the Minister paid his visit, had he shaken hands with any of them? Did they do exercises?

When I got back to Mount Jewel Josie served me lunch.

'How is the Colonel, Master David?

'He's a bit out of sorts.'

I went to Dr O'Shea at his consulting rooms in Mauricetown.

'...Silver Meadows suits Jack, and I am pleased with the nursing facilities. He is under proper supervision.'

'Will he have to stay there for ever?'

'I am sorry to say it seems likely. I have known people like your uncle survive in this condition for years. I blame modern medicine for prolonging life far beyond its appointed span.'

'You believe that three score years and ten is long enough for anyone?'

He smiled grimly. 'Perhaps a year or two more than that. Perhaps they should issue a silver bullet to everyone collecting their pension for the first time. Or plenty of barbiturates.'

There spoke the good doctor. Bastard.

'...I have been treating the Colonel for years. The way it is,' he pointed a finger at me, 'nothing will ever kill him off.'

'He doesn't seem a total zombie. He is able to read a book. The other day he was reading *Out of Africa*.'

'David, he can hold a book. That means nothing.'

'So you are saying he is going to have to stay in that basement for ever?'

'David, control yourself.'

'I don't like the idea of watching him slowly die.'
'We are all slowly dying. And your uncle is in his twilight years.'
'Twilight years is a horrible phrase.'
'Many accurate phrases are horrible.'
'Does it cost the same living downstairs as living upstairs?'
'Of course.'

Lady Marsden was back in Silver Meadows. Before going down to see Uncle Jack I called into the sitting room on the ground floor. The usual dozens of old people were reading and talking; a group were doing exercises under the direction of a physiotherapist. Music played, 'Tea for Two'. 'Up, down, sideways' – wrinkled old arms moved.

I remembered in what now seemed the good old days when Uncle Jack was talkative, he told me me how a crinkly old lady was said to have run or marched over twenty miles, the distance measured on a pedometer. She was given a little silver cup and a new pair of running shoes and there was yet another photograph for the local paper.

'Of course she died the week after.'

Exercise was voluntary; when Uncle Jack was asked if he would like to join in, he said, 'Not bloody likely.' Lady Marsden said the same thing more politely.

There she was, sitting in the window playing cards with another merry widow whom I was on nodding terms with. I went over and greeted them.

Mrs O'Brien was playing cribbage with Lady Marsden – bridge had gone when Uncle Jack vanished. When Mrs O'Brien addressed her as Daisy – Lady Marsden frowned; she did not consider her nearly smart enough to call her by her Christian name.

'How is Jack?' Lady Marsden asked.

I said, 'He's downstairs. Have you ever seen what's down below?'

She shook her head.

'You've no idea what it is like? It's terrible.'

She put her hand up to her neck where the silk scarf she wore must have been hiding a scar.

'I don't know what you expect me to do about it.'

'You could have a word with Mrs Freebody. You could complain.'

'What good would that do?'

Mrs O'Brien said, 'Jack's a lovely man. Always a joke. Always makes one laugh.'

Lady Marsden said: 'Your turn to deal.'

A forgotten name, a missed birthday, an unexplained misquotation, an appointment not kept, or any small episode of forgetfulness draws old people towards the terror they try and reproduce in horror films. So does the word they can't think of, and the longer time it takes to slip back into the memory.

After sixty the memory starts to go, and then the worst begins to happen. Those are just the preliminaries and the chances are there is violence to come.

'The lamps are going out over Europe,' said Sir Edward Grey in 1914, but it is the lights going out in the brain that makes the elderly shake with fear.

Suddenly I was desperately sorry for my uncle. For the first time since childhood I felt guilty for all the thoughts and feelings I had directed towards him. Since I was eleven years old, standing at attention in the hall for two hours after I had kicked one of my uncle's Labradors. I remembered thinking, as Uncle Jack shouted at me to stand under the stuffed head of an antelope shot in Kenya, I wish he was dead. The first of all those yearnings that he would die and leave me everything. I had them most of my life. I had them in Sydney when I was swimming at Curl Curl. I had them at Sammy's funeral.

I remembered his energy, striding around the estate or going off with his Purdey to shoot something. He was always a keen shot. His path through life was littered with dead pheasants and dead woodcock. His instincts were those of a hunter gatherer. He had poured scorn on me for my reluctance to go near any gun, or fishing rod.

Now he was condemned to a dungeon, reduced to throwing books at Mrs Angelica Freebody.

Old age, someone said, is the time when you are punished for things that are not your fault. Someone else wrote, ask not for whom the bell tolls.

CHAPTER SEVEN

I began to visit Uncle Jack more often, twice or three times a week. In spite of what Dr O'Shea said, I brought him books, picture books mainly, and old copies of the *National Geographic. Lions of the Serengeti...Seeking the Elusive Okapi*. He opened them. Did he read them? I didn't know.

I discovered that since he went down to the basement of Silver Meadows my uncle's main interest, was not looking at photographs of zebras and lions. It was food.

These days, since he had tumbled into hell, he had this one compensation. He seemed to think of little else but food. He got animated at the call for lunch. If he happened to be asleep he stopped snoring, woke instantly when the meal was announced, got up, abandoned the television, dropped the book or the magazine that might lie in his hands and rushed for the dining room ahead of other greedy old maniacal inmates.

The dining room down below was just as sombre as the rest of the basement, and so dimly lit the old creatures could hardly see what they were given as they settled down at the long grubby trestle tables. Towels were tied round their necks, not always clean towels,

Uncle Jack ate and ate.

Whenever I encountered Mrs Freebody she reported at length about his amazing appetite.

To reach the basement I had to go through the main hall upstairs before making my descent. After a nurse let me in, Mrs Freebody would make a point of coming out of her study and greeting me, before giving me any faintly positive news about the old man.

'How hungry he always seems to be! More than most of my other patients...such a pleasure to watch the Colonel tucking into an Irish stew. Or queen of puddings, his favourite. He is never ready to give attention to anything else until his plate has been cleaned!'

Did she make a point of standing and watching him? After he had finished and wiped his mouth on the towel, I was sure she called out: 'Good boy, Jack!'

Perhaps she gave him a chocolate. He was a special client.

'...How he loves his food! Roast beef and Yorkshire pudding on Sunday, and he gobbled it up...'

'...You are not his only visitor, you know.'

'Oh? Who else has been?'

'Mr Cook, the clergyman from Castlepaul sees him regularly.'

But inevitably old friends ceased to come and see him. No more Trigger or Gusty or Beaky or Duffy.

'Poor old Jack' they must have been saying to one another, relieved that they didn't have to visit Silver Meadows ever again.

'And poor Daisy. Did you hear what he did to her?'

Hazel took a risk in insisting on coming to see my uncle. Maria, the Filipina who seemed to spend much of her time looking after him, described to me what happened.

'Woman priest come. Say hello. White collar. Say Our Father. Colonel see her. Colonel shout. Colonel chase her. Woman run.'

After Hazel's swift departure Mrs Freebody arranged for my uncle to be given more tranquillisers to bring on the deep sleep that lasted between mealtimes. But he always woke up in time to eat.

I began to time my visits to late in the afternoon when he had finished his lunch and the effects of these tranquillisers had worn off to some extent. I also found that arriving after lunch meant that it was less likely that I would run into Mrs Freebody who would be making her stately inspections of the rooms above. Quite often I was able to sneak past her office and downstairs without running into her.

Usually after he had eaten his massive meal Uncle Jack went into boa constrictor mode and fell asleep in front of the television. Occasionally he woke to watch, particularly if there was a nature programme about Africa.

'This young male is in a state of mast...'

Or there would be chimpanzees or gorillas, very like human beings to look at, but not as pretty.

But most afternoons I would have to prod him awake and take him to the farthest corner of the room to give him news of Mount Jewel. I made a point of keeping him in touch with his old home, although it was difficult to tell how much information sank in.

Every morning I walked around the estate with Massey.

'Tell the Colonel the barley's in...Kelly will be coming round with the harvester for the wheat...ten bullocks is due to go to the sales... Melissa is covered by Murtagh's stallion...Flanagan seen to that...'

I would relay Massey's news. 'Uncle Jack...Melissa's in foal to a horse belonging to Willy Mullins. The winter wheat has been sown...'

I would speak loudly in order to be heard above the television. He nodded dreamily each time I finished a sentence.

Dan Hennessy rang me.

'Look here, David, we'd better get power of attorney so that we have control over the Colonel's expenses.'

'Go ahead.'

'The trouble is, he will have to sign a couple of documents.'

'I don't know if he is up to that now. You don't realise that he is under sedation most of the time. It is pretty well impossible to get any sense out of him.'

'I should have tackled him earlier.'

'Yes.' So you should have.

'David, if I give them to you, could you make an effort to get him to put his signature on them?'

Solicitors. There's a special circle in Dante's hell for them. Lower than the basement of Silver Meadows.

The television was roaring and the old women were asleep. A couple of nurses stood sentry, giggling by the main door. Filipinas, but neither one was Maria. Uncle Jack, was also asleep, snoring gently, wearing his great coat. The old lady beside him woke up for a few minutes to watch the nature programme playing on television. A man in a diving suit announced: 'I am swimming among socialising sperm whales.'

My uncle's eyes were closed and he reminded me of a crocodile submerged in an African river. I could hear the gurgle of his breath, the usual in, out, in, out, as I watched the twitch of his moustache when he moved his mouth.

'Uncle Jack?' No answer.

I sat for some moments wondering what to do. My plan was to talk about some neutral topic like fishing which should interest him – if he understood. Then I would bring out Hennessy's document.

'Uncle Jack?' I bellowed. This time he moved, opening a watery eye.

I tapped him on the shoulder and the other eye opened both focused on me.

'Why are you here?' The sour words came out slowly with a struggle for breath.

'I have a small favour to ask you, Uncle Jack.'

I opened the envelope and bring out Hennessy's piece of paper. He tried to take it but it dropped on the floor.

'It's most important.' He gazed at me with a look of incomprehension. I took his hand gently and he offered no resistance.

I had come prepared with a pen which I placed between his arthritic fingers.

'Please, Uncle Jack...'

I was still pressing his fingers over the pen when one of the Filipina nurses appeared behind his chair.

'Is not allowed.'

Soon I was upstairs in Mrs Freebody's study.

'Who gave you permission to bring in this document? ...I do not care if it was his accountant...come now, David, your uncle is a very confused and sick man...it is quite against our rules.. please be more considerate to us...I would hesitate to call in the police...'

Next day I called on Dan Hennessy at his office in Laurence Street.

He said, 'Mrs Angelica Freebody is a foolish woman. She must know the importance of gaining power of attorney.'

Hennessy was wearing a dust coat over his clothes to prevent specks of brown powder settling on his clothes. Before him on his chaotic desk were papers detailing the expenses of Mount Jewel and the Silver Meadows account.

An accompanying letter from Mrs Freebody sought immediate payment. Hennessy handed it to me and I skimmed through it. If a cheque was not sent straight away, Silver Meadows would be unable to keep Colonel Hilton any longer. There was a shortage of beds and a waiting list of victims. She did not use that exact word.

She suggested that in future the bill might be paid quarterly which would save considerable inconvenience.

Hennessy shook his head as he inspected the line of figures. I had a suspicion he was looking at them for the first time.

'Silver Meadows does seem to be expensive. As much as a five star hotel. All the extras...snacks...laundry... Pears soap, Kolynos toothpaste – I suppose Jack could use cheaper brands? – tranquillisers, sherry...'

'He doesn't get sherry down where he is.'

'Oh...we'll cross that off then.' Hennessy drove a vigorous line through the item with a biro.

'I suppose we'll be able to continue for a few more months. Thank goodness your aunt in Spain has passed away.'

'Oh? Aunt Maud?'

'She was in her ninetieth year. You have no idea how much the Colonel was paying her every year for her upkeep.'

"I wonder what happened to her dogs.'

'They were put down. Six of them.'

The only positive feature of Uncle Jack's life in the dungeon was the good care Maria took of him. She rubbed him down when he showered. She put paste on his toothbrush, polished his shoes, mopped his face with a sponge, arranged for his jacket to be cleaned, and hung his trousers on the tin coat hanger provided. She sewed back the buttons which he tended to pull off back on his shirts.

How did I know this? She told me. Looking at Uncle Jack's shining shoes, and his clothes which were usually clean, I had no reason not to believe her.

How old was Maria? Mid-thirties? Her hair was shining black, not a grey strand in it, but she could be dyeing it. In her forties, at a guess, with those wrinkles, and the gold gleaming in her mouth when she smiled.

Three days before Christmas the basement room was filled with the usual sleeping old women. Beside them the Christmas tree, similar to the one they had upstairs had far fewer ornaments. Maria and another Filipina nurse were putting up some meagre paper streamers.

When I arrived, the Revd Charles Cook was reading Uncle Jack a passage from the bible. Nothing to do with the infant Jesus or glad tidings.

'And the Lord sent down an angel which cut off the mighty men of valour and the leaders and captains in the camp of the King of Assyria...'

There was more. Every now and again my uncle gave a grunt.

'And when he came into the house of his God, they that came forth of his own bowels slew him with the sword.'

Mr Cook looked up and gave me a smile. 'I thought the Colonel might enjoy this particular reading...nothing like a good battle scene to revive old memories.'

After he left, I took his place.

'Uncle Jack, the men at Mount Jewel all send their best wishes...'

My uncle said: 'Cigars.'

'What?'

'Bring me cigars.'

Maria climbed down from the ladder on which she had been balanced and beckoned.

'Colonel like cigars. You bring Christmas present?'

'How can he smoke in here?'

'I arrange. No one see.'

If that was what he wanted...

I drove the Rover up to Dublin to obtain boxes of La Gloria Cubana. I paid for them with almost the last of the salary I had managed to squeeze out of Dan Hennessy. I put them into the usual Supervalu bag – quite like old times – together with a bottle of Bushmills and a bottle of eau de cologne. On Christmas Eve I managed to slip the bag into Maria's hand.

In the upstairs sitting room at Silver Meadows a Christmas tree glittered with glass balls and twinkled with multicoloured electric lights. A mass and a Protestant service took place in the dining room, after which upstairs inmates were provided with crackers and presents, small ones donated by Mrs Freebody. She made a sunny little speech wishing everyone glad tidings.

Downstairs they dispensed with nearly all of that sort of celebration – although a priest appeared and mass was said. The Reverend Cook did not bother to reappear and Hazel was well out of it. The mad old women were given paper hats. Upstairs and down the inmates were served turkey and plum pudding and Uncle Jack, who also wore a paper hat, ate and ate.

At Mount Jewel Cook and the maids went home to their families. UNPAID I thought as they departed. I spent Christmas alone.

I sat in the kitchen eating the chicken Cook had left me, throwing pieces to the cats and dreaming about Australia.

I had been back in Ireland for a horrible year.

What a dreadful festival Yuletide was.

I went back to Silver Meadows just before New Year.

Uncle Jack said, 'Thanks.'

Maria managed to get him to smoke – perhaps in the yard of the

91

basement, or some storeroom. Nor did I know where she hid the cigars. In the old days when he was upstairs, he used to squirrel them away in the chest of drawers he was provided with.

Maria said, 'Very nice perfume. I like very much o de colon.'

'You must miss your family at Christmas.'

'I miss. But I send Manila much money.'

Mrs Freebody appeared in the basement, all smiles; snorers stirred.

'Your uncle had a really wonderful day. How he enjoyed his Christmas meal! I think if we had let him, he might have eaten the whole turkey!'

I suspected that soon there would be formidable money problems. Meanwhile, as New Year came and went, it was becoming clearer to me that Uncle Jack was not all that daft. We began to have regular talks.

'You liked your Christmas dinner?'

'No cranberry sauce.'

'What did you have for lunch today?'

'Cottage pie. They make it with horse meat.'

Conversations got longer.

'I'm not taking those bloody tranquillisers.'

'You're given them to stop you hitting people over the head.'

'I pretend to swallow them.'

Since I found it increasingly difficult to talk to him over the noise of the television, I would lead him into the dormitory where he slept. We would draw the curtains around the bed with the iron head and foot, and sit on it. I had brought along a patchwork quilt from Mount Jewel to make the cubicle a little less dismal. Beside the bed Maria kept the shelves immaculate, everything folded carefully, shirts, regimental tie and underwear.

Maria would be standing there keeping a watch for Mrs Freebody or some other nurse superior to her. Inmates were not allowed into the dormitories during the day time.

'He talk better,' Maria said.

It was true. Uncle Jack's speech improved every time I came.

'Maria's a grand girl...cuts my moustache. Of course, she has one of her own...'

On this visit when I was leaving, he said: 'Find out about Mary Attridge and Pauline O'Grady.'

'Who are they?'

'Bridge partners. They owe Daisy and me a fortune.'

I asked the Mrs Freebody about Mrs Attridge and Mrs O'Grady.

'Sadly, they have both passed away.'

Uncle Jack said, 'Inspectors were here yesterday.'

'Inspectors?'

'Always showing up – supposed to catch people by surprise.'

I looked down at the weeping slate floor. 'Do you mean to say they passed this basement as suitable for people like yourself?'

'Mrs Freebody bribes them. Gives a great deal of cash to her friend the Minister... She sleeps with him.'

Later he said: 'Shame the way I tackled Daisy. Going for her like that got me down here. It could happen to a bishop.'

Maria called out: 'Mrs Freebody come this way.'

My uncle dived towards the lavatory. I was left sitting on the patchwork quilt wondering what lie I could tell. But it was a false alarm – only another nurse who came in for a moment and addressed Maria in Spanish.

Uncle Jack emerged. '...They don't bother giving you proper lavatory paper – strips of newspaper...the *Independent* – not even the *Irish Times.*'

'Not true!' said Maria. 'Toilet paper good!'

Later she called out, 'She come! This time she here!'

Mrs Freebody appeared. My uncle stopped talking and let his mouth droop open.

'Maria, you should know better.'

'Colonel want come here.'

Mrs Freebody's frowned. 'You know that is forbidden. I have told you may times.'

'David, the Colonel must stay in the main downstairs living room during the day.'

She gave one of her smiles. Not the usual beam, but something more like ice.

'And please remind Mr Hennessy that he has not settled the monthly account.'

CHAPTER EIGHT

Hennessy said, 'There's a problem.'

I learnt that the estate had been losing money.

'The easiest option is to sell off more Guinness and Bank of Ireland shares.'

'I thought my uncle managed his business affairs with his dowser.'

Hennessy cackled. 'Seems that dowser had not been doing its job for some years.'

He added, 'Seriously, David, we are going to have a little difficulty continuing to pay this sort of bill...'

'What are his sources of income?'

'His pension – he gets a small one from the British army... dividends, of course, but they have dwindled sharply. What the farm makes – E.U. subsidies... They still don't add up to enough to pay Mrs Angelica Freebody. We can use that money – but not the income from his stocks and shares without his signature.'

Whose fault was that?

'I suppose we couldn't look for somewhere cheaper for him to stay?' Another cottage home or somewhere that offered sheltered accommodation.

He shook his head; snuff whirled. Someone once told me that King Charles II was an avid snuff taker who paid twenty pounds a year for snuff when twenty pounds would buy a house.

'I understand they would be all more or less this sort of price. I don't think we could consider any of those institutions run by the Department of Health...'

'You mean the County Home?'

'Wouldn't do at all.'

I doubted if the whole of the castellated asylum outside Mauricetown would be much worse than the basement at Silver Meadows.

'What's to be done?'

'You could start sacking some of the staff at Mount Jewel.'

'Most of them have been there for as long as I can remember.'

'Time Roycroft retired – he must be the same age as the Colonel. You don't need a cook and two maids to look after you.'

'Cook has been at Mount Jewel for over forty years.'

'Does the Colonel belong to the Masons? They are good at looking after their own.'

'He had a row with them.'

'Even so, they might be worth trying. The British Legion?'

'Yes he does belong to the British Legion.'

'They would hardly come up with enough money to pay these fees. I shouldn't think the Masons would pay for them either.'

'What about the Trust?'

'While you're uncle is alive the Trust can't be broken.'

'So as things stand Mrs Freebody is gobbling up the family money.'

'Put it like that, yes.'

'Couldn't we remove him, bring him home? Have round the clock nursing?'

Hennessy polished his spectacles with a grubby handkerchief. 'You'd have to get Dr O'Shea's permission – and probably some other doctor's as well. And it would be almost as expensive.'

'He's not nearly as daft as O'Shea makes out. I am able to have perfectly rational conversations with him.'

Hennessy grunted in disbelief. 'Don't forget he's nearly killed two women. Look here, David, I'll pay this current bill. After that we will have to consider something drastic.'

'Like what?

'We could sell some of the land at Mount Jewel.'

'Can that be done without power of attorney?' Your fault we don't have it. 'My uncle's permission? I doubt if he would be up to giving it.'

'We'd manage something. We would have to look into the medical situation. And you might have a talk with that ancient cousin of yours – she's the only surviving member of the Trust.'

'You mean Cousin Helen?' I had not seen her since I was a child.

'She might have some ideas about breaking it up – it's costing her. She seems to be the only one around who might have some cash.'

A maid answered the door of Cousin Helen's terraced house in Dun Laoghaire. Like Uncle Jack, she had two maids and a cook. Like our indoor staff, they lived downstairs in a kitchen with an Aga – Cousin Helen spent much of her time down there keeping warm, chatting to them and doing the easy crossword in the *Evening Herald*.

Visitors like myself were entertained in the drawing room which was large and cold, the dividing doors kept open. I was led past the tumbling group of stuffed monkeys into the drawing room where Cousin Helen crouched over a small fire, her yapping Yorkshire terrier in her lap.

I glanced around at the things that used to fascinate me as a child. The little gadget for holding up crinolines above the mud. The portrait of her great-grandfather wearing a luxuriant dundreary moustache; he had been a slaver in Barbados. On the floor was the skin together with head and open jaws and teeth of the tiger that had eaten Cousin Bartholomew in Bengal. A photograph of the six maiden aunts who had gone to Zanzibar as missionaries. On the walls were pictures of Louis Wain cats and portraits of King George V and Queen Mary half throttled with jewellery round her throat – I was reminded of Uncle Jack and what he had done to Daisy.

A tray of orchids flourished. They were descended from some obtained by a great-uncle who travelled to Tibet in search of plants. He sold a lot of them and made a considerable amount of money. He brought back a Tibetan prayer wheel which was in the corner cabinet along with a lot of simpering china figures of shepherdesses and suchlike.

In another corner was Cousin Helen's harp. On every St Patrick's Day she used to make her panting chauffeur carry the instrument up to the summit of the Hill of Tara together with a little stool. On the great mound overlooking the grassy plain her diminutive figure could be seen, wind tossing her hair, as, ignoring flurries of rain, she engaged the strings. Her tinny repertoire, watery notes of Thomas Moore, blew over royal Meath.

Cousin Helen's family had started off poor – so poor that her father and uncles could not afford retrievers when they went shooting. Instead, their sisters were dressed in bathing suits and sent into the bog after dead snipe. Alice, Cousin Helen's sister, managed to marry a rich man – the poor fellow never realised until too late that Helen was included in the liaison. He and Alice were long dead, but Cousin Helen was still sound as a bell. No need for her to be considered as an inmate of any place like Silver Meadows. She worked in her garden and helped out numerous charities. Everyone who met her was charmed by her kindness and gentleness. How she came to be involved in Uncle Jack's Trust was a mystery especially after he had once accused her of stealing a bottle of sherry. But relatives stick together.

We sat together trying to keep warm while the maid brought in tea scones and Marietta biscuits. 'Who is Marietta?' I ask idly.

'What rather than who,' Hatta replied. 'It's a town in Georgia where they make them.'

I tried to describe Uncle Jack's financial problems.

'Don't mention, such things, my dear boy,' she said, delicately pouring out Earl Grey.

She was old fashioned enough to believe that everything could be left in the hands of your accountant and solicitor. They would look after everything and each year dividends would magically appear. I talked to her about the Trust but she did not seem to understand. Uncle Jack was a sweet old fellow lucky enough to have inherited a considerable fortune.

'Didn't one of his horses win the Gold Plate at Ascot?

'Gold Cup. No it didn't.'

'Why don't you talk to Mr Reeves?'

'Who is he?'

'Mr Mark Reeves. My solicitor. Such a pleasant man!'

I tried again to persuade her that a portion of the Trust might have to be sold to cover the expenses of Silver Meadows.

'What a pretty name!' she said, handing me another buttered scone.

I phoned Hennessy. 'She says to talk to her solicitor.'

'What's his name?

'Mark Reeves.'

'That's unfortunate.'

'Why?

'He is in Venezuela.'

'What's he doing there?'

'Don't you ever read the *Irish Times*? He fled there with eighty million punts of his client's money. They've been trying to extradite him for months.'

'I wonder if any of the money he has is Cousin Helen's.'

'Highly likely.'

'Should she be told?'

'David, we have enough problems.' He added, 'You know, it has occurred to me that you could sell your uncle's horses. If you did it privately and not through any blood stock sale they could go as farm produce. Hasn't the Colonel a friend who is keen to buy them?'

'Harry Andrews. I suppose it's worth a try.' For a long time Harry had expressed an interest.

My uncle called Harry Andrews the Runner when he abandoned his home in England after the war for the dubious delight of living across the Irish sea. Ireland offered an alternative to the Labour government and the huge taxes Harry was forced to pay to Mr Attlee. Around 1950 he settled happily on a large estate not far from Mount Jewel. Uncle Jack met him on the hunting field.

The arrival of Harry and his family in the neighbourhood was generally welcomed. His estate gave plenty of local employment, and when he took over from Uncle Jack as Master of the hunt, he poured money into the upkeep of hounds. When he wasn't on horseback wearing his red coat he roared around Meath and Louth in his Mercedes. People who lived by the side of the road rushed out to glimpse him pass by.

After Hennessy's suggestion, I invited myself to lunch, giving heavy hints about selling horses. In the dining room I sat with Harry, Kitty, his wife, tall and elegant with splendid legs like the high kicking chorus girl she once was – and two sulky teenaged sons. A silver fox was placed in the centre of the table. The food was served by an English butler. Kitty described her flat in Chelsea in a way that made me suspect she was on the verge of going the way of Harry's previous wives. Irish winters were cold and boring.

'You don't hunt?'

She smiled at me as if I had asked a silly question.

Harry's small piggy eyes were shining with pleasure at the thought of buying my uncle's horses.

I told him: 'Last year Uncle Jack put Open Skies and Knockout into Goffs but neither of them made their reserve.'

Harry said, 'Never be so sure you can sell at the right price...the market is almost flat.'

The offer he made for six of Uncle Jack's horses was miserable.

'I'm afraid that's the best I can do,' he chortled. I saw his sons exchanging glances. 'It's a lot of money.'

'I doubt Uncle Jack will agree.'

'If he doesn't he is pottier than ever. He's enough problems without thinking of horses. He should have given up the idea of keeping them long ago. They are too expensive and for a man in his frail physical condition it's far too much for him. I tell you I am doing him a favour.'

I assumed that bargaining as if he was in an Egyptian bazaar was one of the reasons why Harry had become so rich. It helped that he had inherited a fortune from a firm that sold soap – Wrights Coal Tar, Sunlight, Pears, no one could remember.

'Trade!'

What did he know about Ireland or people like my uncle? Another wealthy English expatriate with his fat portfolio, and now Master of our local hunt.

The derisory offer the Mount Jewel horses would cover three months stay at Silver Meadows.

'I particularly want Caviar Coast.' This was an animal that had won as a two year old and was the only one of my uncle's horses to be currently showing form.

'I'll discuss the possibilities with Uncle Jack.'

'I thought he was senile.'

'Not at all,' I said coldly.

'I'm sorry to hear it,' Massey said when I told him.

'We'll have the yearlings still with us.'

Massey was silent. He did not think much of those yearlings. Then he said, 'Mr David, the Coast is due to be running on Saturday.'

'Is he entered?'

'He is. Did you remind the Colonel?'

Now I remembered that before he had been taken to Silver Meadows my uncle had entered Caviar Coast for a race at Leopardstown.

'The papers are good. All in order. Paid up. If you have the Colonel's say-so we'll send him down Wednesday.'

I hesitated before I lied, 'I told the Colonel, and he said go ahead.' I knew that Massey had put his heart into training this particular horse and reminded myself that Uncle Jack was in no condition to roar at me if things went wrong. And if the Coast was entered and fees were already paid…

So we all went down to Leopardstown: outdoor staff, Cook and Josie. Bridget had left Mount Jewel because she had not been paid. Paddy O'Mahony, the jockey, wore my uncle's colours, the same as his regimental tie. Massey was there, of course, wearing his pork pie hat. Why do National Hunt trainers wear them? One of the great mysteries never tackled by Dick Francis.

I betted heavily with my last remaining punts. So did the rest of the staff of Mount Jewel.

I could not bring myself to watch the race, which reminded me all too much of the fatal race meeting I had attended in Australia and the flawed advice of Cousin Desmond.

Here at Leopardstown at first it seemed to be a rerun of that miserable occasion in New South Wales. There was a terrible five-minute wait before the win was confirmed, similar to the occasion when Shining Angel lost by a head and Cousin Desmond threw me out of his house.

But this time things went well. At Leopardstown Caviar Coast won. The roars from Mount Jewel went up into the sky.

We celebrated; I had never seen Cook drunk before. The Coast's win was just as well, since no one at Mount Jewel had been paid for weeks.

I rang up Harry Andrews and told him I would accept his offer provided he paid a bit more for the Coast after his win.

'No David. We agreed. A deal is a deal.'

'All right, then.' What else could I say? There would be some money to send on to Silver Meadows.

'You've talked to Jack?'

'Oh yes,' I lied.

'Under the circumstances you are wise. Keeping so many horses these days needs a great deal of capital and experience.'

'Shocking business,' Flanagan, the vet, said when he came to check the health of the animals before they departed. 'And the Colonel doesn't know? He'll not get over it.'

I did not tell him there was no need for the Colonel to know at this stage, if ever.

But that evening there was a phone call; a woman's voice in distress. I didn't recognise it at first.

'Oh, hello, Kitty.'

'Harry is in hospital – that bloody Mercedes...he crashed...' A broken pelvis. No more would his Mercedes roar through Louth lanes.

The deal was off.

The smile on the face of Massey when I told him reflected my own feelings.

But the bills continued to arrive. The special delivery letters brought to the door of Mount Jewel almost daily, had glaring notices on the envelopes. I avoided the usual trick of stuffing them into a Chinese jar and just threw them down on the rent table.

I lay awake and worried. If the staff of Mount Jewel continued to be unpaid they would leave one by one the way Bridget had. How we had jeered Bridget for a fool when we celebrated Caviar Coast's win in that Dublin pub near Leopardstown! Could the Coast be entered in another race as Massey had been urging? Uncle Jack would have to sign something... Those horses cost a fortune – poor old Runner had been right. Must remember to ring Kitty to find out how he was...

The money obtained from those winning bets on the Coast would not keep people here at Mount Jewel happy for more than a month. One thing, I was not going to sack anyone myself. I didn't want to be responsible for dismissing anyone – I wouldn't like to end up like Captain Boycott.

If Uncle Jack had allowed me to help run the estate, I might have had the responsibility...

Since Bridget's departure the house had not been dusted or swept – Josie thought such tasks beneath her. I could do them myself – perhaps I would make a start tomorrow. At least pick up the messes left by Edward and Albert...Cobwebs...

Power of attorney? Now that Uncle Jack was more cogent might I persuade him to sign something relevant? Hennessy could try – he could go down to Silver Meadows and make the attempt, instead of me. Mount Jewel's financial problems were partly his fault.

I thought not for the first time: could we remove my uncle from the place, bring him home and provide round the clock nursing? Might he get violent again? Would we really have to get Dr O'Shea's permission? Yes we would, Hennessy had said so. Could we find a more complacent doctor? Did Daisy have any grounds for suing Uncle Jack? Or even Hazel? Yes they both did.

Those bills – piling up day by day... Phone calls with angry demands – best not to answer it... One of these days the phone would be cut off. The cost of petrol...I still persuaded Hennessy to give me a small salary which went largely on petrol for the greedy Rover. For how much longer?

I heard a ghost walking on the upper landing. Stamp...pause... Stamp...The one legged ghost – the ancestor who had his leg taken off after the battle of Vittoria. Albert barked.

Could Mount Jewel be sold? Why not? For more than three hundred years we had lived through times of trouble. The estate was an anchor to our presence in Ireland; we could pull it up.... So many others had... Poor old Runner had bought his house from the O'Briens who went off to live in sunny France... Must ring Kitty – Runner had been tough about Coast and the other horses – must not think serve him right...

So many of Uncle Jack's friends had downsized. Pug Hardy had been broken by Lloyds. Squirrel Donogue had become bankrupt by his love of horses. The Butlers had got rid of their cold castle which had been turned into a convent. Manners Fitzherbert had also lived too well. The last of the Montgomerys had decided to uproot themselves from their mansion in Offaly and their land had been taken over by the county council for housing.

Not a big house left among them. A convent here, an hotel there, ruins elsewhere. All these owners of big houses – few as big as Mount Jewel, it had to be said – and their wives – or widows – drifted towards bungalows.

Rats leaving the sinking ship Uncle Jack always said.

If he were saner Uncle Jack would never agree to the sale of Mount Jewel – but he was not in a position to make a decision. Was he sane at all? Dementia?

Perhaps he never needed to know – which brought us back to the problems of power of attorney...

Signatures?

Already there had been signals and the word had spread that Mount Jewel might come on the market. Last week a Volvo had driven up to the porch and a cheeky young man enquired if the place was for sale.

'Go to hell !' I must have sounded just like Uncle Jack.

I watched the man look startled and retreat down the steps back to the car. His piggy face had blotched red.

'You think you can still treat people like that?'

How much was Mount Jewel worth? I had looked at the Thursday supplement to the *Irish Times* which featured property...must cancel the *Irish Times*...not much of a saving, but an expense none the less. A million? There would be no difficulty in selling an estate of this size and importance... More – six hundred acres. Two million? Uncle Jack's permission...Uncle Jack would live in clover for the rest of his life, surrounded by nurses...well into the twenty-first century. Would there be anything left for me?

I must get hold of an estate agent – not the fellow in the Volvo...

I thought about Australia and how I would love to be back in Sydney.

Dawn. The rooks were calling.

In the basement of Silver Meadows there was no sign of Uncle Jack among the sleepers. One of the Filipina nurses was overseeing them.

'Outside.' She gave me a shifty grin.

I searched round the place looking beyond the floribunda roses. I spotted him in the little summer house which Mrs Freebody called her temple. He was with Maria; I could see his arm around her waist. Were they trying to keep warm? He kissed her on her cheek. He looked up and caught sight of me.

'Clear off!'

I went to Hennessy at his office in Drogheda, and we discussed the possible sale of Mount Jewel.

It was the usual conversation.

As ever any sale would depend on getting Uncle Jack's permission. Documents for him to sign. You go and see him, Dan and see what you can do. He is as sane as I am. Not possible, David. Up to you. I'll think about it. The situation has become desperate. There is just enough money for the current bill. Otherwise...I'll think about it...

At Mount Jewel at last Cook and Josie felt it was time they departed. They went without telling me, left no note, merely some tins of cat food on the kitchen table. The cats vanished after the Aga went out. I had no idea how to restart it – that was a job usually left to Manzie. But Manzie had also gone; like Cook, he had a pension waiting for him.

I went to the hen run, threw some feed down, and, using a spade, just as I did as a boy, lifted up the rump of a hen to collect the egg beneath her. There were a couple more. In the cold kitchen I cooked myself scrambled eggs on the electric ring that was installed for summer. I opened a couple of tins of cat food and gave the contents to the dogs.

Next day, when I arrived at Silver Meadows I found the chaos of fire practice. Old women wandered around very slowly. Those who were arthritic crawled at a snail's pace, leaning heavily on their sticks. Crutches and zimmer frames were being dragged around the tarmac. An east wind shrieked; rain threatened.

Nurses rushed about and the air was full of cries, commands and complaints.

'We'll find your glasses, later, Patsy...'

'I've only the one slipper on.'

'Mrs Brennan, Mrs Brennan, come here, out of the way!'

'Where is Miss Kenny?'

'Where is Sister Anastasia?'

'Angelina, go and fetch Sister Anastasia! She'll be at her prayers in the chapel.'

'Sophia, get Mrs Corrigan off the stretcher – we need to take it back inside for Maureen.'

'What do you want to go back inside for?'

'I'm so cold!'

'Nurse, you've trodden on my dentures!"

'I hadn't my lunch finished!'

'Mrs Mulligan never came out.'

'Holy Mother of God! Go back and fetch her! Hurry! She must be still seated on the toilet.'

'Get Vincent to help!'

The kitchen staff appeared, fresh from washing up the last meal, impatient to lay out the next. An old lady in a wheelchair sat praying, moving her rosary around.

I glimpsed Lady Marsden, exquisite as always in her fur coat and hat, a silk scarf twisted around her throat.

A group of the patients from downstairs, the loonies, supervised by a nurse, were sitting on the tarmac. They were all dressed in dressing gowns and slippers.

Mrs Freebody stood at the front door, unlocked, wide open, as nurses and patients hustled past her outside. She had a notebook in her hand and her finger was pointing all over the place. She was counting; there was something frantic in her actions. No one seemed to be prepared to return to the warmth inside.

It was a chilly day to be organising a fire practice.

A shrieking noise came from outside the gates and in drove a fire engine which braked sharply just in time to avoid running over an old woman in a flapping dressing gown. Uniformed men jumped out and ran to the back for a hose. Only then did I notice smoke rising from the basement.

Where was Uncle Jack? I caught sight of him where I had seen him before, down at the summer house, Mrs Freebody's temple. Maria was beside hm. He was too far away for me to see whether there was a look of guilt on his face.

CHAPTER NINE

The tarmac had been cleared of old women by the time I drove out through the gates of Silver Meadows. I hoped from the bottom of my heart that this was for the very last time.

The firemen had rushed down to the basement and squirted the hideous curtains in the main room which Uncle Jack had set on fire. The hose poured onto the television which was already ruined together with the rest of the rooms contents. Dürer's hands had gone up in flames.

Uncle Jack was beside me, a rug over his knees, his blackthorn stick impeding my gear changes. Maria sat in the back among bags and suitcases. Although at Silver Meadows most of the rooms downstairs had been damaged, the dormitory where Uncle Jack slept in his iron bed had not been affected by the fire and his possessions were retrieved intact.

'Bad Colonel. Why you not call me and smoke cigar outside? No trouble then.'

The basement would not be in use for a long time. The loonies would have to go upstairs and share the space up there with the respectable and sane. Or go elsewhere, away to other places specialising in patients with dementia, Heather Lodge, Mountain View House, Riverside Home, and all the other care homes, with rural names, and waiting lists, friendly and welcoming, their well-trained staff in charge, and group activities listed for every day.

For a fair amount of time during the foreseeable future Mrs Freebody would be deprived of a certain amount of fixed income.

Almost before the fire was declared extinguished and the fire engine had departed, the shivering inmates, chivvied by nurses, had begun to trickle back inside, nearly all of them calling out how much they needed a nice cup of tea.

Mrs Freebody turned her wrath on my uncle.

'There is no question of Colonel Hilton staying any longer at Silver Meadows.'

At the same time that he was thrown out of Silver Meadows Maria got the sack.

'Not for another minute...'

Maria protested. 'You not want me here. I not going...'

'Oh yes you are,' said Mrs Freebody like a panto dame. 'Your behaviour has been inexcusable. What do you think our patients would feel if they knew any of our girls carried on like this?'

'Colonel fault. He kiss me.'

Mrs Freebody had heard enough.

'I want you to leave at once!'

'Please, can wait until tomorrow?'

'No it can't.'

Maria stared at her in silence.

'Puta!'

If Mrs Freebody could not understand Spanish the meaning was plain.

'Either you go now or I will call Vincent.' I doubted if Vincent would have been much help.

Mrs Freebody retreated inside the house as I packed the car. I noticed her looking down at me through the window of her office before I drove off, her cropped blond hair and watchful expression lit up by the evening sun. Then I drove away from the grey house with its fake battlements.

Our first stop was the hostel which housed the nurses, who worked in Silver Meadows. Nearly all of them were from the Philippines. A minibus carried them to and fro every day. Maria got out and went to fetch her belongings. Uncle Jack sat without saying a word, his face a mask of indifference to the trouble he had caused.

Maria reappeared carrying a shabby suitcase which I threw into the boot. We drove in silence, bumping our way down country lanes scattered with the bodies of crows and, once, a dead cat. We passed piles of sugar beet like piles of skulls. We drove through Mauricetown and along the road to the entrance of Mount Jewel.

'Very big gate,' Maria broke the silence.

Past the ruined gate lodge, shrouded with ivy and up the twisting drive. It was late in the evening and the men who still worked on the estate had gone home. There would be some explaining to do tomorrow morning.

'Very long way.'

The drive was well over a mile. The car came up the last curve and I parked as near to the porch as I could.

'Very big.'

Uncle Jack woke up. 'The fourth biggest house in Ireland.'

'Maybe too big.'

My grandfather had thought the same. Sixty years ago he had decided: 'Best thing for this house is to knock it down and use the material to lime the ground.' But he died before he got around to putting his plan in action.

Uncle Jack and Maria climbed out of the car as I went up and pushed open one of the heavy front doors.

'You not lock door?'

Uncle Jack said, 'Never.'

'Not like Silver Meadows.'

'Not like that bloody prison.'

Since my uncle had inherited the place, Mount Jewel had always been open and accessible. It was assumed by him that with staff wandering around inside and outside the house would keep it safe from thieves. This was in spite of the dining room burglary which had taken place during the lunch party held to mark his resignation from his position as Master of Hounds.

The Runner was taking over from him. Old friends had all turned up, the usual, together with the odd wife; in addition, the usual widows had attended; after lunch, when they all moved next door into the drawing room for coffee, burglars swooped. None of the coffee drinkers heard them at their work, sweeping off the plates and spoons and carrying the fine eighteenth-century mahogany table to the long window, pushing it outside and into the waiting white van.

The thieves took a couple of pictures as well, including one of Aunt Maud riding side saddle. Unaware that portraits by Alfred Munnings were worth a good deal, Uncle Jack had considerably underinsured the painting. Ignorance is bliss; he had been delighted with the amount he received for its loss. From that time onward the perpetually unlocked doors were to encourage more burglaries and more insurance.

Albert and Edward rushed out wriggling, howling in ecstasy, leaping up on Uncle Jack.

'Good boys!'

They spent a minute reaching up to lick his face between their roars of joy. Then they turned their attention to Maria.

My uncle hobbled over to where she was lying on the gravel. 'Are you all right, my dear?'

'Dirty dogs. Like in Manila.'

'Come inside out of the rain. David, get everything out of the car.'

I began to carry in his belongings together with Maria's suitcase.

If only I had been given some warning. There had been no opportunity for getting the place clean – my efforts at sweeping and dusting had been feeble. There was no question of signs of welcome like freshly cut flowers.

The hall was dark and big. At the far end the staircase rose and divided. The grandfather clock struck the hour with its usual echoes.

In the dusky light Maria looked around, at antlers, the tiger skin, the stuffed bear, the prints of the Doneraile steeplechase, the groups of swords and spears, the stand for sticks and umbrellas gouged out of the leg of an elephant which had been shot by Uncle Jack in Kenya, and the mildewed portraits of ancestors staring out of carved gold frames.

'Very cold.'

'My dear, you're too used to the fug in Silver Meadows.'

'In Philippines always warm.'

The dogs were running round lifting their legs, continuing to make sounds of happiness.

'Josie? Bridget!' Uncle Jack called out.

Panting from bringing in the luggage, I gasped. 'They've left. Cook as well.'

'What would they want to do that for?'

He could never understand why any of his employees would ever wish to leave Mount Jewel. Similarly he considered that anyone who voluntarily left Ireland for good must be deranged. England was bad enough; as for going further afield, to Spain, he thought Aunt Maud must have been out of her mind. Or in pursuit of lovers. And Australia – only fit for convicts. After his time in Africa and his years as a soldier he had become convinced that there was no place in the world to live in outside Ireland.

'They weren't being paid.'

'Humph.' His stick banging on the parquet, he stumped his way across the hall, Maria following timidly, making big efforts to keep out of the dogs' way. I was in the rear.

The study was dominated by the piles of bills and all the angry correspondence I had left lying on the rent table. The shutters were drawn. I switched on the light, thankful the electricity had not been cut off.

The chandelier, whose glass bits and pieces were long overdue for a dip in hot soapy water, gave a sullen illumination. In the light my uncle noticed Maria was shivering. 'Here, my dear!' he threw her a hairy dog's blanket which she took and wrapped round her shoulders.

'Get the fire going, will you, David.'

He settled down in the armchair he had used for the past fifty years. 'Ah! Good to be home!'

'Not warm!' Maria shivered in the dog's blanket.

'Get a move on, David!'

The dead fire was under a chimney piece with a fine marble depiction of Apollo in his chariot. It had been somewhat ruined by Uncle Jack some years ago during a row he had with Massey when, wielding his blackthorn stick, he had struck off Apollo's nose. The grate was filled with ash and a huge half-burnt log that a week ago had tried to burst into flame and had given up. A pile of logs, which had been cut from a recently felled tree and had not had time to dry out, waited consumption. Four turf briquettes might have helped to create a blaze. There was no kindling, no coal and there were no firelighters.

I did my best, making several trips to the yard and the coal house to scrape up a few pieces of coal lying in corners, and a fortunate discovery of a few sticks that passed for kindling. I kicked the dogs out of the way and borrowed Uncle Jack's matches – the same he had used in his efforts ot burn down Silver Meadows.

It was a long time before I managed to get a miserable fire going with the help of old copies of the *National Geographic*.

'Always rain here in Ireland. More rain than monsoon.' Maria wrapped the dogs' blanket more tightly around her shoulders.

Uncle Jack stretched out his arthritic legs and put his spotty old hands up to what could hardly be described as a blaze. A little flickering flame may have offered some warmth.

'Give us something to drink, David.'

In the drinks cupboard little remained. There was some Baileys Irish Cream bought to give Cook and the maids their Christmas tipple when they got their annual present – an extra weeks' wages. The stuff at the bottom of a bottle of crème de menthe must have dated back forty years.

'Not that muck.'

But it was a success with Maria.

'Peppermint – I like.'

Uncle Jack sipped the Baileys wrinkling his face with a suggestion that he was drinking poison.

'Get dinner, will you, David!'

Could he have shed dementia like an old overcoat? How recently seemed the time when he sat among mad old women, silent, his mouth open.

In the kitchen I found the last two eggs I had collected from the hen run. I would have to boil them. Some old bread – I would have to toast it. Half a jar of Cook's home-made raspberry jam – that would taste all right after I scraped the mildew off it. In the back of a cupboard I discovered a tin of peaches and another tin of sardines. The peaches would be dessert. All would be washed down with tea which Uncle Jack would drink out of his huge tea cup. Pity the milk was slightly off.

The sardines would have to be for me; I opened the tin and wolfed them while the eggs boiled.

I took the loaded tray upstairs; this was what Josie had to do every day. I staggered across the hall to the study.

Uncle Jack looked at the meal I had prepared in silence.

Down again to the kitchen I filled all the hot water bottles I could find, four, two stone, and two rubber. I climbed to the first floor carrying luggage – it took three trips up the great divided staircase, around and up again.

The sheets upstairs in the huge airing cupboard felt damp; the signs of mice had to be ignored. Why were the cats never allowed up here to hunt them? So many of the bedrooms containing the uniforms of past dignitaries who had been family members were locked, that there were only a few spare rooms.

Maria could have the room at the east end to which rare visitors were assigned. It had not been slept in for many years. The sun shone straight in during the morning, and there was a view of river and mountains. Water colours, painted by maiden aunts, failed to hide the brown streaks running down the walls. Damp would be Maria's lot; damp sheets, blankets, towels; nor would the hot water bottles chase away the moisture of the mattress.

The one electric blanket in the house belonged to Uncle Jack; I had been using it while he was away. I tore it off my bed and installed it in his giant four-poster, before making that up with more bedclothes which were also damp I managed to find his bed socks. Damp.

In the sitting room Uncle Jack and Maria had finished their boiled eggs and drunk their tea.

'Not much of a meal.'

Food had been my uncle's obsession at Silver Meadows.

The fire was nearly out. Uncle Jack got up stiffly out of his chair.

Maria trailed up the stairs behind him and the dogs. I led her to her bedroom at the east end. The light was dim; the kerosene in the heater, which had added very little warmth to the room smelt strongly.

CHAPTER TEN

Next morning I peered into Uncle Jack's bedroom to find Maria lying beside him.

Some time in the night she must have wandered across the wide acres of the first floor from the east bedroom.

The embroidered curtains of the four-poster framed her small frowning face. She had metal curlers in her dark hair. She lay staring at Uncle Jack's coffin stretched at the far end of the room.

"Is there anything you want? ' I asked.

'No thanks,' said Uncle Jack.

They got up around noon.

Maria came downstairs and went straight to the telephone in the study.

'You find me Silver Meadows number.'

I knew it by heart.

Uncle Jack and I stood by as Maria dialled.

We could could hear Mrs Freebody's penetrating voice, stammering with anger.

'No, you certainly cannot come back...no question... I do not not need untrustworthy people like you working here...irresponsible...of course you are dismissed as I told you yesterday...do I make myself clear? '

Maria put the phone down sadly. 'I stay here.'

'My dear, you should be happy.'

'This house cold.'

Uncle Jack changed the subject. 'Time for breakfast.'

I said, 'There isn't any.'

'I gathered that, you fool. We go to Dennihy's.'

'I haven't any money.'

'Have you never heard of putting things on the slate?'

So we went to Dennihy's in Mauricetown and ordered full fries. The dining room at the hotel was warm as we sat and devoured sausage, bacon and eggs, black and white pudding, mushrooms, tomato, toast, marmalade and coffee.

Uncle Jack had a second helping. And a third.

'No problem, Colonel.' The manager of Dennihy's was happy to accept a delayed bill.

After we had finished my uncle said, 'Drive to Drogheda, David. I have to talk to Hennessy.'

'The car has very little petrol.'

'Fill her up at Redmond's... I'll pay later.'

'Certainly, Colonel,' they said at Redmond's.

I was not allowed into Dan Hennessy's office since my uncle made it plain that he considered his dealings with his solicitor were none of my business. Like old times. His ruling did not apply to Maria and I felt a stab of jealousy as he escorted her up to Hennessy's chaotic office.

I was left to slouch in the driving seat of the car, parked with difficulty in Laurence Street. I recalled Uncle Jack sitting in Mrs Freebody's basement in front of the television, asleep, his jaw dropped open, one of many insane snorers. Had that daily sleep been a long pretence?

Was it safe for him to be on the loose or should we be looking for another tranquil nursing home where he could stay? Or was he a pariah for such places and doomed for a lengthy stay in the castellated horror in Mauricetown?

Money, money, money.

After more than half an hour Uncle Jack and Maria came out of Hennessy's office and crossed the road.

'Wait there!'

They were away, braving the east wind.

I wondered if I had time to go up to Hennessy and consult him. But here was the man himself coming out of his office. He too, crossed the road and I wound down the window.

'Every thing is fine, financially, David. Your uncle's off to the bank to get a bit of cash. Amazing what a few signatures will do.'

'What do you think of his state of mind?'

'He doesn't seem to be the slightest different to what he was last time I spoke to him.'

'Are you sure? Do we need medical opinion? Should I ring Dr O'Shea?'

'Leave O'Shea out of things for the present. As long as the Colonel does not clobber any more women, or try to burn down any houses he should be able to stay out of places like Silver Meadows.'

'How did you hear about the fire?'

'Mrs Freebody was on to me.'

'Could he be sued by her?'

'Not for the price of a couple of curtains.'

'The television went as well.'

'Oh yes, and a few other things. She's sending me the list. But not enough has been destroyed for her to go to court. She'll be heavily insured. The Colonel's been unlucky as an arsonist.'

'What do you think of Maria?'

Hennessy gave me one of his winks. 'She's a level-headed girl and Jack is quite a handful.'

I should have questioned him some more, but he was off; no one wanted to linger in that wind.

I had never heard Uncle Jack call anyone my dear. He never addressed Aunt Maud like that.

Uncle Jack and Maria had seemed affectionate enough this morning when I found them in bed tucked up cosily under damp blankets. They reminded me of that Irish peer who became infamous for using his maid as a hot water bottle. Uncle Jack seemed to be employing similar methods of keeping warm. But more likely, the fault was with Maria, complaining of cold.

I continued to worry about my own position at Mount Jewel.

I thought wistfully of Australia. I longed to be there.

Here were my uncle and Maria, walking back towards the car, Maria carrying several large carrier bags containing new clothes.

Uncle Jack said: 'Drive to a supermarket David.'

They did a colossal shopping. I trailed around after them pushing a trolley. Maria bought spices of the type that had never been seen in the kitchen of Mount Jewel.

'I also find coconut.'

Tins of dog food, chicken, rice, noodles, cake, coffee, tea, more cake, chocolate biscuits; the trolley piled up. Uncle Jack bought three bottles of Bushmills and plenty of cigars. They were nothing like as splendid as those sold in Fox's, but enough to be going on with.

'Never going to be caught short again.'

Back in Mauricetown Dennihy's and Redmond's were paid and I was ordered to get a bag of coal.

'Just to go on with. Don't forget firelighters.'

At Mount Jewel the dogs were barking at Dr O'Shea who sat waiting in his BMW. When he got out of his car, he ignored my uncle and addressed me.

'David, I have been able to find another nursing home specialising in dementia which is willing to accept the Colonel.'

'He'll be perfectly all right here.'

'I am not prepared to give my permission for him to be outside a proper hospital or nursing home.'

Uncle Jack shouted, 'Clear off!'

Dr O'Shea continued to ignore him.

'I'll give you the name of the place I have found – with great difficulty, I may add, since not many homes want to admit patients who have a history of violence. You can expect their ambulance to be along in the next couple of days.'

'O'Shea, you swine, that's what you did before – and I ended up in that ghastly hole.'

'Colonel, you were sent to Silver Meadows for your own good.'

'You seem to have the idea that Silver Meadows is run by Mother Teresa.'

'I will not give my permission for you to be without proper medical supervision.'

'You can't wait to put me in a straightjacket.'

The dogs were showing their teeth.

From the safety of his BMW Dr O'Shea called out to me: 'David, the Colonel will be collected in the next few days and taken to new premises – the Purple Heather Nursing Home outside Trim.'

Before he started up, he paused and addressed Maria, shouting above the barking dogs 'As for you, Miss Fernandez – Mrs Freebody has spoken to me about your behaviour which seems to have unaccountable for someone in a position of trust. There is no possible way you can continue to work in Ireland and she is taking steps to see that you are deported back to the Philippines as soon as possible.'

In the hall Maria put down her carrier bags and burst into tears.

'You not let me go from Ireland?'

My uncle put his arm around her. 'Don't believe a word of what that fool was saying.'

'I work. I need. I send money to Manila. To my family...'

'My dearest, you never need to work again.'

Maria went upstairs and put on a red woollen shirt waister which she had just bought. It was the first time I had seen her out of nurse's uniform.

Uncle Jack said, 'Come with me, my dear, and we will tour the estate.'

'Over her new dress she put on an ancient tweed coat, a grey woollen scarf and a matching hat like a tea cosy, ancient clothes which had belonged to Aunt Maud. She rummaged in the box under the hatstand in the vestibule and chose a pair of gumboots too big for her little feet.

Uncle Jack strode ahead, the happy dogs running beside him, and I went along as well, carrying umbrellas. I felt superfluous as I showed Maria the steward's house, the laundry and the line of stables. I pointed out Aunt Maud's famine pot and the empty greenhouses. Maria made it clear that none of these things were interesting.

Massey and the two men still working the farm greeted Uncle Jack in astonishment.

'Good to see you, back again, Colonel,' Massey said, and the two men with him gave a sort of half salute and mumbled something similar. Their voices sounded cautious; they had heard that Uncle Jack was mad and they had seen him behaving in a peculiar way.

Their glances veered towards the tiny oriental figure beside him muffled up in moth-eaten clothes.

'Many horses.'

So there were, some whinnying, some putting their heads out of their stable door to peer at their master. Thank goodness they had not been passed on to Harry the Runner.

I remembered that I had never rung up Kitty to find out how Harry was – dead or alive. There was a lot to tell Uncle Jack.

Massey opened up the bottom of one stable door, brought out Caviar Coast and led him up and down. He looked splendid.

'Very big horse,' squealed Maria, running to Uncle Jack and seizing his arm. The men looked on.

Massey said, 'He's in good heart since his win.'

'What win?'

All eyes turned on me. I had to say, 'He won at Leopardstown ...I forgot to tell you...'

Massey said: 'He could do with another race.'

'I'll see to it.' My uncle added: 'Come up to the house. Seems you all may be due some back pay.' He was smiling.

Money made him happy all the time.

He moved on, together with Maria, trying to hang on to him and avoid puddles at the same time. Massey followed and I brought up the rear.

We crossed the lime avenue to inspect the Kerry herd, small and black with pointy horns.

'Many very pretty little cow.'

'Pedigreed,' Uncle Jack said proudly. He asked Massey: 'Is Murphy's still taking their milk for ice-cream?'

'Yes Colonel.'

The money for that had gone straight to Dan Hennessy, a drop in the ocean of what had been owed to Silver Meadows.

We left the Kerry cows and walked past the small lake where the swan lurked. Maria gave a scream as it flapped and hissed.

I pointed out the ruined dower house. 'That was where I lived when I was a small boy.'

'Old building. Not good. No roof. All fallen down.'

I considered that it served her right when Albert ran into her and she fell into nettles and weeds.

'New dress all mud.'

Back inside the house Maria grumbled as she set about wiping down the red shirt waister. After the salvage operation on her clothes she called out: 'Now I cook.'

I took her down to the kitchen and showed her the electric ring.

'Why not that?' She pointed to the Aga. 'Keep kitchen warm.'

'I don't know how to light it.'

'You fool like Colonel say.'

'I'll get Massey.'

There was nothing that Massey could not do. He had the Aga lit in no time and soon the usual old warmth permeated the kitchen.

Maria sorted out the food that had been bought that morning.

'Get me apron.'

I found one in a drawer.

'Now go. I cook.'

Upstairs, having paid Massey, and given him the back wages of the other two men still working on the estate, Uncle Jack was contemplating the bills on the rent table.

'Explain!'

He proved as acute as any accountant – I wished that Dr O'Shea were there to hear him querying one overdue account after another. There was no trace of dementia in the way he ripped open each envelope and absorbed its unpleasant contents.

He spotted that Hennessy had been paying me a salary.

'If you want to continue with that, you will have to continue to act as my chauffeur. I don't feel up to driving any more.'

For years he had dreaded the moment when he would be unable to drive. Few old people are so miserable that they plan to stick their heads in a plastic bag when their driving license is forfeit, but the prospect is always there, like death itself. It is unfair, considering that the elderly, or most of them, are not reeling out of pubs in the small hours.

'And light the fire.'

Spicy smells were coming up from the kitchen.

Uncle Jack waved at the bills. 'We'll go back to Drogheda tomorrow and get Hennessy to deal with this stuff. Maria will need more clothes.'

Maria appeared at the study door. Dinner was eaten by the fire, a proper fire this evening. Filipino food. Under Maria's direction I brought up her chicken which was served with sauce made of liver, sugar and spices accompanied by a pile of noodles.

Uncle Jack fiddled around his plate and found the parson's nose. '*Le nez du pape*. The only thing I recognise.'

'You like?'

'Delicious.' He sounded dubious.

'I good cook.'

Later Uncle Jack said: 'Perhaps Josie and Cook will come back.'

'Who this Josie? Who Cook?'

'They work here – or they used to.'

Uncle Jack and I were silent remembering Cook's queen of puddings and steak and kidney pie. Her Yorkshire puddings which were so light they threatened to fly to the ceiling. Sponges impregnated with cream and home-made strawberry jam.

Maria frowned. 'No need people inside kitchen. Better alone. I do cooking. I give plenty Filipino meals.'

An ambulance came up to ferry Uncle Jack over to the nursing home near Trim. Dr O'Shea drove behind it ready with the usual knockout injection he carried in his briefcase. He had arranged a repeat of my uncle's exodus to Silver Meadows.

The dogs alerted us. We stood at the study window and watched the same two men climb out of the ambulance who had taken Uncle Jack to Silver Meadows a year ago. Dr O'Shea came over to them and there was a muttered conversation.

'I'll shoot them.'

I had been afraid of that. I had removed Uncle Jack's Purdey from the gun room in good time.

A couple of thoughts occurred to me as I hid it in the airing cupboard. One was that Hazel had been very lucky that Uncle Jack merely intended to burn down her rectory. I also considered that while Uncle Jack was in Silver Meadows and I was desperately on the lookout for money I could have sold off the Purdey.

Here was a superb killing machine, slayer of various African animals, not to mention pheasants and snipe on home ground. It had fine walnut verneer and was elaborately engraved, patterned with classic Standard Fine rose and scroll, It would have sold for around fifty thousand pounds

Too late for all that now.

'David, run down and bolt the front doors.'

The house vibrated with the rattle of the great door knocker, the ringing of the bell, and the barking of the dogs.

'Good boys!' Uncle Jack tinkered with his hearing aid.

We watched as ambulance men and the doctor returned to their vehicles and sat and waited. An hour passed – the dogs must have been hoarse with barking.

Massey appeared walking up the drive.

Uncle Jack called out of the drawing room window: 'Massey, tell those fools to get the hell out of here.'

A long consultation ensued before they all started up and drove away down the avenue.

After they had disappeared Uncle Jack said: 'Get that bottle of champagne and some glasses.'

CHAPTER ELEVEN

Maria was sitting up in the four-poster bed, her head festooned with those steel curlers. She looked like a witch. My uncle was lying next to her gently snoring. Beside her was a table crammed with stuff bottles of ungents, make up, make up remover, shampoo, hair brushes, combs, perfumes, and other things to make her beautiful. There was also Viagra.

On the other side of the bed were Uncle Jack's medicines.

'This pill for stopping Colonel getting angry. This pill for stopping heart go pit-pat. This pill for stopping Colonel get up all night for pee-pee.'

She smiled at me – even though it was only eight in the morning, her lips were painted carmine.

Uncle Jack woke up.

'What are you doing here, and where are my teeth?'

They were in a tumbler which stood beside Maria's eye-lash curlers. With some difficulty he managed to place them in his mouth.

'That's a lot better, and now please leave us.'

Was it my imagination that before I closed the door he gave me a leary wink?

A couple of weeks passed and Maria had become a fixture at Mount Jewel. She had moved into Uncle Jack's bedroom permanently. The east bedroom had reverted to its old gloom, damp stains increasing behind the water-colours.

Surely he was too old to make love, even if they continued to go around holding hands? At his age any excitement had to be bad for his heart. Was it only the electric blanket that led her to my uncle's four-poster and his welcoming old arms. In any case nookie would be hardly easy with someone who had all those steel curlers in her hair.

The dogs were evicted.

Maria hissed like a goose.

'Why you keep dirty animals? I slip, maybe break my leg on mess. Big turd...I go round like skiv with bucket and brush...Also make pee pee...'

The old dog blankets were thrown out on the landing and Albert and Edward slept there.

At night new anxieties kept me awake.

How do you solve a problem like Maria?

'Colonel love me. He much better in my care than stay with many silly old women.'

For the sake of argument I contradicted her. 'He was quite happy at Silver Meadows.'

'You liar. You selfish man. You think carefully. Where would Colonel be except for me, Maria? He live and die at Silver Meadows. No memory. Mrs Freebody take his money.'

Uncle Jack beamed as he listened. He disagreed with Maria only about one thing.

'You not like nice Filipino food?'

After another trip to Drogheda to buy more clothes, she agreed to the return of Cook and Josie. They were paid more.

Although Maria loathed both of them and they loathed her, in just a few days they came to a status quo. Maria never gave orders and much of the time she did not go near the kitchen. The cats were back there, the old tabby, a slew of half-grown kittens and the fat old white tom.

Now the smells that came upstairs were of roast lamb, steak and kidney pie and other old favourites. Apple tarts and queen of puddings to follow.

'Ah...'

We ate once more in the dining room, Maria might sulk, but she ate heartily. My uncle gobbled his food in the same way as he used to in the basement of Silver Meadows.

Only on Josie and Cook's days off did Maria descend to the kitchen. The first thing she did was to hit the cats with a broom. They disappeared through the barred windows at the sight of her.

Once a week smells of the Philippines wafted upwards and spices pervaded the house. Uncle Jack would sigh, light another cigar – Cohiba Sublime which he felt he deserved – and brace himself for the weekly Filipino meal.

He resumed his rounds of the estate, annoying the men much as he used to. Every day he inspected the cattle, horses and sheep and consulted Massey who ignored most of what he was told.

Maria seldom went outside with Uncle Jack to inspect the estate.

'Farm no good... Not making money.'

During her trips to Drogheda she bought increasing numbers of shoes, all high-heeled.

'You'll soon have as many as Imelda Marcos,' Uncle Jack said.

'You like all Irish people. They know nothing of Philippines but shoes and Imelda Marcos. She good woman.'

He squeezed her hand. These days her fingernails were painted scarlet.

'She have two hundred pairs shoes. Maybe more. I have eleven pair.'

These days Maria wore high heels when she went up and down the staircase inspecting Mount Jewel's indoor premises.

'This house too big.'

One wet afternoon I accompanied her while Uncle Jack sat in the study swearing at bills.

'Why this room locked?'

It was not easy to explain.

'You tell me. Your grand daddy...'

'My great-grandfather...'

'He lie dead in there?'

'No. Just his uniform…'

'This room here? Why also locked?'

'My great-uncle...he was a governor in Nyasaland.'

'Where Nyasaland?'

'Africa. East Africa.'

'Great-uncle clothes inside?'

'I think so. No one has seen them for years.'

'Not great-uncle in bedroom?

'No. He's in the churchyard in Mauricetown.'

'This room here? More clothes?'

'Yes, as far as I know.'

'Why damn fool arrangement?'

'You'll have to ask the Colonel.'

Uncle Jack was drinking his first evening whiskey.

'We've done it for a long time...shut up a bedroom after someone dies...General Standford...his stuff is in the south-west bedroom...he fought at Vittoria...'

'So much nonsense idea.'

'Not at all. When I'm dead my uniform will be locked in my bedroom in the same way. David will see to it. You won't forget my medals, will you, David?'

Old General Standford was the one-legged ghost whom I used to hear regularly. I never heard him now. The ghosts had departed, probably because they did not like Maria. Since she had come into the house I had heard no footsteps.

'Where keys?'

'Lost.'

'You get Massey open doors.'

Massey was summoned with hammer and tongs or whatever means

he used to force the bedroom locks. We stood in silence as the door of the south-west bedroom swung open. It had been locked in 1836.

Quentin Crisp once wrote that no further dust gathered in a room after it was untouched for four years. He was wrong.

There were quick movements of spiders; the cobwebs that covered the windows left the room in semi-darkness. A pile of garments lay on the tester bed. Grey dust covered the uniform of the something-or-other Foot that had been worn by my one-legged ancestor at the battle of Vittoria. The interior of a chamber-pot, was furred with more cobwebs.

'...Dirty...' For once Maria's often used word was apt. She put a red high-heeled foot on the inside of the room and clouds arose.

'Why you people do this crazy thing?'

Eight further rooms were unlocked by Massey.

Maria decided that I would join her for the great clean up. 'We need new sweeper for carpet.'

The next day I drove the pair of them into Drogheda where Uncle Jack bought a vacuum cleaner.

In the afternoon Maria and I cleaned General Standford's room. Ignoring clouds of dust we got rid of dead birds. Windows were opened; spiders and broken butterflies were thrown out.

'Take clothes away.'

Dust enveloped me as I carried the old uniform and the yellowing sheets and blankets to the attic.

Maria polished the windows, the cracked mirrors and the bulky dressing table.

'Go there...under there – open drawers' – I gained a knowledge of nineteenth century men's underwear. More for the attic.

'Sweep there.' I swept up a hundred and fifty year old dog turd.

'Already room look better...'

By the evening we went down to the study and drank Uncle Jack's whiskey .

'Very good. I need.'

'What have you been doing?' my uncle asked.

'One bedroom all clean.'

Not that Uncle Jack cared. Cleaning rooms and hoovering were nothing to do with him. Women's work. And David could do his bit.

Next day another room was cleaned. And then another. Uniforms, ostrich feathers, clothes medals, were taken to the attic. So were long dresses in the south-west bedroom which may have belonged to a governor's wife or a vicereine.

'Woman sleep here.'

A dark green silk costume pushed out by a bustle was accompanied by a bonnet, long white gloves, and a green umbrella. A bible lay nearby.

'Christian lady.'

Maria rummaged in the drawers of the dressing table and found a jewel box; when she opened it diamonds glittered.

'Very nice...'

She showed the box to Uncle Jack who had no idea who it had once belonged to.

Now it belonged to Maria, together with its contents.

Drawers were turned out; cupboards were emptied of ancient garments. Maria found and saved a mink coat that may have been Aunt Maud's.

Spiders were bashed to death – Maria did that. Bad luck, surely. Jackdaw nests containing dead birds were removed from chimneys. Maria picked up a mummified rat. 'Same Filipino rat.' She added:

'No more spiders webs. No more dust, falling plaster. Broken chairs must go.'

We worked for a week until eight rooms were divested of ghosts and memories and dust. They smelt of Mansion House and Mr Sheen and Windolene and bleach and toilet duck.

Even Josie was impressed.

Maria took my uncle on a grand tour; they wandered hand in hand from room to room. Behind the dogs I followed, brush and pan in hand in case some further piece of detritus needed to be gathered up.

'Very clean. You like?'

After the eight unlocked and newly cleaned bedrooms had been inspected Maria said: 'Now we look at other rooms.'

Many of the other bedrooms which theoretically had been in use over the past decades were as dusty and spider-ridden as those that had been locked and sealed. Up on the third floor were yet more unused rooms, with streams of damp running down the walls and iron beds with yellowing mattresses.

Maria asked. 'How many bedroom altogether?'

'...Perhaps thirty... I don't know.'

'How many bathroom?'

'Three. One on each floor.'

'Difficult for wash or make pipi.'

Uncle Jack agreed.

'House too big.'

Maria went around the ground floor carrying a tape measure. She paid particular attention to the dining room and the ballroom. In the afternoon she put on the flat shoes she had worn as a nurse in Silver Meadows. She did a tour of the estate; it was the first time she had been outside walking the grounds since her first days here. She went around alone, without Uncle Jack.

'You too old for big walk.'

His limit was now the stables and the daily talk with Massey.

I caught sight of Maria walking briskly by the lakes. She was out all afternoon.

Over her evening whiskey she said: 'Farm no good...not making money...'

CHAPTER TWELVE

A few days later I was sitting in Dan Hennessy's office, snatching half an hour while Maria and Uncle Jack went shopping. Hennessy had a piece of paper in his hand. He handed it to me in silence.

'My God!'

Uncle Jack must have written it at Maria's dictation. He proposed turning Mount Jewel into a hotel with a golf course.

To my dismay Hennessy said, 'I don't think it's such a bad idea.'

'You must be as mad as he is.'

'What else can you do with the place?'

'Surely it can continue the way it is?'

'Maria is right. As a farm Mount Jewel is losing money by the minute. And there isn't much to be earned from second-rate steeplechasers.'

'For God's sake, Dan. Ireland is full of luxury hotels and one more building will only add to the useless pile.'

'The location is good. The country can't have too many golf courses.'

Hennessy and I stared at each other across his littered desk. I hadn't come in to his office to talk about this monstrous idea. Mount Jewel would become another trophy castle for rich Americans to stay in. Our private family home would join Disney extravaganzas.

This was not the time to start discussing my own family position.

I had hoped to talk about family funds and suggest that Hennessy should ask Uncle Jack for cash to repair the double staircase and the pillars in the ball room. All he could talk about was financial liquidity and balancing the books. He retrieved Uncle Jack's letter.

'Think about it, David.'

Things moved quickly. The outdoor staff – just two men, since Massey stayed with the racehorses and refused to cooperate – were summoned inside the house to strip it of much of its contents. With the aid of Fitzpatrick and Duffy, out went saggy old sofas and ancient heavy silk curtains that had been in place for over a century. Carpets would be replaced. The iron beds had to be removed, together with damaged old mattresses. One by one, out they all came from the third floor, down the great staircase and out the door and into the back of the farm tractor. Then, as Maria stood on the porch and watched, they were taken away down the avenue to the dump at Mauricetown.

'Too much mice.'

Rentokil was called in. Many mice, and plenty of rats were exterminated. It was difficult to get rid of all the vermin in such a large house.

'We leave historic things.'

Paintings survived, dozens of portraits and miniatures, the hunting prints, the water colours that hung in spare rooms, and some that Maria thought could have been valuable.

'We need plenty money.'

An authority from an auction house in Dublin was called in to examine them; he did not think much of them.

'I knew you were wasting your time,' Uncle Jack said. 'The good stuff was sold off in 1928. I think there was a Rembrandt. Of course we kept the Snaffles and the Lionel Edwards.'

Both the auctioneer and Uncle Jack proved to be wrong. So did those who made estimates in 1928. A dim portrait in the dining room, a faintly moustached lady with ballooning bosoms, turned out to be by Peter Lely. Selling her would provide enough money to equip most bedrooms with ensuite bathrooms.

She would not be missed. However, Uncle Jack had a quarrel with Maria as to whether to get rid of so many prints that featured horse races. They never argued for long; the adoring look would come back into his eyes. Maria was persuaded that hotel guests would appreciate all the leaping horses as well as the cock fights.

The Purdey was sold as well.

The grandfather clock was retained; so was the elephant's foot for sticks and umbrellas. Rusty pieces of armour stayed on the walls, together with the obligatory Irish elk horns in the main hall.

'Very big horns.'

A week later the cry was 'too many books'. There was another argument about the contents of the library, at the end of which Maria agreed that guests would spend many hours reading bound copies of Scott, Dickens, Thackeray and P.G.Wodehouse.

Several times a week I drove Maria and Uncle Jack into Drogheda to interview Hennessy. I parked the car in Laurence Street as they crossed the road – I was never allowed to accompany them. But I knew what was happening. They were hard at work turning the new venture into a company. Maria's name headed the list of directors.

'Nothing I can do about it, David,' said Hennessy when I sneaked into his office to find out what was happening.

I protested that I was Uncle Jack's heir.

'Doesn't look as if you are any more.'

I could hardly argue that Uncle Jack had gone crazy when true love had lifted him from the menace of dementia. His besotted lovesick mind had saved him, and at his advanced age, he enjoyed living with this grasping woman.

He never gave me a thought. Whatever decisions were made were my uncle's – and Maria's. Not mine.

Should I throw in the towel? Accept that I was never going to be Uncle Jack's heir, and that Mount Jewel would never be mine? Make my way back to Australia?

Not yet.

As more men were hired – soon there were a dozen – Mount Jewel was being transformed into a hotel.

Yet another new face appeared daily at Mount Jewel. Jimmy O'Hara was not only a professional golfer, but also satisfied after he had walked around the estate that there was plenty of opportunity to make a championship course.

'I'll do the designing. No need to call in Jack Nicklaus.'

Maria agreed with his plans.

'Mr O'Hara cut down many trees.'

Under his direction, the men on the estate were put to work building a fairway to Heaven. They started with the second oldest oak tree in Ireland which came down with a thunderous crash. Uncle Jack smiled as he inspected the great trunk lying its full two hundred foot length.

Maria was convinced that a golf course would add to the reputation of Mount Jewel. 'Nine or eighteen holes?'

'Eighteen.'

Trees continued to be felled. The men were kept busy. Soon putting greens were almost ready for play.

I was beginning to agree with Maria. Perhaps her plan of converting the house into a luxury hotel did not seem so outrageous.

It was not difficult to convince her that I had changed my mind.

'You like to become trustee?'

So, in her company and together with Uncle Jack I made another trip to Hennessy's where I signed a number of papers.

Maria was triumphant. 'Now you see. I am right. I am Filipina – all good business people. No lazy, nothing like Irish.' She was annoyed because Josie and Bridget had given their notice once again. Their salaries had to be further increased in order to persuade them to stay.

One evening as we sat in the dining room and Josie served Cook's Irish stew, I listened to Uncle Jack and Maria.

'I not want lazy people around me…'

'No, my dear.'

'Irish always enjoying themselves.'

'Yes, my dear.'

'Very good my family come here and help make big hotel. Help make money.'

'Your family?' I asked. This was the first I had heard of any of Maria's relations.

'They come from Manila. My brother, his wife and daughter. I invite them.'

'When?'

'Soon. They stay here for nice long holiday.'

'Can they speak English?' I wondered, inconsequentially.

She turned on me. 'What sort of people you think we are? We very smart, speak plenty languages. Tagalog. Spanish. At home my family speak Bisaya. We all go to mission schools. Irish priests. We learn English. Good English.'

Uncle Jack paid the fares of Maria's relations and Hennessy arranged for visas. Tickets were dispatched, a date was fixed, arrangements made, bedrooms prepared for the newcomers who would soon be flying here from Manila.

'We meet at airport. David drive us there.'

Maria insisted Uncle Jack should get new clothes to meet the arrivals. This necessitated a journey to Dublin to a tailor for the first suit Uncle Jack had bought in twenty years. Harris tweed.

'Nice shirt – washed and ironed. Good tie.' She picked out his regimental tie and made him pin on his war time medals. He was persuaded to wear the bowler hat he wore at funerals.

'I tell my brother Rodrigo you important man.'

She plucked white hair out of his nostrils, trimmed his eyebrows, took the greasy hearing aid out of his ear and cut away more hair that blossomed in there.

She herself chose to wear her favourite new tight-fitting red dress and a big hat decorated with feathers. Her shoes had higher heels than ever. She carried a bunch of red and white roses with a long label saying WELCOME TO IRELAND.

Uncle Jack had not been to Dublin Airport for many years. When he was last in Collinstown as it was called then, the only people who flew were the rich. Uncle Jack and Aunt Maud would wait for their plane carrying their shooting sticks. Those who travelled with them would have been friends who would murmur about the hoi polloi. The women would be wearing hats which sloped to one side of their heads, and fox furs around their necks, stuffed fox heads biting their tails.

Fifty years later things were different. I pushed my uncle in a wheelchair into the arrivals lounge. There was a smell of greasy food.

Uncle Jack sneered at a man who strode past wearing a stringed singlet and jeans with designer holes.

Maria's relations had flown first to London before hopping over from Heathrow to Dublin. Their plane was late.

Three times I was sent over to the arrivals board to check the messages.

At last I could come back and say, 'It's landed.'

More waiting had to be endured as passengers walked slowly past baggage retrieval and customs. Two business men in dark glasses ...families with luggage piled high on trolleys, a wailing baby, a group of schoolgirls, more and more of the travelling mob. None of them recognised by Maria.

A stream of passengers wheeling suitcases were greeted by friends and relations. More waiting.

'Where my people?'

The edge of my uncle's bowler hat had fallen down over his nose. Maria held her bouquet of roses; her face under her feathered hat was transfixed with displeasure.

The wait grew longer. Uncle Jack was dozing.

I felt a straw of hope that Maria's relations might have missed the plane altogether. Or changed their plans, and decided not to come. Perhaps Maria might decide to go home to the Philippines...

At last after a gap when no one had emerged from baggage retrieval for more than five minutes, a small fat swarthy man pushed his way past the screen behind a trolley piled high with black plastic sacks. He caught sight of Maria and smiled in her direction, flashing gold teeth. He was followed by a middle-aged woman, and a boy of around eight years old. The boy was chewing gum. Behind them came a very pretty girl who must have been in her late teens.

Filipinos.

The boy?

'Marco!'

Maria dropped the roses she was carrying, got up, ran towards him and took him in her arms. She splashed his face with a red-lipsticked kiss.

Uncle Jack woke up.

The boy wriggled out of Maria's arms went over to Uncle Jack in his wheelchair and began fingering the line of medals pinned on his coat.

'Marco! My son! My darling son!'

Maria seized hold of of the boy again and held him tightly as he tried to squeeze out of her arms. He wriggled. A bubble of gum had formed in his mouth.

'He tired after flight.' She gave him a slap and he took the gum from between his teeth and began to howl.

'No cry, Marco. Mama love you. Mama pleased to see you.' She announced to Uncle Jack and me: 'He adorable. He very good boy.'

I was wheeling my uncle in his chair, while behind me the small fat man pushed his trolley. There were suitcases under the black plastic sacks and a set of giant drums.

Introductions had been made. Rodrigo, Maria's brother and his wife, Delfina... Attracta, their lovely adolescent daughter, who had shoulder-length black hair and a well-developed bust, carried Maria's bunch of roses.

Maria had done all the talking and introducing. Rodrigo, Delfina, Attracta, my very darling boy, Marco.

Marco? The surprise. Uncle Jack, who, after he had woken up was full of smiles, must know all about him considering he had paid his fare.

I was the only person who had not been told. None of my business.

Uncle Jack had greeted each of Maria's relations with unusual courtesy. Smiles were exchanged.

'Ver' pleased to meet you,' said Rodrigo.

'Rodrigo speak English ver' well,' Maria informed us.

'Marco. My little angel son,' she said again. She produced sweets out of her handbag.

We filled up the car, suitcases, black sacks and drums in the boot, Uncle Jack sat beside me, the chauffeur, while all the Filipinos piled in the back. They only fitted in because Maria held Marco in her lap, lavishing kisses on him.

The relatives sang songs all the way from the airport back to Mount Jewel. Maria joined in heartily. Uncle Jack lay back in the seat beside me and dozed. So did Marco behind us, waking up occasionally to stuff his mouth with more sweets. I watched him in the car mirror and brooded.

When we arrived at Mount Jewel, Massey and the men, Cook and Josie were waiting outside the porch to greet Maria's family. The dogs barked. Suitcases and black sacks were brought in and Uncle Jack was divested of his bowler.

In the study we all settled down for a drink, Coca Cola for Marco and Attracta, Bushmills for Rodrigo and Delfina. They liked whiskey so much they had a second glass, then a third.

'You never told me you had a son.' I tried to make my voice nonchalant.

'Husband die,' Maria said.

'I'm sorry.'

'Bus drive over him. Traffic bad in Manila.'

'Is Marco your only child?'

'No time for more. Not too much time make love. Husband dead too soon. But I lucky. I have my darling boy.'

Maria's relations settled down in Mount Jewel in a remarkably short time. Within a couple of days Attracta was flirting with the outdoor staff. Delfina spent her time relaying gossip about Manila to Maria. Rodrigo played with his giant drums. You could hear the sound of them in the furthermost corner of the house.

'I am good musician. All the time people in Manila pay to hear me.'

The other sound was Marco who was also noisy.

Maria need not have worried about Uncle Jack's attitude towards Marco; he accepted the lad into his household without question. Not only that, but very soon they were friends. On wet days my uncle spent much of his time playing with him in the old nursery wing where there were toys that were over a century old. They included a rocking horse with mane made out of real horsehair which Marco rode with shrieks of joy.

Uncle Jack also found the old Hornby train service I had played with when I was a child. In the large cardboard box there was not only the engine and carriages, but a railway station, bridges, lines of track, a signal box and several tunnels.

With a certain amount of groaning my uncle got down on the nursery floor beside Marco and, cigar in mouth, helped him to put the steel railway tracks together and assemble the train. Soon the line of chocolate-painted carriages were passing through the first tunnel, while the little lead station master stiffly waved his green flag when Uncle Jack gave him a push.

I felt envy; my uncle had never played with me like that. The dogs watched them, happily panting.

Maria was pleased. 'Marco good boy. Make Jack happy.'

A problem occurred when Marco thought that he, too, would like to have a go at a cigar. He must have taken it from Uncle Jack's case; his cries and groans had Maria running to the nursery to view his pale yellow face and mop up. As she held him in her arms it was my uncle who got the blame.

The dogs had not yet bitten Marco although he teased them relentlessly. Perhaps they knew that if they did, it would be curtains for them.

Maria thought that the Brat deserved something more up to date than a Hornby train set, so it was into Drogheda to a toy shop for Lego that was soon strewn in every room.

Rodrigo's wife, Delfina took charge of the kitchen, with Maria helping her. Neither Uncle Jack nor I got used to kare-kare, adobo, lumpia, pancit, and halo halo, for now Uncle Jack and I might sigh for roast beef and roast chicken. Cook and Josie, well paid, were content to sit in the kitchen drinking large mugs of tea, watching the Filipina ladies prepare those meals. They did not have to eat them.

CHAPTER THIRTEEN

But all was not well. Hennessy summoned us to his office, Uncle Jack, Maria, and myself.

'Brace yourselves,' He held up a document. I guessed what was coming remembering the communications we had suffered from the head of Silver Meadows.

'What you mean, deport?' Maria asked. 'My family here for holiday. Go back soon, maybe. My darling Marco stay.'

'It's not them they are after,' Hennessy said. 'It's you.'

'What you mean?

'Maria Fernandez...'

'My name...'

'You have really got on the wrong side of Mrs Freebody.'

He interpreted the officialese in the stern typewritten letter that he was waving in Maria's direction. It declared Ireland did not want her. Mrs Freebody had informed the authorities that Maria Fernandez should be declared persona non grata.

'Why she want this horrible thing? I do nothing. I good nurse.'

'That is not what it says here.'

'Colonel he light curtains with cigar.'

'But you were attending him? You allowed him to smoke?'

'Woman jealous. She not like Colonel love me.'

'She didn't like the fire that nearly destroyed her nursing home. This is the second time Jack has been at work.'

'First time Colonel very angry with lady Reverend. He try kill her. This time Colonel make mistake. He smoke. Big mistake.'

Hennessy read out more.

'Two of the patients at Silver Meadows developed pneumonia as a result of having to wait in the rain while the fire was put out. One was a nun. Sister Agnes.'

'They not die?'

'We are lucky about that.'

'Where did the Colonel get his cigars?' asked Hennessy.

'David bring.' All eyes were suddenly turned on me.

'What?' I had been in a doze, thinking what an excellent thing it would be if Mrs Freebody got her way and Maria had to depart from Ireland.

'All your fault, David. Bad man.' Maria began to wail. 'I not want go back to Manila. I not want to leave Colonel. I look after Colonel.'

Hennessy shrugged.

'What to do?'

Uncle Jack was smiling. Another of those smiles that were not directed at me.

He took Maria by the hand. 'Simple, my love. We'll get married.'

There was a pause. Hennessy's features took on a glow of admiration. 'Wait a minute.' He was taking snuff by the handful. 'Not so fast...'

'Of course...fast...we marry very quickly...'

'We will have to deal with a few problems.'

'What problems you say?'

'You are Miss Fernandez?'

'I Missus Fernandez. I show you passport...'

'And your son?'

'Marco darling son...'

Hennessy asked, 'His father?'

'Father die...'

From her bag Maria produced a yellow silk handkerchief by Hermès as tears began running down her face.

'You tell, David.'

'I understand Maria's husband was killed in a traffic accident in Manila.'

'Quezon Avenue...near Diliman Square,' Maria sobbed. 'He walk across road. Bus go too fast.'

Hennessy frowned and took another pinch of the dirty brown powder which dribbled down onto his collar.

'You have proof of your husband's death?'

Maria delved in her bag again and brought out a passport.

'We will need further documentation.'

'You write Philippines very quick.'

Hennessy was left with multiple tasks. In addition to sorting out the legitimacy of Maria's widowhood he was instructed to prolong the visitors' visas of her relatives. Maria wanted moral support from people she knew. More important still was the position of Marco. Her darling.

I knew that Hennessy had taken her side. As we left his office he did not even have to say – 'She's a remarkable woman.'

He did. 'Maria, you are a remarkable woman.'

Uncle Jack said: 'Get on with it, Hennessy.'

We drank champagne that evening before the Filipinos went up to their bedrooms, and Maria retired to Uncle Jack's four-poster. Marco was sharing their room.

In my bed, my thoughts dwelt on giving Uncle Jack a push down stairs before any marriage could take place.

I heard the rooks calling outside as dawn approached and thought of Hitchcock's birds turning nasty and murderous. I devised a new version of Daphne du Maurier's horror story which began in the beech trees surrounding Mount Jewel. Black wings, a phalanx of tearing beaks swooping down, caws of rooks, the tenants who never paid rent...

It did not take long for Maria to plan a huge wedding. Already she had the idea of tripping down the aisle on Rodrigo's arm.

'Organ play here comes the bride...' It seemed that even in the

Philippines the tune of Treulick Geführt was familiar at weddings.

'We put big announcement in paper. David, you arrange.'

I contacted Hennessy.

'No announcement. Things must be kept quiet for the time being. You have to understand that this threat of deportation is very real.'

Phone calls from Hennessy rang day and night, as he struggled to sort things out. He was also ringing the authorities in the Philippines.

A church ceremony was planned. Which church? Catholic or Protestant? What sort of priest to be contacted? Father Doran at St Ignatius?

'Not the ghastly Hazel,' decreed Uncle Jack.

He and Maria squabbled over the problems that arose from a mixed marriage.

Maria liked the idea of sprinkling Uncle Jack with holy water. She would obtain a blessed bottle and let it trickle down his face.

'I make you Catholic.' She purred with pleasure. 'No one can change you once Catholic – not even Pope.'

Uncle Jack poured out another tumbler of Bushmills. 'Sometimes my love I think you are a fool.'

'We go Holyhead – get married in Wales.' That might be one way of avoiding complications. But when Hennessy was consulted once again he advised against crossing the Irish sea.

'You're best off with a civil marriage. In a registry office. Forget about religion. And we will have to hurry up.'

Phone calls were made to the registry office in Dublin.

'People not helpful.'

Three months notice was required by law. With the notification came the notification fee, another cheque provided by Uncle Jack.

That was the start of things.

'...passport...birth certificate...evidence of name, address, age, civil status...nationality...'

Back in Manila poor deceased Señor Fernandez continued to cause trouble – first of all by marrying Maria, then by tripping under that bus. Not only was there the problem of his death certificate, but the original marriage certificate of his union with Maria had to be sent for across the continents.

'Which will not be valid if either party is already validly married,' Hennessy roared down the telephone.

Would one of the party intending marriage be incapable of understanding the meaning of marriage because of mental handicap?

'Put that to one side,' Hennessy said. He was enjoying the challenge.

We learnt that a man might not marry within the forbidden degrees of kindred. Marco, who had picked up more English, got hold of certain details and went around the house reciting.

'A man may not marry...his daughter's daughter, his wife's daughter's daughter, his brother's son's wife, his grandmother...A woman may not marry her grandmother's husband...'

'Shut up!'

'...her father's brother...her mother's brother...'

The days passed and Maria had more big plans. For the start, she needed a wedding dress. She could see that the usual long white garment down to her feet, with attached veil and bouquet was not suitable for this occasion.

'I wear white dress for first wedding. Good Catholic wedding in Philippines,' Maria remembered with nostalgia. 'Not heathen like this new marriage. Proper priest and church. Plenty people, plenty friends. Not like getting married in office without priest.'

A dressmaker from Navan was recruited, and with the aid of a copy of *Harper's Bazaar*, Maria told her what she wanted. Cream-coloured silk, figure hugging, down to her knees. A new pair of shoes, white shoes, the heels very high, which would bring Maria's little figure almost up to Uncle Jack's shoulders.

When Uncle Jack said, 'Imelda Marcos would like them', Maria lost her temper and Rodrigo and Delfina were not amused. The linking of the ex-president of the Philippines with her shoes continued to be a source of irritation.

Even so, Rodrigo recalled with pride: 'Many pair Madame Marcos buy...two thousand seven hundred...maybe more...'

Maria and Uncle Jack continued to go around Mount Jewel hand in hand like young lovers. From time to time Uncle Jack leaned down like a stork and gave his little fiancée a kiss.

'So happy...'

The weeks passed, always with tension, aggravated by Hennessy's fears. Would his paperwork be sufficient and in time? Would Mrs Freebody get there first, and recruit the authorities in charge of deportation? Would Maria and her relatives – who had visitors' visas – be cast into outer darkness, on the long journey back to Manila's suburbs?

'Wedding soon...' Maria was reconciled to the Registry office, sooner and safer. Rodrigo, Attracta and Delfina would not have to attend some dark satanic Irish church.

But three months was a long time.

At last it was possible to announce the impending marriage between Colonel Hilton, M.C. and Mrs Maria Jesus Fernandez. The notice in the *Irish Times* surprised Uncle Jack's friends who kept ringing me up.

'No sex in it,' said Blanco.

Gusty breathed down the telephone. 'For God's sake, David, don't let this take place.'

Trigger advised, 'Give the gal some money and she'll go away.'

I tried to explain that Uncle Jack was in a state of bliss.

'Randy old goat...You can't let the poor old bugger be whisked into matrimony by this particular little foreign hussey...'

Beaky said, 'I suppose she's told Jack she's a widow.'

'Her husband was run over by a bus.'

'That's her story. Jack must be out of his mind. The way he's been all the time.'

Trigger said, 'Of course it's only that she's after his money.'

Blanco said, 'I suppose she's half his age.'

Beakey said, 'Foreign girls are a good deal more demanding. She must think he's a millionaire.'

Beakey's wife said, 'Jack ought to be locked up again in Silver Meadows.'

Maria said: 'Telephone ring too much.'

She was thinking incessantly about another kind of ring.

I had already gone with my uncle up to Dublin to the Happy Ring House in O'Connell Street for a plain gold wedding ring.

'No good without engagement...big diamond.'

'How's that going to be paid for?'

'Colonel have money.'

Another trip to Dublin was arranged. Rodrigo came along.

The taxi took us the short haul up to Grafton Street where Maria had located a quiet discreet premises surprisingly full of sparkling jewellery. She had done her homework.

In no time the delighted young salesman was showing us trays of huge flashy rings. Rodrigo was eyeing them with what seemed to be expert scrutiny.

'My sister want something very big. Good value stone. No swindle.'

Maria pointed out a ring with a diamond just about as big as South Africa could produce, surrounded by a lot of little diamonds.

'How much?' Rodrigo did the asking.

The salesman's smile turned into a grin. 'Two thousand.' He kept his eye on that vulgar piece, thinking perhaps that foreign men like Rodrigo with his heavy black sideburns and cowboy hat, together with the rest of us, posed a security risk.

But it was only the first ring that was considered.

They dithered for hours and the pieces of glittering jewellery that Maria thrust upon her finger had bigger and bigger stones. So did their prices. I grew bored hearing how brilliant they all were – marked with superb clarity, flawless symbols of true love. Exquisite. Rare. Incomparable.

The ring that was finally chosen was very expensive. It was bigger than the one habitually worn by Lady Marsden. It was so big that Maria could scarcely lift her left hand.

'We don't often have a diamond of this quality in stock,' cooed the salesman.

Maria said, 'I like.'

'This good ring,' Rodrigo considered. 'Best from de Beers.'

The old man signed the cheque. He was squeezing Maria's hand so persistently that he could scarcely detach his own to write his signature.

'Better spending money this way than on fees for Silver Meadows.'

The day had come, the big one. Another trip down to Dublin. The ceremony could have been held in Drogheda, but Maria chose Dublin as an easier venue for important guests. She had hired a large white stretch limo with darkened windows to take us from Mount Jewel to the registry office in Lombard Street.

We waited in the hall. My uncle, dressed in formal morning suit, his medals on his chest, a top hat beside him, was sleeping in a chair.

'Wake up, Uncle Jack.'

His eyes opened and he glared in my direction. Maria placed an arm around him.

'Today we get married, Colonel.'

I was also dressed in a morning suit. Rodrigo wore an outfit that resembled a gaucho. Marco was fitted out with a grey suit studded with silver buttons. Attracta and Delfina wore peacock blue. Maria was in her new cream-coloured silk, topped by a huge hat scattered with coloured feathers.

We all climbed into the limo which was soon filled with the crush of scented bodies and the jabber of Spanish. I sat beside Uncle Jack, while Maria sat in front beside the driver.

Rodrigo opened a magnum of champagne. The driver was given a glass, as he speeded down to Dublin, and he, too joined in. By luck he avoided the garda.

We had finished the magnum by the time the limo drew up beside the registry office. We all clambered out unsteadily.

The wedding party reached the entrance to the registry office. Inside, people were waiting to witness the ceremony. Uncle Jack's old friend, the Bishop glared at him disapprovingly. Dr O'Shea was present. Beside him sat Hennessy, and beside Hennessy, Patsy Massey and Jimmy O'Hara.

My uncle's old friends were assembled elsewhere, Trigger, Gusty, Duffy, Rabbit and Blanco and their wives sitting in another line.

As he limped up towards the Registrar, carrying his top hat and leaning on a gold-topped malacca cane, – the usual blackthorn stick had been discarded for the occasion – Uncle Jack was beginning to enjoy himself. He looked younger. He smiled at people he recognised, proving that his false teeth were firmly in place. His bald head glowed sunset pink. Several times he waved at a friend with his cane.

Rodrigo followed the bridal pair in his gaucho gear, tight black leather trousers and shiny boots. Dressed in blue, Attracta and Delfina were also looking colourful. But it was Maria that everyone wanted to see. In her high heels and low-cut glittering cream dress, topped by her feather hat, she caught all eyes.

I saw a group of women sitting in a group together. Surely not? I looked again and slowly the truth dawned on me. Mrs Freebody in a frilled black dress, her white hair with its familiar crop, sat with an assortment of nursers and carers from Silver Meadows.

So it seemed there was no question of Mrs Freebody trying to arrange for Maria's deportation. Hennessy had won that race. She must have thought, if you can't lick them, join them.

Three of the carers present were Filipinas who waved and smiled at Maria before they stood up and clapped. Lucky Maria, they were probably thinking – even an old man was a good catch, especially since he was the means by which the fortunate girl could stay in Ireland legally. Plenty money.

Mrs Freebody muttered and gave them a warning frown which made them stop. But by now the clapping had become general; there was a great burst of applause as we lined up at the front, Uncle Jack and Maria in the centre, the Filipino relatives to right and left grinning broadly.

I sat next to Uncle Jack since I was carrying the wedding ring; after he had dropped it twice, Maria thought it would be better if I took charge of it. For the present the big diamond engagement ring was on her right hand. Next to Maria sat Marco, chewing bubble gum. From time to time during the ceremony there was a slap as a little pink balloon issued from his lips. Rodrigo had been whistling under his breath; Uncle Jack cleared his throat and he stopped.

Behind the table containing an Irish national flag and a bowl of red and white roses. The registrar who conducted the proceedings was a woman who wore gold-rimmed glasses perched on the end of her nose. The ceremony was exceptionally short and less than five minutes seemed to pass before Colonel Jack Hilton and Mrs Maria Fernandez became man and wife.

I handed over the wedding ring. Maria helped my uncle put it on her finger, before transferring the great engagement ring from her other hand. For a moment Uncle Jack looked vague as if he had forgotten why he was here, but he sprang to life when he heard another burst of clapping. He bent down and gave the bride a big kiss on her brightly painted lips.

Maria burst into tears.

'Don't worry, my dear!' Uncle Jack said, 'This isn't the end of the world.'

But perhaps Maria thought it was. She fell down in front of the registrar in a faint.

The Filipina girls who worked for Silver Meadows rushed up to give aid; one of them patted Maria's cheeks, another lifted her by the shoulders. Behind them loomed Mrs Freebody. Maria opened her eyes and catching sight of her late employer staring down at her, gave a shudder as Mrs Freebody bent over and sprinkled her with eau de cologne.

It took time for things to calm down. Behind Maria's prone figure, among Uncle Jack's friends was an abundant rolling of eyes and people tut-tutting. The Bishop had closed his eyes and seemed to be muttering a prayer. He clutched his golden cross, evidently thinking, why am I here? Sighs appeared to be coming from Gusty and Blanco. And groans from their wives.

At last the new Mrs Hilton, drenched in eau de cologne, staggered to her feet and took hold of my uncle's hand.

All was well that ended well. The nurses began laughing and throwing confetti towards the couple until the registrar, who had been wringing her hands for the last fifteen minutes, told them that confetti was forbidden. Too late; it was scattered like a snowstorm.

Uncle Jack and Maria went up to his friends and shook their reluctant hands. Trigger, Gusty, Duffy, Beaky and Blanco, the Bishop all looked grim. So did their wives.

Had Maria truly recovered? It seemed so. 'So happy!' she declared over and over again as she shook hands one by one with her guests.

Hennessy said, 'Congratulations, Mrs Hilton on becoming an Irish citizen.'

Maria adjusted her battered hat. 'So happy.'

Guests had been asked to attend a wedding feast at a nearby restaurant. Maria and Uncle Jack sat at the head of a long table, Delfina, Attracta and Marco beside them. Uncle Jack's friends, were all still expressing their disapproval with glowering faces. At least they had come to the reception.

A Filipino flag flew from the bunch of flowers in the centre.

The meal had been devised by Rodrigo, who also had a hand at the cooking. He stood directing the waiters. Chicken adobo had appeared, along with bistek marinated in soy sauce, kare kare, and paksiw na baboy which I knew was vinegar stew with pork hocks and banana.

I heard Trigger say, 'What muck', as his wife said, 'Shh...' I watched Mrs Freebody being served with crispy pata, fried, heavily flavoured garlic pork knuckles, which Rodrigo had given us several times at Mount Jewel, until Uncle Jack had called a halt.

A few people liked what they were eating. Hennessy for example, Blanco, and surprisingly the Bishop who took a second and then a third helping of crispy pata. He beckoned Rodrigo and asked for the recipe. The girls from Silver Meadows ate a lot.

Marco was clutching his stomach. The new Mrs Hilton had to leave her seat beside Uncle Jack and take him away to be sick. When she returned, having given the Brat a good slap, pudding came around, simipit and mamoncillo, pitsi pitsi, halo halo and sapin sapi.

'A lot of coconut!'

Everything could be washed down with champagne. There were no speeches.

At the end of the meal Mrs Freebody came up to where bride and groom were seated and kissed Maria on both cheeks.

CHAPTER FOURTEEN

Congratulations...An unusual and delightful occasion...Your charming wife...Such a pleasure to meet Maria...

From the insincere letters written to Colonel and Mrs Hilton by guests which Uncle Jack passed on to me to read, you would not have thought that there was anything unusual about the nuptials.

These days things seemed very quiet at Mount Jewel. There was no honeymoon and the newly married couple settled down to gently abusing each other. Uncle Jack's intake of cigars increased. Attracta persuaded one of the farmhands to take her to the Emerald, the dance hall at Mauricetown.

The golf course was not ready yet; plans very similar to those of Jack Nicklaus might be lying around, more trees might be felled, but Jimmy O'Hara maintained that there was a good deal more to do in that direction.

Uncle Jack's finances continued to be a mystery. For a start he was able to arrange for Maria's relations to stay on. They did not show any enthusiasm.

'They are bored,' Uncle Jack said. He was not bored, he was reading. In addition to the usual books on Africa he was reading *Uncle Fred in the Springtime* yet again.

'Is time for my people to see Ireland,' Maria declared. She did not mean that her relations should be going to Killarney or the Cliffs of

155

Moher. Her family would not be ordinary tourists.

'Summer here. They see holy places.'

She had mapped out a tour that stretched from Lough Derg to Knock going on to Croagh Patrick.

'All places for pilgrimage.' Her eyes turned towards her husband, who had fallen asleep. 'Colonel pay.'

'Pilgrimage! Lough Derg! Knock! Crow patrick...'

Rodrigo, Attracta and Delfina began to show the enthusiasm of children who have been promised a trip to Disneyland.

Someone would accompany them on their Irish tour. They needed a guide.

Maria said, 'David go.'

'No!'

She took hold of my arm and clutched it tightly.

'Do not frown.'

'No! You'll have to find someone else!'

'I look after Colonel and pay bills and now when I ask for one small thing this helping my family, too difficult for you?'

'I don't know anything about Lough Derg or Croagh Patrick.'

'Lough Derg all people go out in boat. Pray in bare feet. Eat nothing. All peoples like to fast and pray.'

Maria continued to demonstrate how much she had learned. 'Knock holy lamb on side of church. Croagh Patrick all climb Sunday in July. Best in bare feet – St Patrick like very much people climb in bare feet.'

'It's not the sort of thing I want to be doing.'

'Why not, David?' Maria fluttered her eyes in my direction. 'You not believing man?'

'No.'

Uncle Jack woke up.

'David, you do whatever Maria wants.'

I was further badgered into acceptance by Rodrigo, Delfina and Attracta. 'You help, David. Ireland holy country. We like.'

'I go too,' Marco clamoured.

'No.'

'I want.'

'Too young for prayer. Too young to go barefoot on pilgrimage.'

'Not too young,' Marco wailed.

'Pilgrims must be fifteen years old. You small boy.'

Marco and his mother shouted at each other in Spanish – whatever they said must have been unpleasant if the reactions of Rodrigo, Attracta and Delfina were to be believed.

'Ah...ah...' they chorused sadly.

Maria reverted to English and a threat that had become frequent in the past weeks.

'Be quiet or you go to boarding school.'

She had rented a bus which came with a driver who was specially recommended by the parish priest of Mauricetown.

'Bus driver name Brendan.'

Brendan's minibus appeared at the front door of Mount Jewel. Inside on the dashboard was a small blue-robed Madonna. On the back window a sticker showed the image of Padre Pio.

'You go ten days,' Maria told me. 'Afterwards maybe my family return Philippines.'

If that was the one reward I would get out of accompanying her family all over Ireland, it would be worth it.

Maria and Uncle Jack stood on the porch waving us goodbye, the dogs beside them, giving the odd bark. Marco stood sulking at the far end of the colonnade.

'We say many prayers for Marco,' shouted Rodrigo as he lugged a suitcase over the gravel.

I sat in the front beside Brendan who started up the bus which receded down the drive. Maria waved her arm, my uncle, his stick. We could hear screams from Marco, growing fainter as the bus moved on.

I learned from Brendan that days before he and Maria had made out the itinerary which was to begin in County Cork.

'Cork? I thought we were going to Knock?'

Brendan said, 'I suggested an added destination.'

On this first day we drove past Dublin down south; it took all morning and early afternoon to reach the banks of the Lee and beyond. After a break for lunch the bus pulled up beside half a dozen people who were standing and kneeling beside a white concrete railing. A line of blue lettering read IMMACULATE CONCEPTION.

'Here we are, lads and girls. Curtain raiser,' Brendan said. 'Ballinaspittle.'

'Where statue?'

'Up there!'

So she was, a blue and white representation of Our Lady about twelve feet up from the road, in among bushes, trees above her, standing before her little cave. We could see that her head was surrounded by unlit electric lights that formed a halo.

'Someone see Our Lady move. By herself. Miracle!'

'Many people see!'

'Statue move! Maybe!'

Reluctantly I climbed out of the bus and left Brendan sitting at the wheel keeping warm, and listening to a game of football.

Perhaps Our Lady liked a bigger crowd than the meagre gathering which was doubled by our number.

Rodrigo, Delfina, Attracta and myself sat down in a line on a wooden bench. The Filipinos took out their rosaries and prayed, all the while keeping an eye on Our Lady. I felt hungry. Rodrigo had a camera with him, and angled the lens upwards towards the life-sized figure.

It began to drizzle.

An old man drove up, got out of his ancient Morris Minor and came and sat beside me. He knelt for about ten minutes, then sat up and started to talk.

'I come here every day.'

'Have you ever seen her move?'

'I'm here to pray. I don't come here for that nonsense. This place has not been the same since some fool first saw Our Lady giving him the nod.'

'Don't you believe in miracles?'

'Not this one. All that moving about ruined the shrine for people like myself. I like to come along for a quiet prayer. Our Lady did not do us local people any favours.'

'I'm sorry.'

'I suppose you are here waiting for her to make some sort of gesture or movement?'

'No.'

'Then you've come out of curiosity?'

'No, I just brought along this lot.' I indicated the trio beside me, Delfina's mouth gaping wide open, all of them intent on seeing something unusual.

'Foreigners?'

'They are from the Philippines.'

He sighed. 'We've had plenty of them during the past few years.'

'Do you still get a lot of pilgrims?'

'Not nearly so many come to Ballinaspittle these days, thank goodness, although it's never gone back to the peace and quiet we used to know.'

'When did it start? When she…er Our Lady started to move?'

'The first reports began around 1985. And then the country went mad. Of course it's been going on ever since, but not quite as bad as that first year. Even today the BBC in England is planning to make a film about what's been happening around here since the beginning of all that nonsense. When that film's made it'll bring in more of the mob.'

'Does she still go on moving?'

'Oh yes, regularly. A few people have seen her jump up and down. Sometimes she even speaks to someone. But it's not as bad as it used to be. It was terrible. Thousands of gawpers came on buses. I had to come here before daybreak.'

He ignored the rain which was falling harder.

159

'One good thing, she's been earning plenty of money for us.' He indicated the blue box nearby which had two large padlocks.'You'll see to it your people put donations in there. You too, I hope.'

I only had a ten pound note with me and I had no intention of getting rid of it in this particular fashion.

The old man continued, 'I know a few lads around here used to charge five pounds for a place for fools to park their car. Good money. Nothing of that sort these days. But there are a few who keep looking.' He hesitated. 'Church doesn't like this sort of thing. The Bishop of Cork called it an illusion.'

'But the Church surely approves of miracles?'

'Not this one. They'd like to put a stop to it altogether. Although they haven't gone as far as the Pentecostalists.' He described how a group of Protestants came down with hammers to damage the poor statue. 'From the north of Ireland. Where else?'

However: 'She's been repaired. They should have taken off the light bulbs round her head while they were at it.'

It seemed that one in seven of the people who came here saw something. And now was no exception.

Attracta yelled, 'I see! She move! She move!'

The old man sighed. 'Another one. She had better put something decent in the donation box.'

He got up and strolled off as another minibus drew up and more lookers for miracles poured out, came over and knelt on the wet benches. They ignored the rain which was getting worse. Water dripped down the rocks and formed little pools at our feet.

Our Lady was nice and dry beside her little cave.

'Will we be going?' I asked Rodrigo.

But Delfina and Rodrigo made no move. I assumed they were envious of Attracta and wanted to wait around a little longer in case Our Lady did them a favour as well and stirred and wavered.

I went back to our bus where Brendan was still listening to the radio. He was munching a sandwich.

'Any luck?'

I told him about Attracta.

'Excellent!'

The Filipinos continued on the lookout for almost another hour. They were far more persistent in their veneration than the people in the other minibus who soon drove off.

It began to be hard to see the statue in the rain. Why do so many miracles appear in the wettest parts of Ireland, Glendalough, Killarney and Donegal where a seasonal downpour often resembles a tropical storm?

At last the three Filipino pilgrims rose to their feet and each of them went and put what looked like a considerable amount of notes into the donation box. I was not going to check. They came back to the bus in their soaking clothes and Brendan turned on the heater.

Attracta's eyes were shining,

'She shake head at me!'

Rodrigo said sulkily, 'Attracta only think she see miracle. Our Lady not move at all – too wet.'

'You wrong! I see! Our Lady like me – not like you!'

Rodrigo ignored her. He put his camera away and pulled out a cigarette.

'Is very wet.'

Maria had arranged for us to stay in a hotel in Kinsale. Even before we went up to our rooms to change, Attracta, water pouring from her clothes, rushed to the telephone in the hotel lounge. The gabble of Spanish which everyone in the hotel lounge could hear may have indicated to Maria how she had been honoured.

Attracta's ecstasy continued to irritate us all.

'You envy. Our Lady not move for you!'

We all ate an excellent dinner. Nothing like a good miracle to stimulate the appetite and restore good humour.

'Where we go now?' Rodrigo asked next morning, having followed the evening steak with a huge morning fry.

Brendan wiped his moustache.

'Up to Mayo.'

It was a long way from Cork to Mayo. The sun shone, the sky was blue. This seemed more of a miracle than anything Attracta might have experienced the day before. Overnight she had ceased to annoy and all three Filipinos were in good humour. The minibus vibrated with hymns and prayers.

Somewhere near Limerick, after a pub lunch – appetites continued to be good – the singing ceased as Brendan pulled into a lay-by, turned and switched on a microphone. Speaking slowly, so that he could easily be understood, he told us of the miracle of Knock.

Knock had everything that might appeal to those seeking something holy and unusual, the blaze of heavenly light on the South Gable of the church, the Blessed Virgin and her silver rose, St John the Evangelist, St Joseph all in white, the Lamb.

'...And all the time that evening as they stood there under the gable with the holy picture it was raining. The rain fell on them as they marvelled and prayed. But the sacred images did not get wet.'

'Yesterday we get wet, Holy Virgin stay dry. Everything holy in Ireland happen in rain.'

'One hundred years after, in 1979, the Pope came to Knock and gave the shrine the Vatican stamp of approval. Later Mother Teresa visited Knock.'

I resolved not to say anything about a magic lantern.

We set out northward once more. The sun continued to shine. Miracle! We drove past the turning to Knock airport built on top of a bog to the urgings of Father Horan. Another miracle!

At sunset the minibus reached the town of Knock, which bulged with people.

Brendan shouted back to us, 'A million and a half pilgrims come here every year.'

He turned the minibus into the driveway heralded by a sign which proclaimed BASILICA VIEW Bed and Breakfast.

When the landlady came to the door to greet us, Brendan gave her a kiss.

'My sister...'

The place was agreeable; we were offered supper. Once again Rodrigo, Delfina and Attracta were hungry. Once again we had a comfortable night.

Next morning we discovered that two of the other guests were Filipina nurses from a hospital in Dublin. There were shrieks of recognition in Tagalog, the native language of the Philippines. Someone knew a cousin...plenty of cousins...names, and addresses were joyfully exchanged, and Delfina impressed her fellow country women by boasting about Ballinaspittle.

'My daughter see...Attracta see Our Lady moving!'

Too much choice was offered to the pilgrims of Knock: pilgrimage, processions, mass at any of the five churches in the shrine grounds, a visit to the Apparition church, that was for sure, Knock Museum, confessions, general counselling, enrolment encounters with the Knock Shrine Society, shopping...

As a grumpy Protestant I planned to behave like Brendan – leave Rodrigo and company to themselves and their devotions, buy a couple of newspapers, and spend the day sitting in a café.

Further quarrelling. Too much choice. Too many opportunities for pilgrimage and prayer.

Delfina and Attracta decided that the first thing they would do would be to go shopping while thousands of other pilgrims were praying, processing or confessing. They rummaged among resin statues of Our Lady, medals with drops of holy water, holy water bottles, souvenir pins with pictures of the Lamb, calendars, prayer cards, and rosaries galore, made from green beads, red beads, mother of pearl, silver that would catch the eye of pilgrims – who were never to be described as tourists. And candles...and more statues of Our Lady – some in porcelain.

And postcards of Knock and the gable and the shrine and the

basilica to be sent back to friends and relations in the Philippines. And of course, how could anyone forget? a postcard to be sent to Maria, and the Colonel, wishing them well, and telling them they were remembered in prayers, and once again, informing them that Attracta had seen Our Lady move in Ballinaspittle.

The morning had long gone by the time Delfina and Attracta had tottered back to Basilica View with bags full of items they had purchased.

The postcards had to be dealt with, which meant a trip to the café where I was sitting with the *Irish Times*. For me, the idea of sitting down for a leisurely read of a newspaper to the accompaniment of a cappuccino was blown away.

As Rodrigo, Delfina and Attracta drank their coffee, they wrote to their friends.

'Cards must go from this holy place, Knock.'

'Pope come here, also Mother Teresa.'

'Write that down.'

There was no sign of Brendan, so the pleas were directed at myself.

'David, take us to post office!'

Where the queues were long, since pilgrims had much the same idea as Delfina and Attracta concerning postcards to their friends.

During the afternoon there was more to be done. Should the three of them join in a procession of sick in their wheelchairs, or follow a mysterious gaunt man with a long white beard carrying a cross, and go and pray in the Basilica which stood out like a beacon over the surrounding bog land? Or gather with a group of people who were staring at the sun?

'Very bad for your eyes.'

Attracta stared along with these particular pilgrims, and it did her no good. She fainted. One moment she was swinging back and forwards gazing rapturously at what must have seemed to her another miracle and the next she was lying prone on the ground.

When she recovered there was just time before the shops closed to return to the shops and buy more rosaries for friends.

A really nice day.

Lough Derg would not be as enjoyable as Knock.

We spent the night at a bed and breakfast in Pettigo up in Donegal. No breakfast. We had to start fasting from midnight.

Brendan told us how things would be. 'One meal a day for the next three days. Tea without milk. Toast. No butter.'

We would all be welcome on the island in the middle of the lake.

'Whatever our creed!' Brendan glared at me. 'Penance for everyone! Bare feet. The first thing you'll do when you arrive at the island is take off your shoes and socks.'

Rodrigo asked, 'You come as well?'

Brendan said, 'No.'

'Why you not come?'

'I have to look after the bus.'

'You not come any place. Not look and see Our Lady move. Not see holy lamb at Knock. Now not come on holy island.'

'I have done those things before.'

'You only interested in football,' Rodrigo persisted.

Brendan ignored him.

'St Patrick's Purgatory has been going on for a thousand years. Plenty of fasting.'

'When St Patrick visit?'

'He didn't, but the pilgrimage was named after him.'

Rodrigo said, 'No eating. Walking without shoes. I like Knock better.'

I said, 'I will stay behind with Brendan.'

'You come,' Rodrigo said. 'You promise Maria.'

'You go,' said Brendan.

When Brendan drove the bus to the little pier where boats waited to take us to the island, we found many people besides ourselves assembled to go over the lake to holy discomfort. A few we recognized as having been at Knock. Holy tourism. We had to wait an hour before there was room for us on a boat crowded with sinners.

The Filipinos carried a selection of their new rosaries.

Brendan waved us off. 'Have a good time!'

For him it was back to the minibus and the radio, and a couple of days in Pettigo. No bare feet and prayers for Brendan.

The boat steered towards Station Island. As we got nearer the island appeared grey and menacing and I caught sight of long grey stone buildings under the sombre grey sky.

Rain. Attracta took off her sun glasses. Before we reached the little harbour a gale was blowing across the water the noise of it drowning out the sound of prayers. The downpour assumed a pitiless intensity.

We arrived and disembarked slowly.

'You are most welcome,' the elderly priest shouted at the boatload through the rain. He must have said the same thing earlier that morning – twice, since we were the third boat from the mainland – and yesterday and scores of times this one year. And the year before.

And during the twelfth century some other holy man must have greeted pilgrims from all over Europe desperate to escape the fires of Hell.

Today the priest added, 'God willing, after your visit here you will be greatly refreshed.'

Soaking wet, we took off our shoes and socks.

We began three days and two nights with a series of stations to be visited and prayers said. I followed along, walking from bed to bed in bare feet like the rest of them. The beds were stone mounds which, we were told, were the remains of cells used by monks. Pilgrims circled around in silent prayer.

The rain was unrelenting.

We experienced it all – the twenty-four hour vigil from ten o'clock at night, the Lough Derg cuisine, tea without milk and toast without butter, and if you wished for it, water from the drinking fountains and bottled water which could be bought at the souvenir shop.

I endured the masses, the prayers, the mutterings of faith that refreshed the majority of pilgrims. Who could ever have devised such a harsh pilgrimage for lost souls which was more like an army exercise?

By the second day we all had colds. How many people had died, I wondered, over a thousand years during these three days? It seemed that they took your word for it that you were in good health.

Rodrigo suffered the pilgrim experience doggedly; Attracta and Delfina appeared to be enjoying themselves, especially Delfina, ever in pursuit of holiness. Between prayers and penance they found time for a favoured pastime: they made their way to the crowded souvenir shop and obeyed the notice which advised them to take home a little reminder of the island or gifts for loved ones. Holy tourism. They bought more rosaries; by now they must have had a sack full. And images of St Patrick and crosses. A poster. Postcards.

Time passed infinitely slowly. We seemed to have been on St Patrick's island three months rather than three days before we got back our shoes and socks, which were still damp, and the boat took the crowd back to the mainland.

It was midday when we arrived on the mainland, and Brendan was there to greet us. He was chewing a chocolate bar.

CHAPTER FIFTEEN

Who told us that pilgrims who visited the holy island returned refreshed and happy?

Next day ideas of penance were behind us as we stopped and ate a huge meal on our way down to Mayo once more. Maria and Brendan had arranged the schedule so that we would get to Croagh Patrick on the last Sunday in July, known as Garland Sunday.

During the meal the Filipinos began a quarrel. Although they shouted at each other in Spanish, I caught the gist of what they were saying.

Rodrigo had suffered enough. For him the last three days of penitence and misery were quite sufficient and the prospect of clambering up a mountain with forty thousand other people was not inviting.

Delfina and Attracta felt differently. Attracta, who had gained holy benefit from every place we had visited – yes, she reminded us yet again Our Lady had moved for her at Ballinspittle – insisted on making another effort to add yet another notch of sanctity to her holy experiences. Reaching the summit of Croagh Patrick would be something additional to the penance obtained at Lough Derg, at Knock and at Ballinaspittle,

After a long quarrel, Rodrigo's womenfolk won the argument.

'O.K.' he conceded sulkily at last, lapsing into English. 'Not too much prayer?' he asked Brendan.

Brendan poured some oil on troubled waters. 'God bless you! You pray if and when you like. And don't worry about the climb. There's nothing to it, even for a girl. Bring you all nearer to God.'

'You also come?'

'I'm too lame.'

'I not see you limp.'

' I have climbed Croagh Patrick twice already.'

'Three time lucky.'

'Don't worry about me. You'll all find it easy enough.'

'You stay again listen to radio.'

'You'll leap up like mountain goats.' Brendan added, 'Will you be going up in bare feet? The holiest of pilgrims climb Croagh Patrick that way.'

'Like Holy Island? Once again bare feet?'

'Well...yes...'

But the Filipinos thought differently. At Westport the first thing we did was to stop at a shoe shop and buy boots with money Maria had provided. I was treated to a pair.

Brendan drove us across to the hotel at the outskirts of the town where Maria had booked us in. It was lucky she had done so in time, since it was full of pilgrims all set to do the great climb the following day. We were still hungry after the fast at Lough Derg and we settled down in the crowded dining room for another large dinner.

I was tucking into steak when I looked up and saw a small boy coming through the door blowing a balloon-sized wad of pink bubble gum.

Next day, sitting in the minibus which was making its way very slowly from Westport to Murrisk at the foot of Croagh Patrick, I was once again cursing for allowing myself to be persuaded to one more holy nightmare. Not only was I pledged to clamber up a stony mountain, but I was also instructed to keep an eye on Rodrigo, and Delfina. Far worse, this time I would have to take care of Marco.

I went back over the awful sequence of yesterday evening when I had first spotted the Brat. He had been followed by Maria, Uncle Jack and Massey.

Surprise! Surprise!

Chairs were wedged in among us and the Mount Jewel contingent was welcomed with cries of joy as they settled down to eat.

Massey had driven them down from Mount Jewel.

We turned back to our ruined dinner.

'Why you come?' asked Rodrigo as more chairs were found and our steaks got cold.

'Marco wish to climb holy mountain,' Maria said, chopping up Uncle Jack's chicken and ham into small pieces. 'You, David, you watch him.'

That was when I should have made my protest. I should have insisted that Rodrigo take over the awful task. I had endured enough.

I ordered a whiskey.

Early next morning Brendan drove Rodrigo, Attracta and myself along the edge of Clew Bay with one extra passenger.

I should have refused firmly as Delfina had done, when plans and orders were delivered yesterday by Maria. Delfina insisted she had experienced enough holiness. She would stay in Westport and have another day's shopping. Maria would accompany her while Uncle Jack would sit in the hotel lounge with Massey.

'You go up mountain,' Maria ordered me.

As we inched behind the holy traffic jam, cars and buses containing dozens of prospective climbers, Brendan adjusted his little microphone and gave us yet another lecture. Rodrigo ceased playing his guitar, while Brendan spoke to the sounds of Marco slapping gum against his cheek.

'Patrick come here? Truly come here? Not like Lough Derg?'

The minibus jerked forward as Brendan informed us that yes, indeed, Ireland's holy saint had spent forty days on the summit of the Reek.

'What he do on mountain?'

'He prayed and fasted.'

'Like Jesus in desert. Jesus also forty days. Praying all the time. Why forty days so good?'

Brendan did not know.

'One day enough. And no fasting. Enough fasting on Lough Derg.'

The van bumped along another few yards as Brendan told us that people had been climbing the mountain long before St Patrick came along.

'Five thousand years ago. In the Stone Age.'

'What this Stone Age?'

'Before St Patrick. No Christians in Stone Age. Pagans. Heathens.'

'Now all Christian,' murmured Attracta. 'Climbing mountain we get near to God.'

Brendan had told us all he knew. Rodrigo resumed playing his guitar. As we crept along his music grew sadder.

At last we reached Murrisk where Brendan found a parking space wedged between two buses.

'Up there.'

As usual in the Filipino's experience, the weather was not kind. A blanket of cloud obscured the peak of the holy mountain.

'Two thousand five hundred feet high.'

'Very high. '

'Top five hundred feet in cloud.'

'When you reach the summit you can all confess your sins. And a priest celebrates Mass every half hour.'

'What time now?'

'Eleven o'clock. You'll have to get going if you want to hear the last Mass at two thirty.'

'Come! We go quickly!' trilled Attracta.

Brendan had not forgotten to bring Sunday newspapers with him. He waved us off as we queued up with other pilgrims to buy stout hazel sticks from a dealer.

The majestic mountain where the saint had prayed and driven away lingering pagan spirits offered a double penance. We put on our woolly hats and pullovers under raincoats.

We trudged upwards, Rodrigo, Attracta and myself. Marco ran ahead. Again I felt envious of Delfina and her wise decision to remain

171

in Westport. I already felt tired by the time I reached the statue of St Patrick, which was only about a quarter of a mile up the bottom slope of the mountain. The saint, raised on a plinth, held out one stuccoed white arm in blessing. We paused at the casualty station waiting for anyone who had an accident. A lot of people were preparing to go barefoot. We had more than enough of that on Lough Derg. We wore our mountain boots and woollen stockings.

But: 'I also go without shoes!' shouted Marco.

'No you don't,' I shouted. 'You're mother said no!'

Marco tore off his boots stuffed his socks into them and threw them as far down towards Murrisk as he could. He turned and picked his way rapidly upwards over the stones.

'Silly boy,' said Rodrigo.

'Is good boy,' Attracta contradicted. 'Walk barefoot, sins forgiven.'

But she herself was in no hurry to relinquish her own stout footwear.

I went back downhill and retrieved Marco's boots and came back.

We climbed slowly and eventually caught up with Marco, who had not gone far. He sat on a rock, stuffing himself with sweets. Trickles of blood ran down his feet.

'Do you want to go back downhill?' I asked hopefully.

'Want my boots.'

He let Rodrigo mop away the blood with Kleenex – it was not very much, and did not seem to give his any discomfort. He held out his leg for his uncle to fit on his boots and do up his laces.

'Are you sure you don't want to go back to the minibus?' I persisted.

He did not answer, but got to his feet and ran upwards again. The scratches on his feet seemed to have made no difference to his ability to ascend speedily.

Rodrigo, Attracta and I followed slowly, climbing with the aid of our sticks gasping as we passed happy shriven descending pilgrims. We went one weary step at a time, giving the odd groan. The pilgrim route snaked its way upwards; people were coming down, thousands of them, all pleased with themselves and smiling. They had done it. Their ordeal was over. Their sins were absolved.

Pilgrims going up, like ourselves were full of envy, with fifteen hundred feet to climb. We resembled the queue at Chilcoot Pass, going up the Klondyke in that famous photograph taken a hundred years ago.

'Rain!' Rodrigo observed.

For once it was only a shower. It soon stopped and threads of low hanging mist above us cleared away. Suddenly we were enjoying a beautiful day. Above us was the cone of the mountain where all sorts of people were being forgiven their sins and God looked down through a blue sky. Below us a beam of sunshine picked out the islands with their chess boards of glossy green fields.

The sun shone brightly as Attracta began to climb more quickly and eagerly and was soon far ahead. As Rodrigo and I mounted step by step, it seemed hours before we once again caught up with Marco who was seated on a boulder. The sweets he carried had been eaten. He was aiming pebbles at a couple of elderly pilgrims climbing ahead of him.

'Where's Attracta?'

Marco muttered, 'She climb fast. She reach top.'

Casan Phadraig, the steep path to the summit loomed above us. Rodrigo and I were in a state of exhaustion.

'I not climb any more,' sighed Rodrigo, sitting down beside Marco. 'My back ache.'

There was silence as the three of us watched a couple of stretcher bearers coming down carrying a groaning old man. Another stone thrown by Marco caught the hind bearer in the back, but he was so intent on his task he took no notice.

'Stop it!' I shouted.

The Brat grinned, and this time the stone he threw came in my direction.

'STOP IT!'

'We go down? Enough going up.'

We looked up at St Patrick's path and the steep escarpment of rocks and boulders leading to the summit. We knew that up there was a small church. Were we hearing the drone of voices like the drone of bees? Even to me, the most reluctant climber on the Reek, this Garland Sunday, it seemed a pity when we had reached a critical point on the ascent to abandon all at this stage.

A descending stranger sat down beside me, resting his stick at my feet. 'You haven't far to go.'

'What's happening up there?'

'There's a priest hearing confession. He's at it all day. And Mass. I took Mass.' His smile was beatific. He sat for just a few moments before getting up and continuing to make a careful descent.

'We also go down?' persisted Rodrigo.

'Where's Attracta?'

'Up there.'

We found her stretched out on the ground like a corpse awaiting resurrection. Was it all our fault that we had encouraged her in this religious tomfoolery?

The sun was shining fiercely and a group of elderly pilgrims was passing. The murmur of prayers followed them with a clink of rosary beads. They stopped at the sight of Attracta who sat up with a listless expression.

'Give her some water. She's been staring too long at the sun.'

'Oh God, I have no strength.'

Her long black tresses had fallen over her shoulders. Cold water was sprinkled over her head and the pilgrims clapped as she got to her feet.

'I see holy things...' She turned and began climbing once more.

Rodrigo gave a sigh. 'She my daughter. I follow.' He picked up his stick. 'My duty. Maybe I also go to Mass. Maybe I confess.'

Marco went after him.

I knew I should follow, but it was pleasant sitting here in the sunshine admiring Clew Bay and its islands. In a little while...In any case I was not going to be participating in any religious ceremony at the summit of Casan Phadraig.

I waved to another group of pensioners making the descent, muttering their prayers. I sat watching about five hundred people passing me, going up, and about seven hundred going down.

I should make an effort...

How could I fall asleep with so much going on?

'Come, David, you help, come quickly, all terrible...'

Attracta was shaking me.

'My father fall!'

She ran back up Casan Phadraig in her bare feet. I followed, and even with the help of my stick, nearly fell myself.

Rodrigo had nearly reached the summit when the accident happened. He may have tripped before he fell down the scree. A crowd was around him, directed by a bald man who was a member of the Knights of Malta.

He carried a radio. 'I have ordered a stretcher.'

Rodrigo lay groaning. His leg looked odd. So did his face since blood was pouring out of his mouth. He had lost a couple of gold teeth.

Marco sat on the scree at a distance looking frightened.

The crowd that had gathered around Rodrigo dispersed, while the Malta man opened a box and took out a hypodermic.

'Pain killer.'

Attracta knelt beside Rodrigo and held his hand. She said 'I reach top. I do confession. I take Mass. Teeth safe. I find.'

'Too many accidents,' said the Malta man, digging the needle into Rodrigo.

'I'm sorry.'

'Two broken ankles, some severe bruising and a heart attack. Croagh Patrick should not be climbed by those of an advanced age.'

Attracta said, 'My father only forty-three.'

'Whatever his age he should have been more careful!'

For a minute Rodrigo stopped his groans. I noticed he was directing furious glances in the direction of Marco, who sat in silence. It was easy to draw conclusions. But it would be up to Rodrigo to complain if his painful predicament was the result of any stone throwing by the Brat.

He was considered too badly injured to be shuffled downhill on a stretcher. Once again the Malta man spoke into his radio.

'Air Corps helicopter!'

The sun had gone and it was raining again. We waited in the downpour. There was thunder and we could hardly see other pilgrims through the storm.

More time passed before the helicopter landed beside us. It had returned from Castlebar where it had taken the man with the heart attack to hospital.

'You'll be going there as well.'

With a roar the helicopter settled on the scree. A doctor jumped out. Another injection. Rodrigo's leg was put into an emergency splint, he was covered with a red blanket, and placed on a stretcher. Through the rain the doctor, the pilot, the Malta man and myself heaved him inside.

'I go too,' screamed Attracta, but there was no room for her.

The helicopter rose into the rain and pilgrims stopped going up and down stopped and watched.

The downpour had lessened by the time Marco, Attracta and myself began to shuffle downhill. Marco was subdued and limping. He had shown no interest in the arrival or departure of the helicopter.

'What have you done?' shouted Maria.

'Nothing...' But I felt guilty.

Marco also continued to show signs of guilt – that was what I assumed. For the first time since he had come to Ireland he was silent as he watched Maria vented her fury on me.

'You nearly kill brother.'

'I was not there when he fell.'

Uncle Jack had retired to bed in the hotel. Brendan had presented Maria with a large bill. No one was happy, although Attracta displayed less wretchedness than the rest of us. Having fulfilled the demands of every holy place she had visited, it seemed that she even found her father's accident bearable.

Next day Delfina, carrying Rodrigo's guitar and his gold teeth, Maria and I visited Rodrigo who lay in hospital, enduring a leg swaddled in plaster elevated above his head.

'Where Marco?'

'He not come. He stay with Colonel and Attracta.'

'I not wish to see him.'

'Why you not wish?'

Rodrigo caught my eye and shrugged weary shoulders.

'Marco not good boy.'

The doctor pronounced that Rodrigo would need ten days in hospital before he was fit to return to Mount Jewel.

Rodrigo did not elaborate any further about Marco. No one told him, he muttered, that the pilgrimage up the holy mountain could be dangerous.

Maria had brought some snacks – which Rodrigo refused to eat.

'Everything bad.' Maria handed him a small hand mirror. He examined the remains of his face.

Delfina took his hand. 'Soon you play guitar again. Then we go to dentist, put back teeth. Colonel pay.'

CHAPTER SIXTEEN

Delfina stayed in Castlebar hospital with Rodrigo. The rest of us returned to Mount Jewel where a good deal of activity was taking place. The sale of the Lely painting had meant that Uncle Jack's mystery coffers were replenished comfortably and there was money for developing Mount Jewel as a proper hotel.

The bedrooms upstairs were full of carpenters installing en suite bathrooms; the house resounded with sounds of hammers banging in nails. Baths, basins and showers were carried upstairs. On the top floor the barrack room was being converted to rooms and dormitories where staff could stay.

Outside, more park trees had been knocked down as the velvet green of the golf course took shape.

My uncle continued to follow Maria around, smiling and agreeing to anything she said. She was still so annoyed that she would not speak to me.

I knew I had been wrong to lie in the sun dozing just below the summit of Croagh Patrick while terrible things were happening to Rodrigo.

Attracta seemed to have forgotten all about her holy achievements and now spent her time outside flirting with the men who were at work on the golf course.

Marco continued to be in the depths of gloom.

Uncle Jack offered to help him assemble the Hornby train.

'Don't wanna to play with old man.'

But the Brat cheered up when he found some things which he considered more delightful to play with than Lego. Great-uncle Hubert's little Japanese men being tortured were taken out of their corner cupboard and spread all over the floor.

'David, I wish to speak.' Maria summoned me to the study where Marco was playing with the ivory men, arranging in a semicircle on the rent table. My uncle was reading the *Irish Times* and as so often, happened the fiery butt of his cigar was threatening the newsprint.

It seemed that something important was ensuing. A diamond brooch which had belonged to Aunt Maud glittered on Maria's left breast.

She had not spoken to me for a week.

'Now we have important talk.'

She prodded the double page of the *Irish Times* which Uncle Jack lowered. Slowly one lizard eye looked up and met hers.

'David, you know Colonel too old for good sleeping.'

In fact, I didn't. I had only been guessing.

Uncle Jack gave a sigh.

'No proper love… Only holding hands.'

Uncle Jack cleared his throat.

'No children. Very sad. But Colonel love Marco. '

'Yes, dearest.'

There was a pause before she put drama into her voice.

'WISH TO ADOPT! My darling boy become Colonel son!' I watched a smile light up her face.

She repeated 'He will be Colonel son. He will be Marco Hilton.'

'No,' I spluttered.

'You remember, David, we are married now. And Marco will call Colonel Daddy. They play together. You see how happy is Colonel.'

For more years than I could remember I had been Uncle Jack's heir. And now this loathesome juvenile would take my place and my inheritance. I wished I had been able to throw him off Croagh Patrick and get rid of him.

Mount Jewel would be mine. Should be mine. But no more. What could I do? Get Uncle Jack locked up, returned to Silver Meadows? Get this scheming woman sent home, back to the Philippines with her little monster?

'Marco go to good Catholic school and become Irish gentleman. Learn riding horses and shooting. Colonel will be proud of him.'

Such a crazy idea and I could not believe what I was hearing. There is a great difference in inviting people into your house and then finding that all the time they are planning to evict you.

How could my craggy disreputable uncle have allowed himself to fall into such a trap?

'Get me breakfast, will you, David? Black pudding, bacon and eggs.'

When I came back Uncle Jack was reading yesterday's *Irish Times*, checking the death notices. Marco was biting a small half-severed ivory head.

I consulted Hennessy. My uncle was being looked after, he was solvent, and the estate was flourishing largely because of the good fairy – Maria. Soon Mount Jewel would be running as a hotel.

'How's the golf course coming on?'

'Nearly finished.'

'When will the hotel be formally opened?'

'I don't know. Next month?'

'From what I can tell everything is going exceptionally well.'

Miss Switzer brought in Earl Grey served in thick mugs.

'That isn't why I've come.' I was determined to keep my temper.

Hennessy took a pinch of snuff and waited.

'He wants to disinherit me.'

'You mean he is planning to adopt Maria's son?'

'You know about it?'

'Oh yes. I'm arranging Marco's adoption.'

'For how long has this idea being going on?'

'It was planned before the marriage.'

'I'm the last person to hear news.'

'Perhaps the Colonel thought it was none of your business.'

'Damn well is my business.'

'You have talked to the Colonel?'

'To Maria.' I was struggling to find the right words. 'Couldn't we get Uncle Jack certified?'

Hennessy took more snuff. 'David, he is as sane as you and I. He and Maria are married, happily I believe.'

'I don't know about happily.'

'She is taking excellent care of him. He appears to be content.' He added, 'You must see that the adoption of Marcus is a reasonable development, following on their marriage.'

'What about me?'

'What about you? This is something you will just have to put up with.'

'You mean that I am losing my inheritance? Becoming cousin to Marco?'

'You might consider going back to Australia.'

As I left he said, 'Give my regards to Maria.'

Maria was making plans. First of all she spent a lot of time trying to make Marco call my uncle 'Daddy'.

'Why you not like your new daddy?

'He not my daddy. He too old.'

Uncle Jack was dozing outside in a deck chair in the garden.

I tapped him on the shoulder and one eye looked at me from under the familiar Panama hat.

I tried to tell him...legal father...injustice... ignorant...Filipino boy... by succession the estate should go to me...

'Hmm...' He was not listening. He shut his eye, and the sun was warming his old face.

'Ask Maria...'

Marco was tired of Lego and the tortured Japanese ceased to amuse him. He was soothed with presents. Nothing was too good for him, not the new clothes, nor the expensive watch which told not only the time, and the days of the week, but what time it was in the Philippines. It spoke, that watch.

He shouted and hurled teacups on the floor.

'Why not a pony?' I suggested. He might fall off.

'Bicycle better.' They went up to Dublin to buy one which was shining and sleek with many gears. I remembered the rusty old machines I had to put up during my boyhood.

My new task was to teach him how to use it. We needed two horrible days before he got the hang of it and shot off down the drive. He did not break his neck before reaching the front gate.

For the present the bicycle kept him from sulking and shouting inside the house. Now he spent his time outside, swaggering around on the machine burping its silver-plated horn.

'Please Marco, my darling, be careful.'

There were two lakes into which he might fall and drown, but he veered round them.

September came, and the school down the road in Mauricetown was open for business.

'Marco go.' Everyone, was tired of him and his sulks and his shouts. Even Maria.

For a week as the leaves began to turn to autumn colours I drove him down to Mauricetown every morning.

'...Impossible boy – disruptive, rude, endlessly quarrelsome.' That was what his teacher said even before worse happened.

They might have endured him for longer, but he took along Maria's dressmakers scissors in his satchel and while the teacher was (illegally) having a cup of coffee and a cigarette, ran round the classroom cutting off the hair of the little girls in the class. Fair hair, curly hair, dark hair was heaped up in front of the blackboard; a dozen bawling children were as cropped as convicts.

In Castlebar Rodrigo and Delfina were waiting at the hospital entrance, Rodrigo on crutches. As I drew up Delfina gave a friendly wave. He greeted me in a tone that was almost as surly as Marco's. His leg was stiff as a tree trunk.

We drove back in silence, except that from time to time he played his guitar. At Mount Jewel he followed Delfina, slowly manoeuvring his crutches, limping up into the hall where Maria and Uncle Jack waited for him.

Ahead were steps and stairs.

'Rodrigo stay in drawing room,' declared Maria, reverting to her role as nurse.

A bed was brought down from upstairs to accommodate him in the huge cold room, a long away from any lavatory. But Mount Jewel had never been short of chamber-pots.

The men toiling in the grounds of Mount Jewel may have resented Maria's authority, or they may have had mixed ideas about the regular sight of the Colonel, their smiling employer and Maria walking around hand in hand. But they all approved of the golf course, a Garden of Eden. And this particular stretch of Paradise was almost ready for players.

Inside the house things continued to change. The huge room where my ancestors had played billiards was converted into a dining room. Upstairs, comfortable beds had been installed in the bedrooms. New linen and towels were bought from Clery's in Dublin and sent up to Louth in a van.

There was another big clean. Maria stood at the doorways of the various bedrooms her eyes fixed on the activity that was going on.

Advertisements were inserted in *Image*, the *Independent*, and elsewhere. Journalists were dispatched to walk around the grounds, inspect the interior of the house and be offered a good meal.

Ghosts. Ghosts? How had they got into the publicity?

Uncle Jack got the blame.

'Some fellow came along and wanted to know the history of the house so I made up a few yarns.' The figure of a nun flitting up and down a corridor? A headless man? A one-legged man?

'Your talk of stupid ghosts frighten away good guests!' Maria scolded. 'How do we say now not true?'

I knew well enough that all the ghosts had departed when the Filipinos arrived.

The moment came when Hotel Mount Jewel could be declared open. There was nothing formal, only a ring on the telephone.

Someone with an English voice wanted a bed for the night.

The central heating was turned on and Delfina provided a bunch of plastic lilies to decorate the Bishop's Room. A fire was lit in the hall; Uncle Jack was confined to his study. But he would appear later, dressed in his green velvet jacket.

In the kitchen Rodrigo had discarded his crutches and taken charge. He wore a chef's starched linen hat and decided that for this important occasion he would cook pancit luglug.

'Noodles, hard-boiled eggs, vegetables, shrimp, chorizo ...spice... Now you see proper food for cold Irish climate.'

At dusk a lone cyclist was seen riding up the avenue. It had been blowing hard with spills of rain which made it difficult for him to avoid the puddles. Mr Simpson wore a plastic mackintosh and yellow boots. He was a lanky young man, who was investigating Norman castles. He had decided to give himself a treat. His refined voice, which Maria had heard on the telephone belied his appearance and dirty nails. His luggage was a dirty rucksack and a small zip bag full of books.

'He not rich,' Maria muttered after he had been escorted up to the Bishop's Room.

In the dining room candles had been lit and a turf fire burned in the grate. I sat to one side of Mr Simpson, Uncle Jack on the other. Maria had been dissuaded from introducing him as Lord Hilton. Mere Colonel had to do.

The meal was served on gold plates. In Aunt Maud's day gold plates had always been used after so much crockery had been broken by careless maids. After she left, the household had reverted to willow pattern, but the gold service was always there in case of need.

Josie served the Filipino meal Rodrigo had been cooking most of the day. We toyed with it, all of us, while I discussed the weather and mentioned the original castle at Mount Jewel and the surviving shell of the local castle.

'Besieged in 1640. After it was taken all the defenders were hanged.'

'Was Cromwell involved?'

'Yes.'

Mr Simpson took out pencil and paper and made notes. He left a pile of noodles on the side of his gold plate. He did, however, drink most of the bottle of wine we provided and finish the pineapple and coconut Rodrigo provided for dessert.

Next morning he had a hearty fry. I cooked it for him, since bacon, eggs and sausages were not in Rodrigo's remit and Cook and Josie, driven up every day by Massey, never arrived at Mount Jewel before eleven o'clock.

I did not bother about the gold plates; it was back to willow pattern.

Munching his sausage, Mr Simpson asked, 'Who's the one-legged fellow wandering around upstairs?'

'A cousin,' I said firmly.

The rain fell as Mr Simpson cycled away, having obtained directions to the Butler castle. The Filipinos groaned with disappointment.

'No tip!'

'In Manila rich man always leave good tip!'

At least he had paid for his one night stay.

Mr Simpson was the only guest that week.

There was too much rain for Attracta to go out and flirt with the men on the estate; she retired to bed with a book.

'Attracta read lady called Barbara Cartland. She write happy books. Always lady marry at the end. In Manila very popular.'

Uncle Jack wandered around the empty rooms giving advice about the running of the hotel.

'Shepheard's Hotel in Cairo. Now that was comfortable. Always enough waiters. And they had good looking belly dancers.'

'Surely not?'

'Not in the hotel itself. Down the road. Close enough. Very entertaining.'

Maria crossed herself. No more guests.

It seemed she had better things to do at night than stay in Uncle Jack's four-poster.

'Colonel snore. Breath bad.'

Rodrigo offered his usual opinion. 'Colonel too old for sex. Better Maria sleep alone.'

Maria had talked a good deal on this subject before Marco's adoption. But not to Rodrigo – it was scarcely his business. She screamed at him in Spanish and Delfina screamed back.

'Why we stay here?' Rodrigo asked, picking his fat nostril. 'Why not return to Philippines?'

'You go back Manila, you starve,' shouted Maria.

No decisions were made. They would not all go home yet.

Down in the forest below the lake something stirred. It was October, the time when ghostly flocks of spotted woodcock were putting in an appearance. Uncle Jack had not shot at them for many years and perhaps those gullible birds thought life had become safe at Mount Jewel.

The phone rang and a clipped voice asked for my uncle.

'Hello, Jack, glad you're out of that hell hole.'

'Hello Duffy. You mean Silver Meadows?'

'Thought you were there for the long haul.'

'You stopped coming to see me.'

'I was told you'd gone crazy.'

'I'm saner than you are.'

'Listen, Jack...I believe you're running your place as a hotel...'

The phone was passed on to Maria who took down details. Could Duffy and a few companions and their wives stay for three days and have a pop at the woodcock? Could Mount Juliet supply beaters?

'Beaters? What is beaters?'

The phone was passed on to me.

I had to explain the conversation, which went three ways.

'Ah. Men kill birds...'

The phone went back to my uncle and I heard Duffy's voice again. 'Six of us for three days. Look forward to seeing you, Jack, sane or not. '

Maria asked, 'What these birds they want to shoot?'

I tried to describe *scolopax rusticola*.

'You say long beak...black eyes in middle of head...small...why people want to kill?'

'They're good to eat.'

'Who this man Duffy?'

Uncle Jack told her. 'He used to come and see me at Silver Meadows.'

'I not remember.'

'Before I went downstairs.'

'Ah...'

'He's a lord.'

Maria was delighted. 'Very good for Mount Jewel Hotel.'

Uncle Jack lit a cigar and offered another to Rodrigo. 'My advice is to keep off that foul food you like cooking.'

Rodrigo took the hint.

Cook and Josie would supply reasonable dinners and also breakfast. I was told to fetch them both at an earlier hour.

Massey rounded up half a dozen local men as beaters.

'Like old times,' Uncle Jack said.

Massey told him, 'There's not that many woodcock, Colonel. The woods haven't been cleaned out since...before you went away that time. Briars. Branches brought down in that last storm.'

'Duffy can traipse through and blast away. If he finds anything, that's all to the good.'

'There's plenty of rabbits.'

Uncle Jack and Maria waged a silent war.

'We want central heating. I turn on switch, he turn off.'

My uncle always believed too much heat stifled initiative.

'Hotel guests not like cold.'

It took days to persuade Uncle Jack of the necessity of leaving the switches alone. But at last, only a day before Duffy and his friends were due, the heating was left full on. Even in the basement, beyond the kitchen various dark damp rooms felt a whirl of luxurious warmth.

'You are good old man.' Maria gave Uncle Jack a kiss.

It was necessary for her to move back to his bedroom since the one to which she had reverted had to be given over to a guest. She was discovering that taking in guests was not as easy as she imagined, what with beds that had to be made, fires that had to be lit and arranging for food to be prepared and cooked. Once again she had to lie beside a snoring old man.

Duffy and his friends arrived in two Landrovers with their dogs. Duffy was small with the usual thick bushy eyebrows of old age; he sported a bright red nose. Not for nothing did his neighbours call him Rudolph. His wife, Emily, who was a good deal younger, accompanied him.

'Married him for his money,' Uncle Jack had told Maria.

Duffy had invited a couple of other lords, and their ladies came along as well. It seemed the two of them had big houses in the north of Ireland which they had donated to the National Trust, before settling down to live in the wings.

They brought servants who carried in suitcases and guns. They also brought along a case of vintage wine which meant that we could not charge double on our own bottles.

The bath water was piping hot and the rooms were warm as they changed for dinner.

In the dining room candles flickered down the long table and the newly polished silver contrasted with the gold plate. Keeping his seat on a rearing white horse King Billy looked down with a pleased expression. He could put off winning the Battle of the Boyne until we had finished our meal, which was eaten in virtual silence. My uncle sat at the end of the table sawing away at rare roast beef with a blunt Georgian knife. It parted as if it was a slice of butter. He smacked his lips; he had taken out his teeth and put them in the Ming saucer.

A lot of good vintage wine was drunk. Maria and Defina did not sit at the table, but helped Josie to serve. Down in the kitchen Attracta was giving Cook a hand.

Next morning the men came down dressed in baggy tweeds. Their wives, wisely, decided to stay in bed, which meant carrying up breakfast trays. Since the maids were busy, here was another job for me. Up the divided staircase, along corridors and into bedrooms strangely altered by the presence of guests. The day was grey, and the rooms dim and silent except for the sound of rain on the windows.

I had already risen early to fetch Cook and Josie to prepare breakfast; Maria helped Cook in its preparation. Rodrigo insisted on including a Filipino dish full of spices under a pewter cover beside the hot sausages, bacon, black and white pudding, kippers, fried eggs and kedgeree. No takers.

Duffy had cut his chin while shaving and patched it with a wad of cotton wool.

'Pity about the weather,' he remarked sourly, and his companions murmured agreement as if the rain was the fault of the proprietors of Hotel Mount Jewel.

Rain continued to attack the long windows; beaters were waiting forlornly under the porch.

It was not until midday that the shooters prepared to leave. No Uncle Jack, who sat in the study before a big fire playing bridge with the three wives. They played nervously, since they knew what had happened to Lady Marsden. But my uncle was at his most charming, and they spent the afternoon, broken by tea and cake being regaled by tales of the awfulness of Silver Meadows.

'Never grow old,' Uncle Jack said, lighting yet another cigar. 'Three no trumps.' He described that basement. 'Never go mad.'

'Double!' Emily ventured. She and the other women caught each other's eyes; they must have been remembering how these days Daisy Marsden always wore a scarf around her neck.

Outside, umbrellas, shooting sticks and guns could not combat strong winds and driving rain. I was urged to follow the beaters, into the woods, sloshing around in mud and briars. Because the forest had not been cleared for many years, it was filled with thorny briars and branches which formed an almost inpenetrable barrier for anyone trying to get through them.

'What does Jack think he's doing sending us in here?'

In the mist and the rain I could hear the voices of Duffy and his companions. The theme was familiar.

'Who is that foreign woman?'

'Surely he is too old for that sort of thing?'

There were distant shouts and dogs were barking. A shot. Nothing was hurt, not even a bird.

A couple of hours later, apart from two rabbits, the game bags were still empty and the rain was still falling. Wet and dispirited, we made our way back to the house. It had been a miserable day.

'Any luck?' my uncle asked then the bedraggled group of lords.

'I thought you said there was plenty of game.' Duffy growled.

Later the frustrated shooters sat around the open log fire in the drawing room drinking steadily. The prize wine was reserved for the forthcoming meal; now they drowned their sorrows by downing a couple of bottles of Laphroaig Single Malt Scottish whisky, smokey and iodine rich. Uncle Jack was still playing bridge with their wives and after several drinks they ceased to take any notice of me.

Conversation dwelled on their old friend. For many years they had all fished and shot together and shared the same love of sport. Somehow recently this foriegn woman had taken him over and sucked him dry.

'I feel sorry for poor Jack,' said Percy, the lord from County Antrim, and Duffy and the other lord nodded in agreement.

'I'll tell you what we'll do,' said Duffy. 'We'll leave him a couple of bottles of decent wine. The really good stuff. Cheer him up.'

'Bloody good idea.'

Percy had just swallowed two Laphroaigs in quick succession, 'He's not as barmy as people make out.'

It was unfair on Maria who was conscious of the dismal day's sport endured by her guests and had decided to produce a memorable meal. There was caviar, a choice of Filipino delicacies, roast chicken, and a tasty fricassée made from the rabbits.

'Rabbit is only for dogs' said Uncle Jack, who was in a good mood. How pleasant it was to meet old friends who could understand him. A pity about the sport, but it was hardly his fault.

The dining room smelt of beeswax. On the large sideboard dishes of garishly coloured Filipino food was arranged with bowls of flowers. All the company preferred chicken; luckily there were two birds.

Next day at Mount Jewel the wives played more bridge. Outside we could not help the rain. Once again Duffy and his friends and the beaters trudged through the woods behind the wet dogs. The woodcock didn't appear to like flying in this weather and game bags continued relatively empty.

But six birds perished and Cook served them up in the evening. After the flutter and killing she took the day's limp corpses and tore off spotted feathers. The murdered lay, black feet curled, before the guests who picked at little brains and crunched marble-sized skulls. Percy's wonderful vintage wine continued to be enjoyed by the guests. It vanished quickly.

I left them to their meal and went downstairs. In the kitchen, I joined the beaters and the lords' servants who were slouched round the big wooden table together with Cook and Attracta. They were also making merry with Percy's wine while Rodrigo strummed his guitar. There was much laughter as they discussed the floundering peers with their useless guns battling through the thickets of the wood.

'They looked like drowned rats. Wasting their money.'

'Rich men deserve it. We'll all drink to that.'

From the Aga came the appetising smell of steak and chips.

It was while we were all enjoying our meal that Maria appeared in some distress. The diners upstairs needed more wine.

'Wine all gone,' said Rodrigo pointing to a line of empty bottles.

'I say Lord's bottles do not touch.'

'You never did!' shouted one of the beaters. None of the beaters had been tipped.

For the first time in months I was enjoying myself.

'...Mishtake...' A beater with his arm around Attracta's waist was saying when I went down to ask for more.

'Myself I'd prefer a glass of the black stuff,' said another beater, holding up a glass of Chateau Arnauld. 'But this isn't so bad.'

'All gone...very good.' Rodrigo's voice was slurred.

'I have a good mind to report you to the police,' Duffy said before venturing out through the downpour towards his Landrover.

'You no pay bill!' Maria yelled at him.

'Damned if I will!'

Uncle Jack appeared in the hall hobbling along on his blackthorn.

'I say, are you leaving us? What a pity!' He waved his arm in Duffy's direction as the Landrovers drove away.

He was too deaf to hear the last echoes of Duffy's voice.

'You haven't heard the last of this!'

'Too much rain,' Maria kept saying. She did not mention the curtseys she and Delfina had made to Lady Emily. 'No lady' was her opinion. 'Bitch wife.'

She grumbled about other reasons the week had failed.

'Little bird on burnt toast not big meal. Rodrigo stupid drinking Lord's good wine. Lord not happy.'

A phone call came from Hennessy who wanted to see Uncle Jack and Maria. There were urgent things to be discussed.

The three of us went to Hennessy's dusty office, where, as usual he sat with a pile of documents in front of him.

He read out the letter containing the estimate of how much those vintage bottles were worth.

'Not possible, so much.' Maria shrieked. But when Findlaters was rung up and consulted, the value Lord Percy had put on the booze was conservative.

..Donati Claret...Domaine La Grave..Chateau Arnauld...Nuits St George Premier Cru...St Emilion...

'You pay,' Maria told Uncle Jack.

CHAPTER SEVENTEEN

Not many more visitors arrived over the next month. One honeymooning couple; they were splendid guests, since they hardly got out of bed for the week they were here. A quartet of complaining Americans drove up to Mount Jewel at the end of November and demanded a turkey, since Thanksgiving was due. Three priests stayed at the beginning of Advent; Uncle Jack refused to talk to them.

Christmas came and went, enjoyed mostly by Marco whose presents emptied two toy shops in Dundalk. Maria did not do badly either; besides choosing some good jewellery, she persuaded Uncle Jack to give her scent which came in something the size of a milk bottle.

I thanked Maria and my uncle for my tie and shoelaces.

Christmas dinner was Filipino themed. We had enjoyed turkey with the Americans, and now there was an opportunity to empty out the freezer of the uneaten Filipino food that Rodrigo had cooked long ago.

At the beginning of January an Australian pair appeared, having taken a vacation during their summer holidays. It was a pity about the snow. They made the mistake of helping Marco build a vast snowman in the rath field. The wind got to them even before the breakdown of the central heating; they shivered over a couple of days, and then retired to bed. It was the end of January before they departed for Killarney, coughing and wheezing.

Marco? There was far too much of him. A particularly bad day's behaviour wore the household down – Uncle Jack was addressed with a stream of shouted F-words, Maria was called an old bitch, a delicate

Waterford dish was hurled in the dining room, and Marco threw up his dinner.

'School! Boarding school!'

We all held our breath amid Marco's shrieks and wondered if Maria would change her mind.

The selected establishment was far away in County Waterford. I drove Maria and Marco there; the car vibrated with his cries.

I watched him as we drove up the rutted avenue to the grey castellated house which looked like a prison. Silver Meadows was a palace by comparison.

'Don't want to go. Don't want to go...'

Let him suffer, I thought to myself. There was nothing better than an old-fashioned prep school to teach him some old-fashioned manners.

On the front steps the matron was waiting to greet new boys. Some were crying as they waved their families goodbye.

'Don't want to go...' Marco continued to plead as he tightly held Maria's hand. I removed his green trunk from the car.

Most of the small boys who looked Marco up and down appeared to be bullies.

The main hall smelt of antiseptics, rather like Silver Meadows. In the junior dormitory upstairs were two lines of iron-framed beds with red blankets.

The headmaster shook our hands and you could see at once that he was a sadistic monster. His ancient suit smelt of mothballs and he had a hairy upper lip.

Maria said, 'No schools in Philippines like this. Maybe we bring him home?' Luckily her change of mind was temporary. But she gave Marco a wad of money before we left.

'You be good boy and you get more.'

A senior boy was ordered to show the Brat around the school buildings, and see the class rooms where he would study and the exercise yard.

We drove away fast.

There was a wonderful silence in Mount Jewel.

Maria said, 'We make Mount Jewel better. Bigger hotel. Many guests.'

She would like to see how it was done elsewhere. This meant a tour of Ireland. I drove her, together with Uncle Jack and Rodrigo to places of luxury – Dromoland Castle, Castle Leslie, Waterford Castle and others.

'We do like these. We get good cooks. We have good golf course.' She had the work done in a few months. Meanwhile, after nearly two years, the golf course was finished; Jimmy O'Hara had done his job.

'Eighteen holes...'

Many noble trees had been sacrificed. There were not enough left for the rooks to nest in, so they flew away to find new homes.

Teeing ground, fairway, and putting greens wound around what had been a fine park. A helicopter pad was installed where rich golfers could land and it was hoped that celebrities would be enticed to come to Mount Jewel and enjoy amazing golf. Arrangements were made to hire men who had won huge tournaments like Greg Norman or Gary Player.

Maria had wanted to get rid of the horses and cattle so that Mount Jewel could be entirely devoted to golf and nothing else. But she was dissuaded; Massey would leave if the horses went. It was put to her that guests at the hotel might like to go out riding – in fact, we needed more horses, not less. One could hardly use Caviar Coast as a hunter. Not after he won another race at Leopardstown and there was talk of taking him to Cheltenham, which gave Mount Jewel a modicum more publicity.

In the old days golf was one thing Uncle Jack could never stand. He had always believed that there was something dysfunctional in people's minds that made them enjoy chasing a small white ball around the countryside. Men like that could never be trusted, even bishops.

He was fond of quoting P.G. Wodehouse in *The Clicking of Cuthbert*. 'Footling game! Blanked infernal fat-headed silly ass of a game! Nothing but a waste of time... What earthly good is golf? Life is stern and life is earnest.'

And he would add that the only good thing about a golf course was that it could not be built on. There was space for the hoi polloi to enjoy.

But now, as he and Maria wandered around four hundred acres of what had once been a place of beauty, stepping from green to green, circling what had once been a lake and was now merely a hazard, Uncle Jack seemed to accept the ruin of his lovely estate with aplomb.

Maria had used her own methods of persuasion. 'Silly man, we make much money.'

They came out of the rain inside into the study where Uncle Jack sat on a chair with his mouth open. Maria muttered that the Colonel had never done a good day's work in his life, and he still expected money to come rolling in. She was the one who had to show him that the new hotel would attract visitors who would pay for their pleasures which centred on golf.

I seemed to be the only person who loathed the way the melancholy Arcadian parkland spattered with trees and filled with atmosphere which I had known all my life had been turned into a hideous playground. But everyone else seemed to be thrilled at what had been achieved – Massey, Hennessy, the whole population of Mauricetown, the people of Dundalk. In Mauricetown the parish priest mentioned the new golf course at Mount Jewel approvingly in a sermon.

We could forget about Mr Simpson, the historian on his bike, Duffy, the lords from the north and the consumed vintage wine; the visiting Australians who had contracted pneumonia were people of the past.

Trigger and Beakey came to call on Uncle Jack. Like Duffy and my uncle's other friends, they had avoided him during the past year.

Now curiosity had got the better of them.

They may have been startled by what they saw as they came up the long drive – a green to the right of them, a green to the left, a stretch of turf ahead.

'Eighteen holes!'

They came on one of Uncle Jack's good talking days. He was full of smiles. He always liked to boast.

'Cost a bomb.'

'You like?' Maria asked.

'Very much,' Trigger and Beakey lied.

'We have big opening two weeks time. Minister come. You come?'

They were so envious they could hardly reply. They owned houses just as big as Mount Jewel, but it had never occurred to them to put their land into something that could make them proper money.

They looked out of the drawing-room window towards the grounds of the estate spread magnificently before their eyes. They stared at the clipped grass that stretched into the distance.

'You've cut down a lot of timber, old boy.'

Their own estates were similar in acreage to Mount Jewel. Their land and the big houses that went along with them might easily have been similarly transformed into something lucrative by chopping down ancient trees and levelling little places where small white balls could trundle towards their destiny.

The shabbiness and dust that had pervaded the house in the old days had gone for good. Luxury was now offered. Lucky guests, golfers and otherwise, would find their lives temporarily pervaded with comfort which aimed to be combined with old world elegance. Through their bedroom windows it was planned that they could gaze out on the green of the great golf course and meditate on what they would do today – golfing, of course, but other forms of exercise. They were offered hunting, fishing, shooting, and meandering walks down to the lake. They could play golf on a small scale, ignoring the eighteen holes since there was a smaller, miniature course for people who only wanted to do a little putting. Tennis was another option – Jimmy O'Hara rounded up his men and got them to build a couple of hard courts. And people could go fishing – rods would be provided. No need to tell them that the last salmon to be seen in the river was in 1985.

'Steeped in heritage' were the words included in publicity handouts. In the hallway where the long mahogany reception desk had been installed a discreet notice in Gothic script declared Cead Mile Failte. Traditional design was blended with modern amenities, the two elements combined with items that had always belonged to Mount Jewel. In the hall the stuffed bear still stood at the bottom of the stairs and the tiger skin was spread on the floor. Pictures of fighting cocks jostled with steeplechase prints, together with a number of dark uncleaned landscapes. Our ancestors still gazed down at the newcomers, second rate portraits of Hiltons over the centuries by artists whose names would not bring in money unlike the moustached lady to whom my uncle and Maria owed so much. Representatives from Sotheby's had been summoned to confirm that none of the other dirty old oil paintings was valuable.

The seedy and ramshackle interior that I had known since my boyhood had become a distant memory. All the things that had been more or less permanently out of action, wrong or not working, had at last been fixed. Taps no longer leaked; there was no sign of damp even in the remotest corners of ceilings. Old fashioned plug sockets loaded with electric plugs at angles with each other had been replaced.

The drizzle of dust that used to rain down in every bedroom had been spanked off with dusters and feathers at the end of poles by a routine of cleaning which occurred daily, not every six or nine months as used to be the case. The gleaming bedrooms, everyone of which now had a four-poster bed, the newly installed bathrooms enough for twenty-five sweating golfers to shower in and rub down all at the same time, and meditate on their latest hole in one or whatever, all spelled HOTEL.

'Every day I go around and see all things O.K.,' Maria informed Trigger and Beakey. She was taking them upstairs, and I went along too. She was busy telling them how she wore white gloves for her inspection; the daily procession that wandered around the twenty-five bedrooms consisted of a group of chamber-maids dressed in black and white uniforms, girls whom she had ordered to be accommodating and friendly, and offer guests high-end service and hospitality.

Behind them shuffled Uncle Jack, filling the air with the scent of his Corona. He could enjoy the fact that at least he could continue to sleep in his bedroom. His coffin, made by Crowley, and now dusted daily by some friendly maidservant was still under the window, and the bills which were once stored in it had all been paid. The four-poster bed, a third larger than any of those elsewhere, dominated the room and Uncle Jack took up most of it. It was still big enough to include Maria.

I was not so lucky as Uncle Jack. I had been expelled from the room in which I had slept since I was seven years old.

'You go upstairs,' Maria had ordered me many weeks ago, and I obeyed meekly. What had been my bedroom and refuge for twenty years was the last room in the house to be transformed into a place suitable for well paying guests. Spiders had lived there happily until Maria got the broom and the duster in, and threw Dan Dare and dusty Dinky toys and such like into black sacks which I carried up to the barrack room together with my rumpled clothes.

Rodrigo, Delfina and Attracta also had to leave the rooms to which they had been assigned so that more guests could sleep in luxury. Rodrigo was still on a crutch, and the newly installed lift did not go up to the attic. He and Delfina slept in the minute flower room on the ground floor which had a sink; here in the old days Aunt Maud used to spend half her mornings making up elaborate flower arrangements. Like me, Attracta had to go up to spaces of the barrack room where we slept in little padded cells, together with all the new maids and butlers, that Maria hired to be nice to Americans and others.

'Very friendly people, very kind.'

A batch of Filipina girls, cousins of Maria's, were hired from Manila to come over to Ireland and act as maids at Mount Jewel. In addition Maria made sure that other members of the newly appointed staff were Irish with soft sweet accents that the guests would approve of. There were voices from Kerry, from Cork and from Connemara; a couple of intonations among the housekeepers could even be traced to Dublin Four. Plenty of staff; more than one to each guest.

Attracta, whose task was to stand behind the desk installed in the hall and hand out keys with a smile that lit up her pretty face, beguiled incomers with a puzzling pronunciation of English that could be traced with difficulty to the Philippines. Her voice was almost drowned by the noises made by the pianist who sat in the distant corner tinkling tunes from musicals .

The kitchen had been brought upstairs and refitted into the billiard room which was as large as a gymnasium. Sharp knives were bought, and part of the refurbishment included a gleaming batterie de cuisine. Menus were devised, big dinners for hungry golfers and their girl friends, and perhaps even their caddies.

The new chef, Pat Dunne, hired after time working in the Savoy Hotel in London, was in charge. Wearing his tall white hat, Dunne, who called himself Chef Patrice, directed several similarly clad sub-chefs. From time to time he would devote his skill to some béarnaise sauce or put his thumb deep into crème brûlée.

In the dining room roast strip loin of Irish Angus beef, was carved by a specially trained waiter into thin slices, each rare and red. Other items on the menu included monkfish, risotto of crab meat with bisque sauce, Connemara organic salmon – fish caught in rivers, not the wretched creatures twirling around in fish farms.

'Nothing cost under twenty punts,' Maria reported gleefully to Trigger and Beakey. 'All wine good. You drink good bottle?' She had settled them down to a dinner in a corner of the dining room, now named the Earl of Cork Restaurant. Uncle Jack, sat smiling opposite his friends who noted the prices and realised that they were going to pay for what they ate and drank.

Maria had promoted Rodrigo to sommelier; his task was to inflict rich diners with Chablis, Sancerre and Riesling in bottles that cost fifty punts, which meant that each mouthful was a punt.

Trigger could not get away with less than a Sutherland Riesling, and he could hardly pay for just a glass. Sighing deeply, Beakey shared the bottle.

Beakey was especially depressed, since he had recently come across red threads and bulging mushrooms of dry rot in his mansion. He was among those who considered that losing a house was far sadder than losing a loved relative.

'Supreme of roast Doolin lamb' Trigger read from Patrice's menu. 'Creamed potato, garlic and sautéed spinach.' The dish, accompanied by mushroomed creamed potatoes and served from the carving trolley would cost him thirty punts, and would be tender enough not to rattle his false teeth.

Trigger was another fool who had lost most of his money investing in Lloyds, that shiftless rich lazy man's way of earning himself an income. His own house was nearly as big as Mount Jewel, a castellated edifice with a bogus history of descent from ancient Celtic chiefs. He might once have been a good soldier – the fact he had an M.C. was one of the reasons Uncle Jack liked him – but in civil life he was far too cautious. If he had ignored Lloyds, worked as hard as Maria, borrowed more, and installed modern comforts in his mansion, he might now be looking at a way to retrieving much of what he had lost.

Maria ordered the Connemara organic salmon for my uncle whose teeth, as unsteady as Trigger's, were not up to munching slices of lamb.

'With golf we will make much money.' Trigger and Beakey tried to hide their annoyance as they ate their painful way towards the cholesterol-filled desserts delivered to them in clouds of cream.

Uncle Jack drank his coffee amid great puffs from his cigar, the pungent smell of which blew across the dining room, mingling with the delicious odours of Patrice's food. His good humour made Trigger and Beakey more irritable. They preferred the old Jack Hilton of long ago who had been sharp and nasty, instead of the gentle smiling old boy beside them.

Was poor old Jack cuckoo?

'You come to opening?' Maria asked again, when they eventually fled into the darkness.

'No thank you.'

We had already got used to guests and their arrival each afternoon in their sleek hired cars – driving up from Dublin or from the west.

Publicity had induced them to avoid Connemara and come and enjoy the most important country pursuit that Ireland had to offer. Forget the wild mountains of the Kerry and Galway. Forget the lakes of Killarney. Forget hunting, shooting and fishing. Eighteen holes of golf was what they were invited to enjoy.

'We have Minister come give speech.' she told every guest who would listen. 'Very famous golfer. Nicklaus come. Mount Jewel golf course Nicklaus design.' This was not true, Nicklaus had better things to do, but the name had seeped into so many of the news stories that it had been taken for granted. The design came from Jimmy O'Hara – and yes, he had copied most of Nicklaus' ideas.

A tournament was arranged as a preliminary to the opening and metal stands were erected for spectators. A silver cup decorated with golf clubs and golf balls woven into its handle and rims was offered to winners. Over the coming years famous names would be engraved on it. The helicopter trembled as it brought in half a dozen well-known golfers, all of whom were paid substantial amounts of money to attend. Such names are seriously rich, and so are the caddies that accompany them. There are few men who are capable of competing at tournaments all over the world who cannot afford gold taps in their bathrooms.

What was Uncle Jack doing lurking in one of the yard houses used for storing disused cars and machinery? Around the shed were parked a number of old vehicles in what seemed to be a cemetery of crap cars. Among them was a pre-war Ford V8, an old shooting brake and a battered Rover which many years ago he had crashed into a tree.

But his attention was taken by an ancient Ferguson tractor to which was attached a small plough.

I had spent half the afternoon looking for him.

'Why are you here?'

He was dressed in his best suit; on the jacket were pinned his army medals. Why was it covered with smudges of grease? Why was his face feverish and his eyes sunk in his head?

In one hand he held a large spanner.

'I think the gear box has gone. It's an old friend. We bought it just after the war from the North of Ireland. Those Northerners are a clever lot.'

He waved the spanner over the tractor. I noticed that a small plough had been attached to the back of it.

'Uncle Jack, the opening is taking place in half an hour. There's a crowd already at the first green. Maria's waiting for you.'

'Can't you see I'm busy?'

It took ten minutes before I managed to persuade him to drop the spanner and follow me. The Ferguson and the plough remained behind as we walked across the yard towards the golf course. There was no time to change Uncle Jack's filthy clothes. We walked to the first green which had been covered over with a large piece of canvas.

A small green helicopter had landed like a dragon-fly on the newly laid out helipad, and the Minister for Tourism in shiny suit and dark glasses clambered out to be greeted by Maria.

The grounds of Mount Jewel were filled with people, mainly men, gathered in vast numbers so that they could observe a select number of famous golfers aim little white mottled balls. In the crowd were sports journalists, golfers, and more importantly for this afternoon, men holding television cameras. Maria was wearing a sequinned dress which she announced to anyone who wanted to listen that it had cost many hundreds of pounds.

Maria noticed the stains on my uncle's suit. 'What you mean by this dirt,' she hissed. 'Why no clean clothes?' There was little she could do about it at present. The Minister had to be greeted together with other important people.

The Minister was holding some pieces of paper and clearing his throat. It was time for his speech.

A small dais had been erected over the first green which was covered with bright green cloth decorated with a newly designed crest flanked by golf clubs and the name Mount Jewel.

Television cameras focussed on Maria's dress and the Minister. He was a pudgy little man who had been persuaded to attend this moment on the strength of a large donation to his favourite charity from Uncle Jack and free membership to Mount Jewel Golf Club.

As a reward he made his speech very long. He droned on about the refurbishment and the fine hotel and golf club that every guest could see. He wished Mount Jewel every success in the future. Here was a house belonging to the distinguished Hilton family which had royal connections and had been in Ireland for many hundreds of years was ancient and grand, built by Richard Cassels, one of the most majestic Georgian mansions in Ireland.

He talked of this great addition to the county, this place of beauty and peace which offered guests the experience of playing golf on one of the best courses in the country... THE best course, in fact.

Champagne glasses were handed out, filled and raised as a garda gave him the end of the tasselled rope in order to pull back the cover over the first green.

We listened to more applause. Slowly the Minister rolled it back.

There was a stunned silence. People stopped drinking and gazed at the green expanse which was disfigured by raw gashes across the velvety smooth grass.

The plough which Uncle Jack had attached to the back of the Ferguson had done its work well.

In the confusion Maria did not yet guess who was responsible. Marco? But Marco was away at school. The garda sergeant was pointing at green number one and whispering something in the Minister's ear.

Slowly the Minister recovered his voice. In another long inconsequential ramble he mentioned young miscreants who had nothing better to do than cause mischief.

'Don't worry...we will catch them and bring them to the full rigour of the law...'

Maria was looking at the stains on Uncle Jack's clothes.

A tournament had been arranged after the Minister's speech. It was decided that it should take place, even if the first green was unplayable.

At least it was not raining,

Starting beside green number two, golfers trudged around the course, sometimes tapping the balls they hit into the lake, sometimes managing to get them into the holes with the flag in the centre of the putting green. The great crowd followed them over seventeen holes. A fairly famous player, having struggled with the wind, was pronounced the winner and was photographed holding the new silver cup, which was presented to him by the Minister.

When everyone eventually went home, they had been promised that soon there would be similar amazing tournaments played by golfers who were just as famous or more so than the ones they had seen at play today.

And the first green would be repaired.

Maria, Uncle Jack, Jimmy O'Hara and myself waited all the long afternoon to witness this preliminary event. The television cameras bore witness to Uncle Jack's smile and Maria's frowning face. Just as well they did not pick up her mutterings.

'Stupid silly old man...Why you make mess like this? I work for you all day and with golf we make much money... Why you try stop? ...You fool,..Colonel...you not right in head… your fault...'

Sports journalists, adept at describing what they considered a beautiful tournament were taking notes on the way a brilliant golfer had vanquished a number of other brilliant golfers.

They had witnessed the first step of Mount Jewel becoming one of Ireland's premier courses. It had an integration of natural features such as the lakes and any trees that were left standing with golf hazards making the approach to the greens extra tough, exciting and formidable. A perfect environment was offered for golfers young and old to hone their skills.

'Beautiful! First rate!' the guests enthused.

Maria let the police pursue the perpetrator of the crime of destroying the first green. Uncle Jack would not be betrayed – it would hardly help the opening of Mount Jewel. The green was tethered off.

The sergeant told her, 'I have allocated four men to the case.'

And perhaps they were wasting their time.

It would take some weeks for Jimmy O'Hara to get the green playable.

Once again I went looking for Uncle Jack and found Uncle Jack in the backyard.

'They didn't catch me. The Ferguson hasn't let me down.'

'Maria knows, doesn't she?'

My uncle stopped grinning. 'She's not pleased.'

The next day one of the policemen sniffing around the yard discovered the Ferguson and the plough still coated with earth. The culprit was revealed to Maria as my uncle.

'He not right in head. He very sick man.'

Many thanks were offered for all the trouble that the police had suffered. A huge donation from Uncle Jack was given to a nominated police charity.

Maria and Mrs Freebody had become good friends. The relationship blossomed rapidly, arising from Mrs Freebody's observation of the growing success of Mount Jewel as a hotel. Long gone were the memories of the proprietress of Silver Meadows trying to get Maria deported. Instead they now exchanged telephone calls daily, offering each other advice. It was Mrs Freebody who suggested to Maria the school in England to which Marco had been sent.

At least once a week she left Silver Meadows and came over to Mount Jewel where kisses on both cheeks were exchanged. Every week a meal was offered to Mrs Freebody which she did not have to pay for. She was greedy, devouring most of the items on the delicious menu.

There had to be a return visit some time. Silver Meadows loomed.

'David!' announced Maria one day before Christmas. 'We go see my good friend.'

'No bring cigars!' she told Uncle Jack as she wrapped him in his winter coat.

I turned in through the pillared gates and and there was the house, more dreadful than ever.

'Ha!' said Uncle Jack. He had been dozing for most of the journey but as we pulled in over the tarmac the sight of the mansion with its Virginia creeper and fake battlements woke him abruptly.

We got out of the car and walked up the steps, Uncle Jack going bump bump with his stick, holding onto Maria's arm. The door was unlocked by a nurse who greeted Maria with joyful cries in Spanish.

We filed inside.

'Phew!'

The heat hit us. In the hall things were much as I remembered from the past. My eyes caught the Malton prints, the reproduction Paul Henry, the sticks and zimmer frames. Perhaps the artificial white roses were a little grey with dust? The grandfather clock chimed its regular warning. The only thing missing was the wheelchair belonging to Sheila, the old lady who used to sit there most of the day. I remembered she had died. It seemed no one had replaced her.

Here was Mrs Freebody coming out of her office to greet us, dressed in her usual navy blue trouser suit. She gave Maria the peck on both cheeks that these days signalled what great friends they were. In the past, when she was seeking Maria's deportation they might have bitten each other.

Mrs Freebody turned her attention to my uncle. 'Colonel Hilton! What a pleasure to have you back here!'

He growled.

'Come down and meet a few old friends.'

The smell of floral air freshener hit me hard. The heat in the big sitting room was tropical. Nothing seemed to have changed here either, except the portrait of Pope John the Twenty-third was more recent than it had been when Uncle Jack was last here. Now the Pope was shown plump and old. The text was still in place. LIFE IS TOO IMPORTANT TO BE TAKEN SERIOUSLY. On the chimney piece were the usual two jugs of water and the line of glasses. The *Irish Times* and the pile of magazines were on their table. I glanced at them; right up to date. Everything as I remembered.

As ever, the room was full of old ladies, covered in perspiration, who sat sleeping, or knitting or reading or staring at television where the programme showed a woman giving a cookery demonstration. It must have been many years since any of the old dears watching her had mixed a cake similar to the one she was just about to place into the oven. Soon she would be saying, 'Here's something I made earlier.' But no one would hear her, since the sound was turned down. To understand her you would have to lip read.

Mrs Freebody led us through the room in her stately fashion, giving her usual smiles and greetings and how are you my dears. Just as she used to in the old days. We followed. I could only recognise two or three of the old women who used to sit in here two years ago. The rest were strangers.

What had happened to the others, twenty or so whom I had met here when I visited Uncle Jack in the old days? They must have all died. A.P. Crowley's hearse must call in here every few days. Had a few forgiving generous relatives taken some home? Perhaps one or two had gone downstairs? There was no doubt in my mind that the rooms downstairs were still full of the demented.

I glanced at Uncle Jack who for the first time in months had ceased the gentle smiling mood of old age he had been wearing perpetually ever since he had fallen in love with Maria. His face wore the look I had got used to during my childhood.

The old women turned from watching the cake being made, and ceased their reading, knitting and talking. The room filled with a collective gasp.

'Let's get out of here!' shouted Uncle Jack.

Not a chance.

Our group made our way towards the bay window, my uncle swept along unwillingly. Four people sat at a bridge table, just like past times. Two were old men, each faced by women players. One of them turned to look at us.

'Here is an old friend to see you, Lady Marsden!' said Mrs Freebody in her tinkling voice.

Uncle Jack and Lady Marsden spoke instantaneously. They both said together, 'I thought you were dead!'

Lady Marsden had got older, and had shrunk a little. Her hair was immaculate; she must still have the hairdresser regularly. She wore a chiffon scarf.

Sherry was produced. We stood – there were not enough places for us to sit – holding Waterford glasses filled with slugs of Bristol Cream.

The only people who spoke – and with animation – were Maria and Mrs Freebody.

'Like old times!'

'Another glass please!'

The twenty or so old women and the nuns sitting around in the rest of the room looked on.

Not another word was exchanged between Lady Marsden and Uncle Jack. They stared at each other with what appeared to be looks of horror.

We emptied our glasses. My uncle managed to say 'Goodbye Daisy'. Then we left rapidly; his tottering pace was almost like running.

'Cheerio!' Mrs Freebody locked the front door on us as we made our way down the steps and across the tarmac to the car.

I took a moment off to go and peer into the basement. More old women with frenziedly untidy hair were sitting in a semi-darkened room looking at the same programme as the people upstairs.

What did nursing homes do with the old before television was invented?

Uncle Jack was silent as he sat beside me in the car and we drove back to Mount Jewel. As we passed out of the gate he gave a shudder.

CHAPTER EIGHTEEN

It is not easy living in a hotel if you are not a guest. Uncle Jack's study was approached through the door which now had a brass plate on it marked PRIVATE. In there we took refuge. Maria was seldom with us, since she was too busy giving orders to staff, inspecting bedrooms and menus down in the kitchen and generally getting in the way of those who were running the place.

Later Maria would discover weddings and realise that Mount Jewel would be a good place for really expensive nuptials. She was to learn that there was plenty of money to be forced out of greedy brides whose day of flashing celebration might set them and their would-be spouses back twenty thousand punts – or, as the millennium dawned, euros. She was also looking at the possibilities of inviting pop stars down to Mount Jewel to massive three day orgies of singing, thumping musical instruments and taking drugs.

Meanwhile she would carry on with golf.

Another autumn came and the tourists departed with the swallows. Half the staff was dismissed and told to come back next spring. At last we could leave Uncle Jack's study and wander around and almost treat the Mount Jewel as our own. But although there were far less guests staying, local people, together with players from Dundalk and elsewhere, arrived daily and wandered around the course in wind and rain, and, later in the year, even snow. A concession was made to those who lived around Mauricetown who were allowed their golf cheaply.

Maria had less to do, after she realised that wandering around giving orders in a loud voice was a seasonal affair. But if the golf course was aiming to be the best in Ireland, it was time to immerse herself in the game.

She needed the correct equipment. I drove her to Dublin, together with Uncle Jack and Jimmy O'Hara to choose the perfect set of lady's clubs at a sports shop. While Jimmy, Uncle Jack and I were dining in the Shelbourne, she went off and bought herself the right clothes and shoes for the lady golfer.

Over the coming weeks Jimmy gave her lessons, and she turned out to be a good player.

'A natural.'

'Many birdies! I make,' she crooned. Her drives were formidable for a woman and her putting was good; before her the little white ball trembled then raced towards the hole that waited for it.

She appointed herself Mount Jewel's Lady Captain and rounded up a few unhappy women to play with her in competitive roles. Invariably she won.

Winter was passing pleasantly. Was Maria at last drifting away from Uncle Jack?

What was my role here? Not only did I continue to be chauffeur, mostly taking Maria into Dundalk, and to Dublin on shopping sprees, but I kept an eye on Uncle Jack. Maria decreed that he could not be left alone for a moment. She had no time to look after him. She was Mrs Hilton, proprietor of one of the best hotels in Ireland.

In the study, one rainy morning Maria and I had an argument, watched by Rodrigo, Attracta, Delfina and Uncle Jack.

Mrs Maria Hilton and I shouted at each other.

'Find someone else who will combine nursing my uncle with being a chauffeur.'

'Always easy. Anyone do...Rodrigo – he do what I ask...' She barked at her brother in Spanish.

I won. I got a decent salary. Since I had free board I could put most of it away in a bank account. My Australia fund. My running away fund. I planned my return to Sydney, where I would not be staying in any boarding house in Dee Why. Next year perhaps. For the present I would continue to be chauffeur and nurse.

At Christmas guests came again. Many went out in the rain and drizzle to do a tour of the golf course. They were served a Christmas dinner; the dining room was filled with happy housewives who had been let off the awful task of cooking the annual turkey.

The hotel was flourishing. At New Year there was another celebration when assembled golfers and visitors with the Midas touch danced about merrily and sang Auld Lang Syne. Scores of people had made bookings and the guest list for the next spring and summer was nearly full. Another golf tournament was planned that would bring fame and fortune.

Outside the study there was all the hum of the working hotel. It was doing very well; bookings were constant and the place continued to be more or less full even out of season. Articles about the joys of Mount Jewel appeared regularly in newspapers and magazines. An international golf tournament was planned for next summer.

Since our visit to Silver Meadows my uncle had become a sad old man. Albert and Edward had finally died of old age and Maria would not allow him to acquire more dogs. She continued to scold him for destroying the golf course's first green – something that would never be forgotten. Gone was that inane smile which had signified his love for her.

These days the only time he became animated was when Mrs Freebody came to visit her good friend Mrs Maria Hilton at Mount Jewel. And the animation was expressed in fear. His manners were perfect as he greeted her, but his hand trembled as he shook hers.

His distress was worse than those other moods that I had known during my life. The angry uncle, the nutty uncle, the uncle who could or could not have dementia, the smiling uncle in love, had vanished, and now there was this miserable old fellow, crouched by the fire.

For me making my way in the old house I used to live in trying not to bump into the visitors that filled the place. Mount Jewel had become a nightmare. I found no pleasure in living permanently in a hotel, especially in a premises that I remembered as my home. After a few more months I had got tired of the delicious food served by Chef Patrice. I did not even like the great breakfasts to which I was entitled to help myself.

There was no satisfaction in my chauffeur duties, driving Maria and Uncle Jack in and out of Dundalk, down to Dublin, and once or twice taking her and the trembling old man to Silver Meadows.

Back at Mount Jewel outside the study I found it was an effort to show good cheer and politeness to the guests, or help lift their suitcases or answer questions smoothly.

Caviar Coast was cast in his box and died. Massey had a heart attack soon afterwards, although we were informed by Dr O'Shea that there was no connection between the two events. Maria promptly disposed of the rest of the horses, bringing to an end a tradition of horse breeding and racing at Mount Jewel that went back three centuries. The stables were converted into extra guest rooms. Now the hotel could really concentrate on the great game.

I would never inherit Mount Jewel and the place would be left to Marco. I was tired of golf, golf, golf.

I decided I would escape the big house and Maria with her endless commands and my poor old uncle.

I confided in two people. One was Dan Hennessy. I explained my dissatisfaction and the fact that I had endured a good deal.

'I'm not that good as a nursemaid to Uncle Jack. If there was any chance that I might inherit Mount Jewel, I might be tempted to stay. As it is, I think I'll slip away.'

Hennessy reached for his snuff box. 'High time.'

He promised to keep in touch with me and give me every news of what was going on. I left money for him to telephone me. I would come back to Ireland if I was summoned.

I also told Dr O'Shea of my impending departure and made similar arrangements for him to contact me.

'Don't worry,' he said. 'Maria takes excellent care of Colonel Hilton.' I knew that wasn't true but I ignored his opinion.

I did not inform O'Shea that I was the one who spent most of the time looking after him. Nor Maria. Who would take over my role after I had left? Delfina? Attracta? Would Maria call in some Filipina friend or nursemaid? Perhaps get back to Manila to find someone suitable?

I said goodbye to no one, not even my uncle, feeling it would be very hard to make him understand what I was doing. And anything to avoid a confrontation with Maria. No farewells to Rodrigo, Attracta or Delfina.

I left a note on the chimney piece in the study, remembering that my great-grandmother's sister had done the same when she eloped with the groom.

As I walked through the hall of Mount Jewel a couple of women were hoovering and giving the stuffed bear a mild dusting. Sandra, the girl behind the reception desk waved. Outside I made my way to the garage; I had put my bags into the car the evening before. I drove up to Dublin airport and left the car in the airport car park – I had written that I would do this in my note.

I boarded the aeroplane that began the twenty-hour flight to Australia.

CHAPTER NINETEEN

Things went well in Sydney. It was hot, around Christmas time, almost four years to the day since I had departed. Walking in the sunshine, I felt more at home than I had ever done in Mount Jewel. I got in touch with Cousin Desmond and Divina, and made my way across the harbour to Manly and northward to their house. Cousin Desmond had got older and more wrinkled than ever; he talked just as much. I paid back the money I owed them and we became friends. He still had racehorses, and tried to get me to bet – but after the old debacle on Shining Angel when I lost all my money, I declined. So the last time I put a bet on a horse continued to be poor old Caviar Coast.

My friendship with Desmond lasted into the twenty-first century and the moment when he died, a very old man. He departed in a good way, an excellent way in fact, a heart attack while he was sitting at the tiller, steering his yacht. Sad for Divina, but she soon found someone else. I would not have minded marrying lovely Divina myself, even if she was ten years older than I was.

I work in real estate on the north shore. The job is dull, and I could have done the same sort of thing back in Ireland. However, it has brought a measure of prosperity; I have a house in Avalon overlooking the sea and after Cousin Desmond's death I acquired his yacht.

I did not miss Mount Jewel at all. Or Ireland. Or Uncle Jack and Maria.

I was aware Mount Jewel continued to prosper as a hotel and a world-famous golf course. It did better and better. There was an article about the place in the *Sydney Morning Herald* which encouraged Australian people to go to Ireland and up to Louth to try out the golf at Ireland's premier hotel. Celebrities stayed there, not only famous golfers, but film stars and their families. Helicopters were continuously busy. A couple of rooms were booked permanently by journalists so that they could report on the famous.

What about my uncle? Poor old fellow. As far as I could make out when I spoke to Dr O'Shea and Hennessy by phone, most days Uncle Jack slouched by the fire complaining. My conscience struck me every now and again as I felt that I should not have abandoned the poor old fellow. But he seemed sane enough. Hennessy and Dr O'Shea continued to keep me in touch with news about him. I rang regularly. Nothing much seemed to have changed for him except that Delfina was appointed by Maria to look after him. I rang him occasionally. Maria would talk first. Uncle very happy. Then he would pick up the phone and shout over twelve thousand miles.

'What the hell are you doing?'

He sounded as sane and as gruff as I had ever remembered him.

The hotel gave him a great party for his eighty-fifth birthday. Hennessy was there and he described to me guests and staff clapping and singing Happy Birthday to the old boy, after which he cut the colossal cake made by Patrice.

I remembered the birthday he had celebrated at Silver Meadows. This was better. As ever Maria told me, 'So happy the Colonel.'

Could I believe her? What did he do all day?

Nothing much. Sitting by the fire, saving shoe leather, looking at *National Geographics*, occasionally going out in Delfina's company, limping among the guests to the front door, and then a little stroll down the drive.

I telephoned again.

'You've been long enough in that wretched bloody continent. You've had enough of koalas and kangaroos. When are you coming back here?'

'Very soon, Uncle Jack,' I lied.

The hotel continued to prosper and the golf tournaments got more frequent. My uncle continued to wander in and out of the old house.

When I talked to him I thought he might be getting a little vague, every time he spoke. He didn't shout.

'How are you, Uncle Jack?'

'Quite well thank you. When are you coming back?'

'Soon.'

In the New Year Hennessy rang. 'We've had a problem with the Colonel.'

'What happened?'

'He took his passport and his credit card and disappeared.'

'I didn't know he still had either of those things.'

'Bad mistake.'

'They've found him, I presume?

'With difficulty. He flew to Rio.'

'Rio?'

'As in di Janeiro. Quite a business finding him and returning him to Ireland.'

'Where is he now?'

When I spoke to Maria she said, 'Colonel very well.'

I rang Silver Meadows. Mrs Freebody answered.

'He's settling, David.' From twelve thousand miles away anyone could tell that was a lie.

'Can I have a word with him?'

'I think it would be better if you called back in a few days time.'

I phoned Maria who trilled over the line, 'Colonel happy.'

'Why have you put him back in Silver Meadows? You know how he hated the place?'

'Not true. He love my friend Angelica. Good woman. He like everything. But no cigars. They take good care. I see him most days. Rodrigo drive me.'

I phoned Dr O'Shea.

'You have nothing to worry about. Your uncle is in good hands. They take better care of him at Silver Meadows than at Mount Jewel.'

I phoned Hennessy.

'He's fine, David.'

'Have you been to see him?'

There was a long pause.

'Hello?' I roared.

'I'm going tomorrow.'

I rang Silver Meadows again. The minutes ticked by as Mrs Freebody went to fetch him and bring him to the telephone.

'Colonel, your nephew is ringing from Australia. He would like a word with you.'

All I could get out of my uncle was what sounded like a groan.

'What the hell are you doing? Come back at once!'

I counted to ten. What did the old fool want now? Had I become so engrossed in my own welfare here in Australia that my uncle no longer existed for me. I pretended I had not heard him correctly. Surely he realised I was no longer a child to be bullied.

What was he trying to say?

I was selling expensive houses up and down the north shore, and did not like to abandon what I was doing. I might possibly become as rich as Desmond. I was planning to get married.

But now I booked a flight back to Dublin.

I was squeezed into a miserable seat, made smaller by the fat man in front tipping it back, eating frozen food that had not quite thawed out. The long long day was longer if you include air travel as one unit. The stop in Abu Dhabi airport was like a Pressburger set of *Stairway to Heaven*. The difference was that it was full of Arabs in white robes and towels, women in black, with face covering, nothing but eyes visible and anxious Indians and Pakistanis and bearded turbaned Sikhs.

After a couple of hours I was back onto another plane, to find another inconsiderate passenger in front of me, and be offered another soggy meal by another smiling stewardess. And plenty more time to think about Uncle Jack. Twenty four hours of such thoughts did nothing for my jet lag.

At Dublin airport Rodrigo met me. As we drove to Louth and Mount Jewel he described how well the hotel was doing. It had just won a prestigious tourist award.

'We all go to Dublin. Big celebration.'

Who?

'Maria, Marco, all of us. Filipino ambassador attend. Minister, many people attend, say how clever is Maria. Maria given big glass bowl. Waterford glass. Much publicity. All shown on television...'

It was hard to change the subject since Rodrigo was so enthusiastic.

'How is Colonel Hilton?'

'Colonel well, Stay with Madame Freebody.'

'I have come back to see him.'

'He love Silver Meadows. He love Madame Freebody. No need for you to come home.'

Home. Mount Jewel had become Rodrigo's home more than it was mine – or my uncle's.

We drove the rest of the way in silence.

Rodrigo angled the car, a brand new Mercedes, through the front gate of Mount Jewel. There were golfers to right of us, golfers to left of us. A white ball swept through the air carried by the wind. Overhead rattled a helicopter.

'Plenty guests.'

Maria met me in the hotel lobby and offered me a cheek. The lobby was noisy, full of guests coming and going, queuing at the reception desk. There were wrinkles in the flesh that I pecked at with a dutiful kiss. She had dyed her hair the colour of marmalade.

The first thing she did was to point out the trophy that had been presented to her the week before.

'Very nice?'

The thing was huge, the size of the old globes that once stood in the hall in its place. It had been engraved by some careful Waterford craftsman with a medley of stuff – Irish flag, Filipino flag, golf clubs, golf balls.

In the study Marco was using a putter to tap a golf ball into a whiskey glass. He had grown very fat. Surely a youth nearing twenty should not have a wobbly double chin?

'Hello, Marco.'

'Hi, David. Nice to see you.'

'Long time since we met.'

'When do you leave school?'

'In July.'

'What do you plan on doing?'

'I'll help Mummy to run the hotel.'

His voice was standard Bedales – any trace of a Filipino accent was vanquished.

'Clever boy,' affirmed his mother. 'He soon make money. Work with Mount Jewel.'

The study seemed to be very empty without Uncle Jack.

'Colonel well.'

We dined in splendour below the gleaming chandeliers. All the waiters and waitresses were from the Philippines. It seemed to me that a quarter of the forty million people who lived there must have been summoned by Maria to come over to Ireland to work in Mount Jewel.

Maria checked everything that appeared on the menu.

I enjoyed the shellfish bisque with Armagnac.

I asked Maria, 'Is there no way the Colonel could stay here at Mount Jewel?' After all, it was his own house?

'Not his house now. Hotel. He happy at Silver Meadows. He like very much my good friend Mrs Angelica Freebody.'

I asked the question that haunted me.

'Is he upstairs or downstairs?

'Upstairs. I tell you, very happy upstairs. But downstairs now very nice.'

'Maria, I remember very well what it was like.'

'All different now. My friend Mrs Angelica Freebody make basement good for mad people. All dementia people happy.'

'No people with dementia are happy, Maria.'

'Silver Meadows people yes, all happy. Now downstairs mad people have music, exercises, arts, crafts. All looked after.'

'I am glad to hear it.'

'Plenty personal care. Plenty of my cousins come from Manila – good women give mad people personal attention.'

I took a mouthful of chargrilled Irish rib-eye steak. Rare. 'I am glad the Colonel is upstairs.'

'He, too, maybe a little dementia. Maybe he crazy for many years. But no worries. My friend Angelica look after Colonel. Also my cousin Sofia from Manila, she come, she watch him. No need for you to come spending good money from Australia.'

'I would very much like to see him.'

Rodrigo swung the Mercedes into the courtyard of Silver Meadows. Crowley's hearse was parked there.

But things had changed. For a start, the wisteria had been pulled down and the whole house had been painted a gleaming white.

Maria pointed. 'New garden for sick people ...nice smelling plants.'

The downstairs had a new entrance. The bars had been taken off the windows and I could see that inside bright lights were on. I could hear music – Judy Garland was singing 'Somewhere Over the Rainbow'.

Two good-natured dogs – Labradors – waited to be stroked or patted.

Maria said: 'All mad people like reflexology. Hairdresser come every day. Expert people come every day to help give aromatherapy, massage. Patients living in en suite rooms. All happy.'

I got out and went over and peered into the window. The television set, with its arc of old women sitting in front was larger than I remembered.

I came back to the Mercedes. 'I'm glad the Colonel is not down there.'

'No need. He not have enough dementia.'

'I'm glad.

'Maybe one day he go down.'

But I felt somewhat reassured as we sat and waited for today's coffin and corpse to descend the front steps. More work for the undertaker.

Upstairs, too, lights were bright. Mrs Freebody appeared and she and Maria touched cheeks.

The time was June but the central heating was full on. Stepping into the hall was like entering a tropical forest. Australia seemed Arctic by comparison.

How long since I had been here? Five years? Six? Nothing much had changed upstairs in the sitting room, except the television set, which, like the one downstairs, had got bigger. And the people. No one to be recognised, another twenty old women covered with perspiration who were strangers, most with wild white hair, a few with little white beards. So many others had come and gone and died. Except for the two nuns mouthing stuff from their breviaries or whatever who so far as I could remember looked much the same, a little more wrinkled, perhaps, their cardigans grey, their stubbly heads neatly covered with veils. Pray away, sisters, pray hard. Pope John Paul, dead and destined to be a saint, smiled down on them. Pope Benedict was up there as well, beside him.

I looked towards the bow window at the far end of the room. I saw an old man, the one old man in the room.

My uncle's moustache had grown bushier; he had lost most of his hair; the dome of his head seemed like a boiled egg. He sat on the window seat beside a very old woman, very thin, very elegant, her white hair trimly in place, a chiffon scarf around her neck. Her left hand, with the diamond and sapphire ring on her finger (much smaller than Maria's engagement ring) clasped his right hand.